The Other Shore

Tracy A. Ball

Black Rose Writing | Texas

ISBN: 978-1-68433-614-2
PUBLISHED BY BLACK ROSE WRITING
www.blackrosewriting.com

Printed in the United States of America
Suggested Retail Price (SRP) $19.95

The Other Shore is printed in Baskerville

*As a planet-friendly publisher, Black Rose Writing does its best to eliminate
unnecessary waste to reduce paper usage and energy costs, while never compromising
the reading experience. As a result, the final word count vs. page count may not meet
common expectations.

I couldn't go a moment without being thankful for my family. Every day they give me a new reason to be proud. My daughter—The Lawyer (I will be announcing that for the next thirty years!) My grandson—The Summer King, and the newest member of our kingdom, my granddaughter—The Winter Queen are what life is about. And my husband—The Hero, who rescues me daily and makes my stories possible.

***

For Aunt Rita and her quiet bravery.

And, for Wayne, with his unending devotion.

The Other Shore

CHAPTER 1

From the top of the gangplank, Captain Burrell Shoemaker watched his lead stewardess juggle her purse, travel bag, and a prize from a coffee shop on her way to port.

"Running a little late, aren't you Keira?"

"Sorry, Captain. It won't happen again."

She shook the hair out of her face and he noted, not for the first time, the level of her attractiveness: top shelf. Being thirty years her senior, he'd never admit it, but her curves played a part in his decision to hire her. "So you say."

She flashed a row of almost perfect teeth. Running late was so much a part of her routine, Keira's boarded a half hour ahead of everybody else. "You ever have one of those days?"

"About every six hours." He relieved her of her travel bag, and they set off down the corridor. "What's wrong?"

"For one thing, this isn't my assignment. Mona called me this morning to switch and I'm not fully prepared."

"Well, in that case, you're not late. What else?"

"Ugghh. My father."

"Careful. He and I are about the same age."

"Yeah, but you're smart and handsome. He's just a dad."

"Look at that. You're ten minutes early. Keep going."

"He accused me of staying out all night."

"Aren't you twenty-three and all grown up?"

"He's in a snit because I didn't answer the phone. That happens sometimes when you're asleep. He's convinced I'm seeing someone he wouldn't approve of."

"Back to that age thing. You are legal."

"I'm also not interested. I already broke up with the guy he's worried about."

"Are you heartbroken?"

"Nope. Not at all. Next on my list is a real man." She gave him a sideways glance. "Mrs. Shoemaker couldn't have gotten the last one."

"What's it to be, promotion or a raise?"

. . .

"Ta daaa..."

He uncovered her eyes, and Angela blinked the scene into focus. "Oh, Mitch! Are you kidding me?" Her mahogany lipstick formed a glossy O. "That's a yacht." The sleek water vessel resembled a small building; bright lights and music floated down in invitation.

Mitchell Pointe brushed his wife's hair back—she wore it natural with soft spiral curls—and kissed her cheek. "It's your yacht tonight."

"You rented a yacht?"

"For you. Adds three more romantic days to our vacation. We'll hit La Habana and fly home from Florida." He tugged her forward.

"This must have cost a fortune."

"For you, anything."

She paused, one foot on the gangplank. "But Cancun is already too expensive. Sailing across the Gulf —"

"No ma'am. No buts. The world stops right here."

She wanted to protest, but she was tired of fighting off gifts. She was tired of a lot of things. Wasteful or not, it wasn't as if they couldn't afford it. Looking at the sincerity in his deep-set amber eyes, the absolute conviction in his stance, and the determined tilt of his very stubborn chin, she silenced her objection.

Her cell phone rang. If it were anyone other than Deidra, it would have spoiled the moment.

"Five dollars."

"No bet." Angela shook her head. They each reached for their phones. Angela, to be sure they were correct in their suspicion; Mitchell, to shoot a text to his sister-in-law.

"Hello..." Angela disconnected. "She's not there."

Quit butt dialing. Mitchell texted Deidra, then put his phone away. "That interruption is on you."

"Me?"

"Your sister. Your phone. You owe me. Come on." He clasped her fingers and tugged.

She loved holding his hand. His skin tone was darker than hers. Together, they were beautiful. She let him lead her forward. "Our clothes?"

"Already onboard. Had them packed and sent over while we were at lunch." Victory danced in his tone. "You most likely won't need them anyway," he whispered into her ear as they boarded the Siren's Fire–*Love of the Sea*.

The initial tour was an exercise in luxury. The yacht had a salon, a dining room, a galley, a Jacuzzi, a gym, three staterooms, and a bar. For added entertainment, there was a fishing boat, windsurfing and diving equipment, and jet skis. Keira, their stewardess, showed them so many perks, they couldn't take it all in. In addition to the captain and his four-man crew, the *Siren's Fire* traditionally carried four to six guests. However, this weekend Mitchell and Angela Pointe were traveling exclusively.

CHAPTER 2

The dimly lit bar boasted a lavish combination of wood, leather, and glass that made Mitchell thirsty, like he came to the right place. The bartender came over the second he picked a stool. He was a tall man with a neat ponytail of dreads hanging to the center of his back. "What can I get for you, Mr. Pointe?"

"I'll take a beer."

"Right away, sir."

Mitchell noted the sincerity. He liked being called 'sir.' A not-quite-thirty-year-old black man with his list of accomplishments earned the right to be addressed as *'sir.'* He appreciated the recognition.

"Is everything all right, Mr. Pointe?" Keira leaned against the bar.

"Keira. I didn't see you."

"I'm your stewardess, Mr. Pointe. It's my job to be close," she smiled, "but not in your way."

"Never." He returned her smile. "Care to join me?" He indicated the stool beside him.

She shook her head, prepared to decline.

"Please, I insist."

She hesitated for a fraction of a second. "One beer. Nate-Nate, you got any Corona?"

"For you, Keira, my love." The bartender popped the cap and slid the bottle across the counter.

"Thanks, Nate." She caught the bottle and took a swig. "You never answered, Mr. Pointe. Is everything all right?"

"Perfect. We're having a blast."

"That's our goal." She pushed her hair behind her ear.

Mitchell thought the move was attractive. He wasn't interested, but Keira was a beautiful woman with thick, cinnamon brown hair that hung down her back in waves. She had chocolate brown eyes and sun-kissed skin. It made him wonder. "Are you from this area?"

"No. I'm from Hawaii. Been around water my whole life."

"Hawaii. Makes sense."

"Pardon me?"

"You've got that mysterious…" he rolled his finger, trying to find the correct wording. "Appeal. Like you're some island princess."

She leaned away from him with a curious arch to her eyebrow.

"No, no." He held his hand up in surrender. "I'm not trying to come on to you. Not that I wouldn't," he amended, "but I'm happily married."

Keira relaxed. "Speaking of which, where is Mrs. Pointe?"

"Angela is asleep. The busy day wore her out. She's…" He drank his beer, reluctant to say more. "Fragile."

Keira responded to the sadness in his tone. "Oh. Is she ill?"

"No." He rocked his head, weighing his options. "Not really, but somewhat."

Keira remained silent.

"She's depressed." He had another swallow.

So did she. "Can you talk about it?"

He hunched his shoulders. "We've been trying for a baby. But Angela can't. The news devastated her. She hasn't recovered. Not yet. I'm trying to give her some distraction. Sometimes it works." He hunched his shoulders again.

A long moment of nothing passed before Keira said, "I'm very sorry for you, Mr. Pointe."

"Call me Mitchell. Please."

She nodded. "Mitchell. If there's anything I can do to help you and especially your wife, please don't hesitate."

"Thanks. You and the entire crew have been amazing. You've already done everything you can do and more. It's going to take some time. At least that's what her doctor says."

Nate sat two more beers down in front of them. He grabbed a third one for himself. "May I ask you a question, Mr. Pointe?"

"Mitchell, and sure." Mitchell helped himself to the second brew.

"Are you relieved, or resentful? I'm not asking for you to answer, just wondering if your wife is picking up on any of those vibes. Something like that might make her edgy without either of you realizing it."

Mitch thought about it. "I'm no expert, but I don't think I'm compounding the problem. I wanted kids before she did. So she knows I'm not relieved. I tell her twenty times a day it's not her fault. It's just one of those things. She can tell when I'm lying, so she knows I'm sincere." He swirled his beer, watching it slosh around the bottle. "We found out two months ago and I already have us registered at seven different agencies. As far as I'm concerned, this is one route we can't take, but that's all it is. The result doesn't change. We're getting kids."

Keira smiled, drawn to his enthusiasm. "Now we have to convince her that those children need a healthy mother to drive insane."

The idea appealed to him. "I hadn't thought of it that way." He liked how she said "we." For a moment, he wasn't alone in his fight. He lifted his drink. "To my children."

Keira and Nate tapped their bottles to his.

"Highly energetic children," Keira said.

"Lots of them," Nate added.

■   ■   ■

"I hate this. I do. But what can I say? He's doing it all for me."

"If it's killing you, Ange, it's not a kindness. Tell him to stop."

Angela shifted the phone from one ear to the other. "You don't understand, Deidra. He doesn't hear. He thinks my negativity is from depression. He won't give in to it."

"He doesn't hear you because he's not listening. That should tell you something. But never mind that. Contrary to popular opinion, all this activity is stressing you out. When you get home this time, stay home. Tell your husband you need to stay home. If you don't, I will."

"He's trying to help me. It's not his fault nothing will help me."

"Stop talking like that. You've been through a lot. It's going to take more than a weekend full of margaritas to pull through it."

"I better go. If I'm not resting when he comes back he'll think I didn't want to be around him."

"He's be correct," Deidra agreed.

Angela snickered. "It's not true, you wacko. But I am tired."

"Get some rest. Love you."

"Love you too." Angela hung up the phone. The momentary warmth evaporated. She was tired. She didn't want to be around Mitchell. She hated these trips—one surprise after another. She hated surprises. She hated being broken. She hated herself. She was beat up, miserable, and full of hate.

.　　.　　.

Angela looked out over the rail at he beauty of the night. A crisp fragrant wind, and the moon so low it seemed to float on the tide. She thought it may have been a blue moon, but wasn't altogether positive. The mist was invigorating. She didn't see Mitch, but they were on a boat; he had to be close. She tried to sleep, but it was restless. The walk helped—put her in a more positive place. She wanted to share that with him. Her positive moments were so few; he deserved to be a part of every one.

Angela couldn't imagine the toxic dump her life would be without her husband. She wouldn't have a life without him. There were days when she couldn't put two thoughts together. But Mitch fulfilled every need, every minor detail. Their four-year marriage was sacred; their vows, unbreakable.

Looking out into the endless night, she forgot her anxiety. They had a beautiful life. They would get a beautiful child, Mitch would see to it. A baby didn't have to come from a mother's womb to be in a mother's heart. She could almost see her: a pretty angel with bright eyes and a cherubic smile. Or a boy: heart-stealing grin, busy, busy hands.

A tear of hopefulness dripped from her eyelash. Babies were the truest joy on the planet.

"Mrs. Pointe. Is everything all right?"

Angela turned toward the speaker. "Captain Shoemaker. Everything is wonderful, thank you. I'm just taking in this magnificent night."

"It's always magical on the water. Are you enjoying the whales?"

"Whales?"

He came over beside her and pointed. "See there. You can see the spray." While she looked in the direction he indicated, he partook a healthy eyeful of her backside. Standing at six one, he had her by at least five inches. He snuck a peek at her cleavage. She had more than a handful and they were perfect.

"Ahhh," she squealed. "Is it really a whale?"

He switched off the fantasy button. "Definitely. Most likely feeding. If he found a good spot, you'll see few of them by morning."

"I can't wait to tell Mitch. You haven't seen him, have you?"

"I have not, but I'm sure he won't be too hard to find. If I see him, I'll send him your way."

"Thank you."

The Captain moved on. Angela continued to gaze out across the water, excited to see the next plume of spray from the magnificent beast. When it came, she could see it clearly. Angela cast a glance over her shoulder, hoping Mitch would appear. Not willing to move, she reached for her cell phone. She'd take a picture. Or give him a call. Or both.

She dipped her fingers into her pocket, her nail scraping against the case. "Oh." A jolt made her grab the railing. An image of the Titanic popped into her head. Did the boat bump into something? She glanced around and then down, seeing nothing. *Silly. Are you searching for an iceberg in the gulf.* But what did they hit? While the private yacht wasn't the largest of its kind, she was too big for undisturbed waves to bounce her around.

The whoosh was long and haunting. A wall of murk grew out of the water. Five feet, ten… more, much more; it moved upward, blocking the night and terrorizing her soul.

BAM!!!

Angela pitched sideways over the railing. Flying…soaring…falling through the air. Her arms flailed, attempting to catch hold of something. Debris and water rained down with her, drowning out her scream.

She hit cement and plunged downward. Icy cold, black death covered her, dragging her into the deep.

CHAPTER 3

Mitch, Keira, and Nate made a toast. Then hell exploded. There was a loud crash.

The yacht rolled. The floor stood upright. With startled shrieks and angry expletives, they fell to the wall behind Nate. Bottles and glass flew everywhere. The electricity blew. An alarm sounded. Water gushed in, flooding the cabin, filling the space with cold and fear.

Mitch couldn't make it make sense. Everything went dark. He fell on top of some boxes, and other stuff fell on him. He was wet and bruised. Did a pipe break? Did the room break? Whatever happened, this not the place to stay.

"Come on!" Keira yelled.

He followed her lead. Nate moaned but moved when Mitch did.

Half crawling, they stumbled over equipment, broken dishes, decorations, and wine cases, working their way along the tilted bar counter, desperate to escape.

They could barely see, and everything around them was incomprehensible. Part of the boat faced an odd angle. That inexplicable crash came again. The yacht shuddered and gave way in more than one place. The water rose faster now, but Keira had a destination and would not be stopped. Mitchell and Nate stayed with her. Not far away, they heard screams.

The few lights remaining popped and flickered, then died altogether. The nearly capsized vessel lost its remaining power. First one and then the other, Keira and Nate snapped the glow-sticks that hung around their wrists. The neon bracelets were required for all on-duty seamen aboard the *Siren's Fire*. Mitchell wanted one.

They were almost treading the freezing water when they came upon a small boat. Working as fast as possible, they freed it and finally came out of the ocean.

They stared, shocked, expressionless at the chaos unfolding before them. The yacht lay partially on its side with portions sunk, sinking, or floating in the murk. No more screams. Other sounds rended the cold night air. Splintering, cracking, pounding and breaking as if some invisible force had declared war and vandalized the once elegant water vessel.

"Angela." Mitchell called softly as if she would walk in from the next room, sit beside him, and explain it to him.

Angela didn't come. In the long, lonely dark, nobody came. Nobody called. The absence of people—voices—made it unbearable.

"It doesn't work." Nate stared at his cellphone. The icy ocean water had rendered it useless.

Mitchell reached for his phone. He'd call Angela. She would come.

It wasn't there. He checked all his pockets and frantically checked them again. He couldn't find it. Or, her.

"HELLO!" Keira yelled. "Where are you?" She turned to the men. "Guys, we've got to go find them. Get the life jackets. This boat doesn't have a motor. Somebody find the oars. Get the whistle."

Mitchell followed orders, but the life jacket meant nothing to him at the moment. He didn't understand what a whistle had to do with anything, so he opted to free the oars. He rowed in the direction of his cabin.

Nate opened the under-seat locker and gave the survival kit a cursory glance. He passed the whistle forward, and then withdrew into himself, still trying to make his phone work.

Toot, toot, tooooooot, "Hello…" Keira blew two short and one long before she would call out and listen. Toot, toot, tooooooot, "Hello…" It became a pattern. Toot, toot, tooooooooot, "Hello…" Ten, fifteen, twenty minutes passed. Toot, toot, tooooooooot, "Hello…"

No answer.

. . .

Angela's lungs were going to explode. She gagged and struggled for air. The salty water burned her throat. She sank, unable to hold on to anything. Suddenly, her head and shoulders broke through a wave. She choked and sucked in half a breath before going under again. This time she fought for the surface, determined to stay there.

Something brushed past her, knocking her a few feet backward. Even in the dark, Angela made out enough of the shadowy form to identify her attacker. Too terrified to scream, she backpedaled away from the whale, stopping only when her head bumped against something hard. Despite the dizzying pain, she hauled herself upon it—whatever *it* was. Her eyes registered the word, Kawasaki. Her ears rang, like someone blowing a whistle. She wished it would stop. She got sick, threw up, and then nothing.

. . .

More than two hours passed with no sound other than the oars slapping the water and Keira's whistle. It had been a while since she had bothered to call out. No one answered. No one was there. As if it were a mutual decision, they stopped. Mitchell quit rowing. Keira took the whistle from her mouth. They sat in complete and utter silence.

ANGELA

CHAPTER 4

Nolan Woods loved the morning. The predawn hour before sunrise belonged to him. It gave him a sense of peace before anybody had a chance to crap on his day. He readied his speedboat with quick efficiency, having no plans to sail or fish. Today, he wanted to chase seagulls and race the dawn.

For the moment he wasn't Lexie's father, or Jackie's ex. He wasn't the owner of the Summer Shack Bar and Grill. Not today. Not yet, anyway. Today he was Nolan. Wind rider. Dawn chaser.

He pulled away from the dock, heading toward the open sea. Pushing his speed because he could. He didn't have to answer questions or make any decisions other than how hard to mash the gas.

Nolan was there waiting when the sun peeked over the horizon. It was a moment of empowerment; life. He paused, seeing something in the distance he couldn't identify beyond a bulk of bright red, bobbing where nothing should be.

Squinting didn't help. He idled the engine and located his binoculars. It appeared to be a pile of rags riding a jet ski. Why was it there? Who would lose an expensive piece of equipment like that and not notice? He didn't want to leave it floating. It looked new. Somebody had to be missing it. He shifted into gear and angled toward it.

A minute and a half later, what he saw registered. "SHIT!" That pile of rags was a person—in bad shape. He gunned the motorboat.

Coming alongside the jet ski, Nolan saw a woman. He hoped she was unconscious and not dead. She had dried blood, from a gash on her head, caked on the side of her face. She wasn't wearing a swimsuit. He doubted she'd been joyriding. Even torn, speckled with vomit and more blood, her clothes were expensive. A shoeless foot dangled in the water. Nolan thought she was lucky not to be missing a foot.

He pulled her into his boat, relieved to find her pulse. He tied her bright red, makeshift life raft to his boat and gunned it toward Eellek, his peninsula on Stock Island, Lower Keys, Florida.

■ ■ ■

She was drowning, fighting the dark. She couldn't get to the surface. No air. Struggling. Thrashing against the pressure, consumed with terror. She couldn't get out. Couldn't break free...

"Shh... It's all right. Shh... Shh... Calm down. Calm down."

Angela blinked. Nothing made sense. A man. A person. A human. "Mitch?! Mitch?!" Darkness...

"It's okay. You will be okay."

His voice soothed her. Crying, Angela threw herself at him. Grasped his neck, clung to him. She wasn't alone. She didn't understand anything, but she wasn't alone.

He held her, soothed her. Let her cry.

■ ■ ■

It was hot. Smothering. The moisture was gone from her mouth and her skin itched. She couldn't take a deep breath. There was no air to breathe. Angela opened her eyes. It wasn't dark; she wasn't drowning. She was in somebody's bed. The curtains were left open, making the room too bright. She turned her head and blinked several times, adjusting to the light. The walls were a dull, flat grey. A dresser, a chair, a door—it was a room with no identity.

She ran her tongue across her teeth and her hand across her forehead, trying to find some moisture. She discovered a dry, hot bandage. The activity wore her out.

The thoughts and memories that came with alertness took hold, overwhelming her. Tears rolled unnoticed down her cheeks. She cringed, wanting to stop her mind from going back to the last things she recalled.

The bedroom door opened, startling her. A little girl, about eight or nine stood in the doorway. A tight, disapproving frown dominated her face. Her blue eyes were missing their sparkle. Her hair was sectioned into two pigtails. The baby blonde was beginning to grow out. From her crumpled appearance, Angela guessed she'd been in her clothes awhile. She had a torn backpack hanging from one shoulder and a small suitcase at her feet.

They stared at one another for a long minute.

When no acknowledgment came, Angela sized up the situation. She cleared her throat and said, "Am I in your room?"

The child's disapproval became disdain. "Right. I don't care who you are. You ain't that important." She picked up her suitcase and walked away.

Angela stared at the empty spot. "Well, excuse you." She didn't have time to dwell on it. Footsteps sounded in the hall and a man ducked through the doorframe carrying a tray of food.

"Hello. I hoped you'd be awake." She remembered seeing his gentle smile before. He helped her to sit up and positioned the tray across her lap. "I'm Nolan. We can talk while you eat, or I can come back later."

She shook her head. "Nolan. Thank you." She meant for everything. "I'd like to talk."

"Good." He adjusted her pillows to support her back. "But only if you eat. It's been an ordeal for you, Mrs. Pointe."

"You know me?" She picked up the spoon and dipped it into a savory broth. Her stomach growled in anticipation. She looked up, embarrassed.

He moved a small plate of crackers forward. "Yes, ma'am. Your accident is all over the news. Do you recall talking to the coastguard?"

She shook her head, confirming his suspicion.

He reached into his pocket and withdrew her cell phone. "I hope you don't mind, but after it dried, I spoke with your sister. I didn't want your family to worry." He laid it on the nightstand, within her reach. "Deidra is coming down. She said for you to call as soon as you're up to it."

"I'm grateful you did. I'll call her in a minute. Can you tell me what happened?"

"What they've pieced together so far is a whale landed on your yacht and wrecked it trying to get away."

"More than one."

"Judging from the damage, they were big. Sperm or blue. They may have been fighting."

"Two, three. I don't know what kind or how many. But I was right there, in the water with them." She hadn't realized her hands were shaking until he slid the spoon from her fingers and dipped her next mouthful himself. Helpless, Angela allowed it.

He talked while he fed her, treating it as normal. "The boat capsized, It was torn apart."

The images he produced collaborated with her horror. "Where's Mitchell?"

Nolan sucked in a breath. "I don't know."

"He's my husband. He'll be looking for me."

He nodded, not knowing what to say.

"Did they find everyone? Are people hurt?"

"The Captain and one crew member are dead. They're still looking for the others. I found you yesterday morning. It was a damned good thing you found that jet ski."

"Yesterday? I-I didn't go jet skiing." She shook her head. Her last memories did not include anything fun.

"Apparently, it found you. Do you remember how you ended up in the water?"

"I was by the rail, watching the whales." Her tears came again. "Stupid whales. I was going to take a picture. Something hit the boat and I fell overboard. One of those damned things was there—right there. It touched me. I tried.... I tried to get away, to find something to grab onto. That's all I remember." She touched the bandage again. "Did I bump my head?"

"Hard enough to give yourself a concussion. My brother's a doctor. He says you'll be all right. But you need a lot of rest."

They finished the remainder of the broth in silence. He held the glass but let her control it while drinking. She regained enough strength to finish the crackers on her own.

"Did you find me?"

"I did. I like to go boating early. I caught sight of you floating on your jet ski and hauled you in."

"Thank you for saving me." Her eyelids drooped.

Nolan marveled at how fast the medication he put in her soup took effect. He moved the empty tray out of her way and eased her back down. "You're welcome. Try to sleep now."

"Nolan."

"Yes, ma'am?"

"Where am I?"

"You're safe."

"Am I?"

"Yes, ma'am. I'll see to that."

"Thank you." The medicine took over. Angela fell into a blessedly forgetful sleep.

. . .

"How long is she going to be here?" Lexie waited for Nolan at the top of the stairs.

"Did you get unpacked? Got everything you need? Forget anything?"

"I forgot to stay home," she snapped. "Otherwise, I'm fine. Except you have company. How long is she going to be here?"

Nolan headed down the steps. "You hungry? Did you go say hello to your grandmother?"

Lexie followed him down. "You were busy feeding her," she pointed at the tray, "and didn't care if I starved."

"Lexie, honey, I have a house full of food. I picked up all your favorites. You're old enough to say when you're hungry. You can get to Mammaw's house in less than a minute. You'll only starve because you want to. I'm going to make a sandwich. Do you want one?"

"No. I'm going to go say hi to Mammaw."

Nolan watched his daughter leap off the front steps and race up the hill to Mammaw Hilda's house, Eellek Enn. The bed and breakfast was the town's singular accommodation for visitors—not that they got very many. The island was less than a blip on the map with Key West so close. Besides Eellek Enn and the Summer Shack, there were four other businesses on the peninsula: a Ron-Jon Surf Shop, a Quik Mart, KW's Garage, and Eellek Alley—ten pin bowling. The Overseas Highway made all things accessible. The only people inhabiting the bedroom community were recluses or relatives and descendants of recluses.

Lexie got angry when Nolan and Jackie split. She was getting worse with each visit. Every week she would call him wanting to come home. As soon as she arrived, she wanted to leave. He didn't know how to help her.

He wanted to help the woman upstairs. Her helplessness tugged at his heart. He found her, he owed it to her. She trusted him. Not that she had a choice, but she did it with a natural acceptance as if it had always been. He liked it despite the guilt of deriving pleasure from another person's unfortunate circumstance. It seemed kind of low in his opinion. He removed the guilt by ignoring it. He thought about his good deed, instead.

CHAPTER 5

"That you, Nolan?" Hilda's house was echoic without guests. The Enn— she named it—had always been an inn, not some restored manor or converted plantation home. Nolan's great-grandfather blew his bank account purchasing it and the twenty-one acres it stood on for a whopping thirty-six hundred dollars. He was never inclined to do much beyond upkeep. Four generations later, the tradition remained. It had twelve-foot ceilings, archways, brick fireplaces, polished wood floors, a wine cellar, a veranda, and a panoramic view with no equal.

Nolan came in through the kitchen and found the back of his mother sticking out of the hall closet. "What are you doing?" He walked up behind her to look in at a mass of boxes, bags, and other junk.

"Lexie can't find the cord to one of her thingies. If I have it, then it has to be in here."

"Because you put everything in there."

"When I want something I know where to look." Hilda Woods was sixty-two going on sixteen by her reckoning. It made her proud. She loved her hippie-vibe and planned to be buried in a tie-dyed T-shirt. Her marriage to Nolan's father was common law and rocky at best. They were both wild and careless when Nolan and his brother Robert were growing up. After a great while, he became something he called responsible, and she called old. They drifted apart and lived separate lives. When he died from tuberculosis, she hardly noticed, as her lifestyle remained unaffected.

"Do you know what you're looking for?"

"No. But I figured if I come across something fitting the description that I can't identify, I found it."

"Good plan."

"How is Mrs. Pointe?"

"Coming around. I only talked to her for a few minutes. Haven't told her anything yet."

"Poor lady. Last report I saw hadn't turned up anything new. Most likely they'll end the search within the next few days."

"Most likely."

Hilda straightened up with a handful of tangled cords. "These look like anything to you?"

"A mess." Nolan took them from her. "Lexie!" He directed his voice to the high-vaulted ceiling.

While waiting for her granddaughter to appear, Hilda said, "Are you going to call someone to let them know she's awake?"

"Already did. Rob's on his way and somebody from the coastguard will be here in about a half hour. Her sister should arrive sometime soon. That's why I'm here. Keep three eyes on Lexie, would you? I don't know who all will be around. With my luck, one of her outbursts would make the six o'clock news."

"Why are you always talking about me?" Lexie huffed as she came up beside them.

Hilda took it in stride. "Who more important to talk about? Any of these work?"

Nolan held up the tangled mass for Lexie to inspect.

The child hunched her shoulders. "I don't know. I can't tell what's what. It's a ball of knots. Can we go buy me a new one?"

"Sure."

"No."

Hilda and Nolan spoke at the same time. Amid the double glare, he amended. "Mammaw did a lot of work on your behalf. The least you can do is attempt to see if your cord is in here." He handed Lexie the pile. "Go through it. If you can't find it after you've put up the effort, one of us will take you to get a new one."

Lexie frowned. "One of us. You mean Mammaw will take me. If I have to wait for you, I won't ever get to play my game."

"Do you have to have a negative comment for everything, Lexie?"

"Yes." Lexie walked away, the tail of the massive tangle of cords trailing behind her.

"That was positive," Hilda said with a satisfied nod.

. . .

Hilda gave Nolan enough time to get back to his business before she searched Lexie out. The child was in the dining room, struggling to free the cords. "Are you ready?"

"For what?"

"To go get you a new cordy-thing. Unless you want to play with that mess."

"No, but Daddy said I had to try."

"You did. I saw you. Let's go."

Lexie dropped the cords and pushed herself from the table.

The doorbell rang.

"What now?" The child huffed.

"Hold that thought and we'll find out." Hilda did an about-face, intent on investigating.

It was a tall black woman, dressed to the hilt and made up impeccably as if she had come to pose for a magazine cover. "Hello. My name is Deidra Jefferies. I'm trying to locate Mr. Nolan Woods."

"Oh. Yes, ma'am." Hilda opened the door wide. "You must be Mrs. Pointe's sister. Come on in. Where are your bags?"

"Thank you. I have a small case in my car. I'll get it later. I'm anxious to see my sister."

"I imagine so. I'm Hilda." She held out her hand and added, "Nice to meet you," when Deidra shook it. "I'm Nolan's mom. Your sister is down at his house. I'll take you right over." Observing as Deidra stepped across the threshold, Hilda amended to herself that the woman wasn't as tall as she first assumed. However, her shoes were; the lady was strutting about in six-inch heels.

"Mam...maw?" Lexie followed Hilda into the hallway.

"Lex...ie." Hilda imitated her granddaughter's impatience. "What do you want me to do? Leave her standing here until we get back?" Turning back toward Deidra, Hilda said, "This is my grandbaby, Alexis. We call her Lexie."

"Hi, Lexie." Deidra pretended to be interested in the child.

"Hi." Lexie greeted and dismissed her in one word. To her grandmother she said, "Can you hurry up? Please."

"No. My idea. My timetable. Come on, Ms. Jefferies. Follow me."

"Call me Deidra. Please. I appreciate everything you've done for Angela."

"We're happy to help out." Hilda's voice faded down the hallway with Deidra beside her.

Games, cords, and trips to the store all momentarily forgotten, Lexie followed in their wake.

■   ■   ■

"Nice to meet you." Upon Hilda's introduction, Nolan extended his hand to Deidra. The sisters were different, he noted. Similar eye color and skin tone, but Angela was shorter and curvier, with an athletic build. This woman was thin and angular, a blueprint for models. Different, yet both were hauntingly beautiful to him.

She bypassed his fingers to embrace him. "Thank you. Thank you for saving my sister." She immediately began to cry. "I'm so thankful. If…If… Thank you."

Nolan awkwardly patted her back until she pulled away from him. "Angela is fine. She's going to be okay."

Deidra nodded. She wiped at her eyes. "I'm sorry. This is so overwhelming."

"Understandable."

"I want you to know how grateful I am for what you've done. She's the only real family I have."

"She'll be happy you're here. She's medicated, but I'm sure she'll wake up for you."

Hilda entered the conversation. "Some people coming over to talk with her. See if she can help them with the search. It would be better for you to see her first. Help her through it."

Deidra nodded again. "Where is she?"

"Second door on the left." Nolan pointed up the steps, intending for her to ascend alone.

.   .   .

"Deidra!"

"Angela!"

Deidra flew across the room and flung herself across the bed, across her younger sister. "Oh my God, Angela! Thank God you're alive." They hugged and held and cried on each other.

"I'm okay. I'm good. I'm good—"

"I was so scared for you—"

"I'm sorry. I'm so sorry..."

"No. No. No. Don't be. I'm so glad you're okay. I couldn't live without you."

"I'm sorry. I'm sorry..."

Raw emotion covered every thought, colored every word. After several long, hard minutes of acceptance and relief, they separated. Deidra pulled back far enough to focus on Angela's face. They cried and smiled through their tears.

"Mitch?" Nolan didn't have an answer, but Deidra would. There was hope in not knowing. But hope wasn't enough. With her sister's arrival and the flood of emotions, Angela couldn't wait. She needed something more than hope.

A fresh wash of tears trickled down Deidra's cheek.

Angela's heart broke with the realization that she already knew.

"He's gone, Ange. I'm sorry."

Again, they hugged and held and cried on each other. This time without happiness.

CHAPTER 6

The condo was without sound. Day to day to day, Angela hardly ever made a sound. The can opener. The dryer. The shower. Were they real sounds? They only lasted a moment and were gone. Just like Mitchell. She didn't go to work. She didn't watch television. She didn't read or think or make a sound.

Angela didn't know how long she had been a widow. The search had been called off, but she couldn't recall when. She attended the memorial service, although she had nothing to do with the preparations. Deidra or Mitchell's parents—she didn't know who planned it. She didn't know anything. Her days were long and slow, without a sound, without Mitchell, without anything.

.   .   .

The rain came down hard, bouncing off the hood in spiky points and gushing down the windows like a high-powered car wash. She may have been at a car wash for all the attention Angela paid. She hadn't come up with one thought she wanted to dwell on. So she didn't. She didn't dwell. She didn't cry. She didn't remember. She didn't focus. Deidra called it depression. She left it to Deidra's judgment. Deidra told Angela to consider getting away for a while. Angela took it as a directive. She packed—sort of. She filled two suitcases with clothes and toiletries, locked the condo and left. She didn't plan a destination, she just went. When her sister called to check on her before going to bed the first night, Angela didn't mention she'd been on the road for three hours. Nor did she explain she couldn't meet her for lunch the next day. Deidra wanted to eat at one of their usual spots in DC. Angela was currently driving through Emporia, Virginia.

Angela drove. She stopped when she was hungry or tired or in need of a restroom. Sometimes she turned the radio on, sometimes not. She didn't recall tapping the screen. She didn't dwell on it. She didn't know what she ate. She survived by merely repeating to the server the first words she noticed on the menu, then she promptly forgot what she said.

She should have been surprised to turn into the drive, to stare at the antiquated bed-and-breakfast. She may have wondered why she came. She didn't. She didn't care why. She stopped the car and sat there, in the torrential downpour, facing the house beside the Enn without a plan, without a purpose, without a husband, without a thought.

.　　.　　.

Nolan saw the headlights and wondered who wanted what from him tonight. He waited by the door, anticipating the knock. After what he judged to be an adequate amount of time for someone to get from the car to his porch, he opened the door to peek out. "All right," he said to no one. He opened the door wide enough for light to spill out. The visitor could see him waiting. Still nothing. "All right." He stepped onto the porch. The wind blew sideways, pelting him with cold droplets. His irritation escalated. If this wasn't invitation enough, they didn't need to be here. If he came off his porch, they were getting the hell out of his drive. Nolan determined that as he stomped down the steps with his fists clenched.

Right away he noticed the plates. His mind made the connection as his feet pulled him through puddles with quick strides.

Angela watched him advance with distracted curiosity. *He was barefoot.* Belatedly, it occurred to her to roll down the window.

"Angela?"

"Why are you barefoot?"

"Why are you here?"

"I don't know."

His brows furled. "Do you want to come in?"

She didn't acknowledge or respond, but robotically got out of the car and waiting for him to tell her what to do.

Concern surged to the forefront of his consciousness. She seemed to be oblivious to the fact they were getting drenched. "Do you have a bag?"

"Two of them."

It only took a half a beat to realize she wasn't going to add anything. He had to keep them from drowning. "Give me your keys." Her instant obedience prompted him to instruct her. "Go into the house, Angela. I'll get your things."

"Okay."

He had voice control. He spoke, she moved. Nolan popped her trunk and retrieved her suitcases, wondering what made her come to him. This dead woman.

She stood in his foyer.

"Sit down, Angela." Nolan kicked the door closed behind him. "I'll get you a towel." He watched her take a seat and wait for his next command. "Do you want a drink?"

"Okay."

"Relax."

She leaned back into the cushions.

He returned with a steaming mug of hot chocolate in each hand. She accepted the offered cup and drank in silence, unmindful of the heat. She stared out at nothing with flat, dead eyes.

What to do? What to do? Hmmm… what to say? Nolan couldn't answer that question, but he contemplated it, flipping it over in his head as he watched the dead woman watching nothing. He noticed her eyelids were heavy and concluded now was not the best time for conversation. "Finish your drink, Angela, and we'll see about getting you to bed."

She gulped down the remaining three quarters. He hadn't taken one sip of his yet. He got up and offered her a hand, marveling that it only took a second for her fingers to touch his. Her quick response intrigued him. Her mind had disengaged, but she remained attuned to him.

Back in his spare bedroom, he laid her down, tugged off her shoes, and pulled a blanket over her. He wondered if anyone knew Angela's whereabouts, but doubted it. "I'll call your sister."

"My phone is in my purse. Left side pocket." Angela closed her eyes and fell asleep.

Damn.

Deidra's sleepy voice answered on the second ring. "Hey. What's up?"

"Deidra, this is Nolan Woods."

She raised herself into a sitting position. "Pardon me?"

"Nolan Woods, from Stock Island."

"Yes, I'm sorry, Nolan. You surprised me. You have Angie's phone?"

"I do. She's here. Given the state she's in, I guessed you may not have been aware."

"Angela's on Stock Island? Are you kidding me? I saw her yesterday. I talked to her today. She didn't mention flying down there."

"She didn't fly, she drove."

"She drove?"

"She's not functioning well. She may be in a state of shock. If you don't have any objections, I'll have my brother look at her in the morning."

"No, no. That might be for the best. I'm sure you're right, anyway. She hasn't been able to get past the search being called off. Well, whatever, I'll come down to get her as soon as I can arrange a flight."

"No. Don't." He shook his head as he spoke. "Don't upset your schedule. She came here for a reason. Let's wait until we figure out why. At least, wait until we see what Robert has to say. The change of scenery might do her some good."

Deidra thought about it. "The exact advice I gave her. Of course, I wasn't expecting her to act upon it within the hour. But I don't want to put you out. You've done more than enough for our family."

"Nonsense, there's plenty of room. If it helps, it helps. That's what important."

"Thank you, Nolan. And thank you for calling. Will you let me know what your brother says?"

"As soon as he sees her."

"Thank you."

CHAPTER 7

Angela blinked the room into focus. She didn't wonder about being in Nolan Woods' guest room. It was a relief to wake up and not see Mitch's pillows, or his nightstand, or his dresser, or anything that filled her first thoughts with pain. Waking up in Nolan's guest room had no misery attached. She eased out of bed, fearing sudden movement would change the scenery.

The door flung open. Nolan's daughter stood in the frame, Pj's askew and hair disheveled. She gripped a stuffed elephant that had suffered from the acquaintance. Her blue eyes were wide with surprise. The guest room door was open when she went to bed. It should still be that way. She hadn't expected to see Angela. "Sorry," she muttered and shut herself out. "Daddddd!"

Nolan heard her from the back porch. He would have heard her from anywhere in the house. "I'm not deaf, Lexie. Good morning."

"What's she doing here?"

"Good morning, Lexie."

Lexie huffed.

Nolan remained silent.

"Good morning."

"Ah. Much better. Would you like some breakfast? I made some bacon."

"I'll get it." She pouted.

Lexie and her elephant retreated to the kitchen. Nolan shook his head. Her teenage years were going to be hell.

She came back with a bacon sandwich and a glass of milk and sat on the steps watching him clean and organize his equipment from his morning boat ride.

"What are you going to do today?"

"I don't know."

"I'm going to do some crabbing. You interested?"

"That's boring."

"I'll be at the Shack for a while. Do you want to hang down there with me?"

"No."

"I'm glad you don't have plans because Uncle Rob's coming over. He's bringing somebody for you to meet."

"Who is it?"

"It's a kid. Rob calls him Tank. He's about your age. Rob's hoping that you'll make friends with him."

"Whatever." Lexie hated to agree, but there weren't many kids on Eellek. Nobody turned down the opportunity to make a friend.

"Good," Nolan said. "Oh. I don't know if you know, but we have company. Mrs. Pointe is back. I expect you to be respectful to her."

"What'd she come back for?" Lexie understood how it worked. If she wanted answers, she had to use the proper tone.

"I'm not sure. She got in late. We haven't talked yet."

"How long is she going to be here?"

"I don't know. Does it matter?"

"It's my summer vacation here. Not hers."

"She's not interrupting your vacation."

"What if I want to do something with you and I can't because she's here?"

"You can do anything you want with me. Crabbing. Summer Shack. Anything you don't say no to."

Lexie scowled.

. . .

Not long after, Angela stepped out onto the back porch. Nolan noted the dark circles under her eyes. "Good morning. Did you sleep okay?"

"Yes." She looked down. "I slept fine. Thank you. Thank you for letting me stay."

"You're always welcome. Lexie, did you say good morning to our guest?"

"Morning." At first, Lexie didn't turn around. A glare from Nolan prompted her to swing around and ask, "How long are you going to be here... visiting?"

Angela quirked an eyebrow. "I'm leaving now. That should make you happy."

"Leaving?" Nolan repeated. "You just got here. Come on. Let's have a cup of coffee." He climbed the steps and held the door for her. "I'll make you breakfast. Lexie, honey, get dressed. Rob should be here soon."

"To see her."

"He's bringing Tank with him, to see you."

Without another word, Lexie left them.

"Rob is coming by to check on you." Nolan reached for two mugs. "I told Deidra I'd give her a call once he did."

Angela sank into the nearest chair. She didn't like having her day scheduled without her consent. But what could she say? She did drive through five states for no apparent reason. Perhaps someone should schedule her day. "You talked to Deidra?"

He sat her mug in front of her. "I thought she might get worried." He busied himself with toast, preferring to wait until she was ready to talk.

She did not talk, preferring to wait until he asked her something.

He could wait longer than she could. His lack of questions made her eager to tell him. "I don't know why I came down here." She studied her coffee. "I'm sorry for intruding. I didn't plan it, or I would have called. I just got in the car and drove."

"You're not an intrusion." He came over with two plates of bacon and buttered toast.

"Thank you." She gave him a half smile and reached for the meat. "I guess I needed... I don't know what I needed. Maybe to get away. Find a place that wasn't connected to my past or how it used to be... I guess. I wasn't thinking about anything."

"What about now?"

Her smile grew bigger. "So far, no."

He liked her smile. Her lips were full with some fancy lipstick artfully smeared across them. "Not much around here to hold your attention, anyway."

"Your daughter would rather I not linger."

"It's not you, it's me she's mad at."

"She'd rather be mad at you without an audience."

"Her anger is not going to change because you're here; you might as well stay." Nolan had no idea he was going to say that, but the moment he did, he realized it was a good idea.

Their eyes locked.

"I don't even know why I'm here."

"Stay at least until you get that much figured out."

She liked the idea. "I feel terrible, imposing on you like this."

"Not at all. It's nice to have you here. I planned to call to see how you were making out." He didn't know why he told her that, but when her smile touched her eyes, he was glad he did.

"I'm not making out too good."

"Nonsense. This isn't easy for you."

"It's not easy. But it should be something. That's the problem: Nothing means anything. I can't function. I don't fit into my life. I can't do anything."

"You shouldn't have to do anything," he said, "Not yet."

A booming voice calling for Lexie interrupted them. Nolan raised his voice to match. "We're in the kitchen."

Moments later, Rob Woods strolled into the kitchen looking more like a biker than a doctor. His jeans were faded and his leather jacket hung open to reveal a Harley T-shirt. He had the same blue eyes as his brother, although Nolan's were darker. Same hazel-brown hair; Rob's appeared to be under the care of a more expensive barber. Angela guessed their ages to be within a year or two—Nolan seemed older. Rob was taller, but not by much. Both men had a lot of muscle. Hard work and/or hard fun was not a foreign concept to either of them.

A gangly kid whose arms and legs seemed to be growing faster than the rest of him peeked from behind Rob. The child's hair was disheveled. He wore part of his breakfast on his shirt, and he had the wide-eyed wonderment of someone impressed with the world around him. He waved excitedly.

"Hi." Angela fell in love with him.

Rob put a hand on his shoulder, bringing him forward. "Good morning. Tank, this is Miss Angela, and this is my brother, Mr. Nolan. This is my buddy, Tank. He's staying with me for a while."

"Forever," Tank corrected.

"Possibly forever."

Lexie walked into the room. "Why?"

Instead of answering, Rob said, "Tank, this is Lexie. She's my niece."

"I know. You told me."

Tank and Lexie sized each other up while the grown-ups watched. Lexie made the first move. "I have games. Half of them are at my grandmother's, but that's next door."

"We can play."

"Have you ever been crabbing?"

"Uh-uh."

"I'm gonna check my dad's traps. You can come see if you want."

"I want to see."

Lexie turned to Nolan. "Is that okay?"

"Yes, ma'am. I appreciate it."

She nodded and made for the back door with Tank following. She paused at the counter, snagging two pieces of leftover bacon and offered one to Tank. "Sometimes my dad makes a whole pack of bacon in the morning and you have to keep eating it until it's gone."

Tank shoved it into his mouth. "I like bacon."

Rob reached for the coffee. "He likes bacon. He likes anything that goes in your mouth. That kid eats nonstop."

CHAPTER 8

Nolan occupied himself while Rob gave Angela an examination and followed it with a short consultation. While Angela was upstairs, he shared his opinions with Nolan. "Post-traumatic stress. A touch of emotional amnesia. The former is to be expected given her ordeal. The latter is only as it pertains to her husband. I want to watch her for a while."

Nolan made a face. "I was not with you a single day in medical school. What's emotional amnesia?"

"Good thing. Then I would have had to study. Emotional amnesia is when you lose or block the emotions tied to certain memories. In her case, her husband. How it felt when he gave her a back rub or massaged her feet. She can recall the event, but she has no connection to it. Her memories are like a story she's been told, not something she's lived. "

"Does she need any medication?"

"If it comes to it, I'll give her a prescription—something to help her relax. But I'm not ready to do that yet. She said she slept fine last night. Change of scenery might be all she needs."

"That's what I thought."

"I told her she could stay with Mom. She'll be able to rest. I can keep an eye on her and you won't be put out."

"Put out? Why would I be put out? I already invited her to stay here."

Rob arched an eyebrow at Nolan's tone.

Nolan arched an eyebrow at Rob's raised eyebrow. "What?"

"What are you getting testy about? Everybody knows you don't like having people around. Besides, Mom has nine extra rooms and Lexie would be happier having you all to herself."

Nolan did not know what he was getting testy about. The Enn was in his backyard. Lexie *would* be happier with that arrangement. It was the point of the matter. It wasn't Rob's business to reassign his houseguest.

Rob, more astute than Nolan was comfortable with, said, "Your carnal reasons for wanting her here should wait, anyway. She's not ready." He turned away before Nolan answered, talking over his shoulder as he strode down the hall. "I'll keep Lexie with me today. Take them sailing. We'll meet you at the Shack for dinner."

Nolan was still stuck on the 'carnal reasons' comment. He didn't have carnal reasons. Rob was an ass. Nolan put his effort into regaining his composure.

A few minutes later, Angela came down the steps lugging her suitcases.

"What are you doing?" He met her at the bottom step.

"Dr. Rob thinks I should stay here awhile. For some reason, this place soothes me."

He watched her descend and a few carnal reasons flitted through his mind. *She was hot.* "If Rob thinks you should stay, what are you doing with your suitcases?"

"I'm taking them over to the Enn. I don't want to impose on you."

He reached for the handles, covering her hands with his. "You're not an imposition. I invited you."

"You'd be too much of a gentleman to tell me if I was. I'll feel better about being underfoot by not being... underfoot." She amused herself with her wording.

"Fine." He took both suitcases from her. "We'll get you settled in over there, but you can come back any time you want."

"I will keep that in mind." She followed him out.

"Definitely keep that in mind. After two days with my mother, you'll be looking for a place to hide."

"Nolan. Your mother is very nice."

"Most crazy people are."

. . .

Hilda was delighted to have Angela. She shooed Nolan off to work and settled Angela into what she considered to be her best room overlooking both the garden and a peaceful shaded inlet. They shared the dinner chores and chatted while they relaxed in rockers on the front porch while the palm trees dotting the yard swayed in the ocean breeze. Hilda was over-sharing the details of a unique week she spent with a trucker when Nolan pulled into the drive.

"I'm sorry, Angela. I had no idea it was this late." Hilda stood up. "Why did you let me talk your poor ears off? You probably wanted to go to bed hours ago."

"No, no," Angela shook her head. "Is it late? I'm not even tired."

"It's after ten." Hilda nodded her head at Nolan's back. He was hunched over the back seat. "He never leaves the Shack before ten. If Lexie weren't with him, he would have closed the place himself."

Pulling his sleeping daughter from the back of the car, Nolan positioned her over his shoulder with ease. He waved to the women but moved quickly to his abode.

"He loves Lexie more than anything." Hilda leaned against the railing. "He was beat up when Jackie left him, but he puts his energy into Lexie. So I guess that's a good thing."

"She seems like a sweet kid." Angela was impressed with her easy lie.

"Who are you kidding? Lexie is a beast."

That made Angela chuckle. "I was trying to be gracious."

"Don't bother. We deal in reality around here. Don't get me wrong, I love her to death. But they've spoiled her rotten. Especially Nolan. When he and Jackie split, Lexie took it upon herself to beat them both up for it. We love her and let her fight. Sooner or later, she'll get tired of fighting and realize we love her anyway. Oh, as long as you're here—and you're welcome to stay here as long as you like—don't put up with any of her sass. Lexie is not in charge of anything. She needs to understand that on all fronts. She can be mad as hell for as long as she likes, but we don't allow her to manipulate people with it. If we did, she'd never grow out of it and the real world would kick her little ass."

"Thank you. I'll keep that in mind."

"I'm serious. She's only four feet tall. Don't let her forget it."

"Yes, ma'am."

"And on that note, I am going to take my sorry self to bed."

"I'm going to stay up a bit, if that's all right."

"You do whatever you like. You're home. Goodnight darlin'."

Those simple words touched Angela in a way few things had lately. She didn't know where to put her gratitude. "Thank you."

Hilda patted her shoulder in understanding. "I'm so glad you're here." She went inside, leaving Angela to the night and her thoughts.

The sound of the waves was such a constant it was easy to forget. Until all other sounds ceased except the cascading crash echoing… Angela had a new attachment to the water. She suspected it was the primary reason she came back to Florida: to be near the water. She neither hated nor liked the ocean. It was more that part of her was still there, out in the deep, in the dark, trying to find a shore. At the same time, she wasn't going in. She'd never set foot in the ocean again. If she did, it would swallow her, and she'd never get back. Instead of going in, she had to linger on the edge, waiting for herself to find a way out.

Nolan watched Angela from his window. She was so still that he might have thought she fell asleep, except she held herself rigid—not one muscle relaxed. And she never moved. He sensed she needed him.

He came around the side of the Enn and climbed the steps to the wide porch. If his appearance surprised Angela, it didn't show. Her eyes were vacant, still in another place. But she smiled when he called her name.

"Did you fall asleep?"

"No. I wish I could."

"Do you want to take a walk? Stretching your legs might help."

"Sounds good." Angela enjoyed being around Nolan. He made her feel safe.

Nolan's house and Eellek Enn were at the end of the road, a cul-de-sac of sorts. There was a lot of vacant property belonging to the Woods family with palm trees and meadows and grassy fields full of wildflowers and exotic plant life. The next nearest dwelling was at the head of the street. The beautifully landscaped mansion belonging to Dr. Robert Woods dwarfed all the other residences on the island.

According to Nolan, Hilda hated it. She called it the eyesore. She hated the statue fountains. She hated the circular drive. She hated the gardens; all her flowers came from those gardens. She especially hated the pool; she hated it twice a week when she did laps. She loathed his six-car garage. Ever since her last accident, he kept her motorcycle under lock and key. So far, she'd had four failed attempts at breaking and entering.

Beyond Rob's house were the makings of what the locals referred to as the town. The lights from the Quik Mart stood out against the darkness. KW's and Eellek Alley were long since locked up and their owners asleep. Further down, on the opposite side of the road, neon green flashed, signifying that the Summer Shack was still open for business.

They didn't walk that far. Instead, they cut across Rob's impeccably manicured lawn to stroll down the beach. They talked about nothing of real relevance, just odd collections of details that made them who they were.

"We call this the Willow Inlet." Nolan led Angela to a hidden glade behind the Enn that was curtained on two sides by a wall of willows. "You can't see anything from the house and this," he pointed to a tree stump that was as big as a table, "makes for a comfortable place to hide."

"Did you hide here often?"

His eyes lit up at some memory. "Only when I did something I had no business doing. Which was about every other day."

They worked their way back around to the Enn. Nolan paused at the bottom of the steps. "Are you tired enough for bed yet?"

"You would think I would be. I'm going to chill for a few minutes. But don't let me keep you awake. Thanks for walking with me. I had fun." She did. For a little while, she was a normal person, instead of some wretched soul whose life had been snatched away.

Nolan studied her. She was so fragile; anything could break her. As he mused, the realization came to him. "Why don't you come over to the house? You'll sleep better where you were."

"No. No, I couldn't—"

"Try it and see. If it doesn't work, who cares? It doesn't matter which room you use. As long as you get some rest."

Suddenly, she was tired. Hadn't she said she was going to chill because she wasn't sleepy? Not understanding her mind confused her. Nolan's advice was best. She trusted his judgment. "All right. Nothing like going against the doctor's orders and then disrespecting my hostess." She started up the steps. "Let me grab some pajamas."

He caught her by the hand, not wanting her to go into the house for fear she'd change her mind. "Naw. I'll find you something. You can come back over in the morning. And don't worry. All negative influences get blamed on me."

She entwined her fingers through his as they walked across the yard together. "Is that the usual?"

"That's been the usual for almost forty years. Can't imagine it changing now."

■　■　■

Angela slept fine. And so began a routine. Her days were spent reading, exploring, and hanging out with Hilda. Nolan covered her evenings. He put her to work waiting tables at the Summer Shack—something she took pleasure in, as neither he nor Hilda had yet to accept payment for her room and board (Darlin', you're home). She spent every night in Nolan's spare bedroom where she slept great.

The only thing Angela did not do was go on the water.

CHAPTER 9

Lexie watched. From a safe distance, she watched Mrs. Pointe with her dad. Sometimes she watched Angela interact with Mammaw, Uncle Rob, and Tank—Tank loved her. But mostly she watched Angela with her dad. They stayed up late, talking on the porch and the pier while he crabbed or fished and she flipped through magazines. Curious to know what went on when she wasn't around, a few times Lexie pretended to go to bed early to eavesdrop. To the best of her discernment, they didn't act any different when they were alone.

Lexie couldn't decide how she felt about Angela. She wasn't too annoying. She wasn't often in the way. Whenever she, Lexie, wanted someone's attention—her dad's or her grandmother's—Angela left the area. Even after Mammaw told Angela Lexie did it on purpose, Angela smiled and said it worked for both of them. Lexie wasn't sure what she meant, but Mammaw laughed, so it was most likely an insult.

Overall, Lexie couldn't find enough to dislike about her. Angela was black—she didn't know if that made her beautiful, but she seemed pretty enough, with brown eyes and thick spirally hair. Angela's hair was dark, not blonde like her mom's. It wasn't cut in layers, so the red highlights showed through. Lexie didn't think her mother was pretty anymore. Her hair wasn't soft and shiny like it used to be and her teeth were kind of yellow. Jackie's rounded belly stuck out. Instead of exercising she got high and watch TV. Sometimes, she didn't smell good.

In that area, Angela had her beat. Angela had everybody beat. Lexie would never admit it, but she thought Angela smelled like a flower that she wanted to keep inhaling. Sometimes she would sneak into Angela's room to spray her perfume and catch a whiff. When she grew up, she would get that exact scent, and she would wear it every day for the rest of her life.

There was one other thing perplexing about Mrs. Pointe. She didn't disregard Lexie. She wasn't inviting, but she never told her to go away or ignored her. Sometimes her mother ignored her, but whenever Lexie asked Angela a question, she got an answer. Not always a nice answer, but then, her questions weren't always nice either.

. . .

Angela opened the bathroom door and jumped a foot off the floor. Lexie stood in the doorway, her blue eyes wide and her frown prominent. "Good Lord, child, you almost gave me a heart attack."

Lexie didn't comment.

"I suppose you want something." Nolan's house had two and a half bathrooms. Each room at the Enn came with one, and there was one downstairs. It wasn't as if Lexie had to wait to pee.

"Dad and Mammaw and Uncle Rob and me and Tank are going down to the beach. Maybe some snorkeling. Dad told me to ask you if you wanted to come."

Angela, still trying to get her heart rate down, took a deep breath. "No, but thank you for asking."

"Dad told me to ask you."

"You did us both a favor by listening. If he had to do it himself, he wouldn't have taken no for an answer. Then we would be stuck with each other all day." She stepped around Lexie and moved off without a backward glance.

"What are you doing?"

Angela glanced up. There was Lexie. "Did you knock?"

"This room didn't use to belong to anybody."

"While I'm here, it belongs to me. I expect people to knock and wait until I invite them inside."

Lexie reached behind her and knocked twice on the now open door. She waited.

Angela smashed her lips together. She did not want to encourage the brat.

Still, Lexie waited.

"Are you waiting for me to say come in? A little late for that."

"They're your dumb rules." Lexie came further into the room. She didn't say anything as she inspected the walls. Only two pictures were hanging. One was an autographed group shot of the '72 Miami Dolphins. The other was of a Tequesta village. "I have an uncle who slept in this room for a while."

"Rob."

"Not him. He's a doctor. What would he need to stay in this rinky hole for? I meant my uncle Travis."

Realizing Lexie wanted an audience, Angela closed her book. "I haven't met him. Is he your mother's brother?"

"Eww. No. He was a surprise from my grandfather."

"I see."

"He was supposed to be getting to know people, 'cause Pop-pop was dying. The only person he wanted to know was Mommy. They spent a lot of time smoking pot and taking… naps." The very words insulted her.

"Is this something your dad would want you talking about?"

Lexie set her face in an arrogant sneer. "It's my family's business. I can tell it to whoever I like. Mammaw says, don't do it if you have something to hide."

Angela hunched her shoulders. It wasn't as if she had to care. "Is this why your parents got divorced?"

"Mostly. At first, we lived in Orlando. But then Uncle Travis started taking naps with other people. Then we moved to California. Naps. That's what they told me."

Angela studied the child. This was an intelligent kid. Even at nine, or however old she was at the time, she wouldn't have appreciated down-talking. "I wouldn't have gone for it either. Maybe they couldn't think of a decent way of putting it."

"Maybe they shouldn't have done it."

"You're right."

Lexie stared at Angela for a long moment. Then, without another word, she left.

That was Lexie's routine. She would appear, start a conversation, drop it, and disappear.

Angela was getting used to this tactic. Still, it made her frown. "Creepy," she mumbled and returned to her book. Her phone rang. The ringtone made her smile. "Hey, Deed."

Deidra was talking, but not to her.

"Also creepy." She hung up the phone.

.   .   .

Angela came through the living room, dusting. She used the orange polish for the coffee and end tables, drawn to the deep rich wood.

"Why are black people different?"

That came from nowhere. "Lexie?" Startled, Angela searched for the child.

Lexie pulled the curtains back from the bay window seat.

"Girl."

"I can see your skin, but why are Black people different?"

Angela sat the polish down. "Everybody is different. All races have their things. But, as a general rule, back people aren't different. White people are different."

Lexie snapped to attention.

"This is an overview. I'm using very general terms, understand?"

Lexie nodded.

"Generally speaking, there are two kinds of white people. One kind is just like everybody else. They try to love themselves and other people too. They listen and talk, learn and teach. They help and hurt—all the normal stuff."

"What's the other kind?"

"They don't understand everyone has equal value. A homeless man and a doctor are worth the same."

The kid squinted her brow. This was news.

"Some people get their value from devaluing others. They see things in terms of comparison: this is a better house, this is a better job, this is a better person. They can't win the competition unless they find or create a loser. They don't listen. They don't learn. And they don't help." Watching Lexie absorbing knowledge was the most rewarding thing Angela had ever experienced. "People from all races can be mean like that, but white people have the unique power to cause harm—that's what racism is. It's not saying, I hate black people, or Mexicans, or white people. Racism is having the power to harm an entire race. If they are the kind of white people who get their value from devaluing others, they cause a lot of harm. The problem, for people of color, is figuring out who's who because you all are white on the outside."

Lexie contemplated a moment, then made a face. "Mammaw said, yesterday, white people gave black people a rough day on purpose. It lasted four hundred years and still going. Today, black people ain't here for white people's shit. So don't try it."

Angela pressed her lips together to hold in her laugher. "That too."

"I read about slavery. Daddy told me what redlining was. I'm not here for white people shit either." Lexie closed the curtain.

"I appreciate it," Angela said. "Stop using swear words." The grin escaped, and the reprimand was lost.

.   .   .

To his credit, Nolan did not force a relationship on either of them. Angela accommodated Lexie's mood swings. Lexie usually remembered to be polite, and she was less guarded around their guest. It helped that Tank was an appendage—an appendage that could eat his weight in one sitting. The ten-year-old kept the balance of time and attention even.

Angela had been there for almost three weeks. It wasn't getting old at all. Thanks to her, Nolan began to enjoy the simple pleasure of living. It was pleasant to share his thoughts with her. Or listen to her ideas. It was nice to agree and fun to disagree every once in a while. Race was a vast frontier for them to explore. Learning to blur the lines might be hell for the country, but arousing in his house. It was good to be around a woman, catch her laughter, watch her eyes sparkle, inhale her perfume, and imagine how soft she was.

The experience was good for Lexie too. They didn't exactly get along, but he wanted Angela's influence for his daughter.

CHAPTER 10

Nolan lost count. He shoved the stack of tens he separated back into one pile and started over. *Ten, twenty, thirty, forty...* He watched her clean tables. Good. *Seventy, eighty, ninety...* He never had to ask her to do anything; she always worked. *One-twenty, one-twenty-five, one-thirty...* She leaned forward, soapy sponge in hand, scrubbing as if she thought she might uncover gold. *One-fifty-one, one-fifty-two, one-fifty-three...* She did all her chores that way. Each detail was important, she didn't overlook anything. Her energy was enough to make a person tired. *One-fifty, one-fifty-one, fifty-two, fifty-three, fifty-four...* She was lovely to watch. All curves and muscle and soft femininity. She had the best fitting jeans he'd ever laid eyes on. He laid his eyes on them every chance he got. *Crap.* He had to start over again.

"Oh, just go get it. You're starting to drool." Joey, his second in command, breezed past carrying a tray of glasses. "I'll lock up."

Angela's jeans made him impulsive. "Deal." He threw the money into the drawer and slammed it shut. "Hey, Angela, are you about ready?"

"Wow. You're done? I have four more tables to wipe down."

"Leave it. Somebody will get it. If not, they'll be here in the morning."

"You're the boss." She threw the sponge in her bucket.

Five minutes later they bid Joey and the remaining staff good night. Outside the air was mild, blowing in from the marshes.

"Are you tired? Do you want to go home?"

"I'm up for anything. I'm lamenting not grabbing something before the kitchen closed. I haven't snacked in at least an hour. I'm starved."

"You've got the right guy. I know a place that has excellent cold cuts and beer on hand."

"I'm not going to mess up Joey's kitchen."

"Not there." He nodded at the pub. "There's another place. It's about two minutes away. The best part is it's free."

"Mmmm. Sounds good. Where is this quality establishment?"

"Rob's house. He's not home. We can leave him the dishes."

"No dishes? In that case, lead the way."

. . .

He gave her a tour of his brother's estate. They raided the refrigerator and hung out in his game room playing table football.

"You're good at this," Nolan said after her second straight win.

"Every single group home Deidra and I lived in had at least one."

From the interviews after the rescue, Nolan knew she had no other relatives, but she hadn't spoken about it before now. "How many homes did you live in?"

"Six or seven. I don't remember." She moved over to Rob's ping pong table.

He followed her over and served first. "May I ask about your family?"

"You may." She slammed the ball hard enough to make him stretch. "No clue about our dad, or dads. One day, our mother took us to Social Service. She sat us in a chair and said she was going to the restroom." The ball bounced back and forth between them. "Or so we've been told. I wasn't quite a year yet and Deidra was two. We were lucky. They kept us together. We don't have any hard feelings or psychopathic tendencies I'm aware of. Just one of those unpleasant happenings in life."

"You seem healthy. Not a psychopathic tendency in sight." His serve whooshed past her.

She gave a girlish squeal that made him chuckle. "Healthy lungs too."

"I'll get you for that!"

The game ended when the last ping pong ball rolled under the sofa. "Do you want to move the couch, or move on to the next game?"

It was a three-piece reclining sectional. "No, thanks." She laid her paddle down and pointed to the pool table. I have no clue how to play this game, but I'm going to brutalize you."

"Brutalize me?" The idea wasn't at all unpleasant to him.

"Oh yeah. I'm dangerous."

It wasn't long before he discovered how dangerous. She repeatedly knocked the balls off the table and once lost her grip on the pool stick.

"You're not dangerous. You're a menace."

She laughed, agreeing with his assessment. "Mitch tried to teach me once. You can see how that turned out. That was before we stopped having fun." She paused. Her wood-brown eyes, glossed over with unshed tears, took on a smoky hue. "I'm sorry. That was ungracious of me." She laid her pool stick down and turned her back to him. "I shouldn't speak ill of the dead."

Likewise, Nolan set his stick aside. He joined Angela on her side of the table, leaning against the rail. "You're not ungracious. It's all right to speak the truth." He touched her shoulder. "Even about the dead."

Angela glanced at him and then away.

"Do you want to talk about it?"

She sighed. "I shouldn't think negatively about him."

"You can't feel guilty about that. He was human and so are you."

His compelling tone drew her in. "I had a great marriage. That can't be denied but... but sometimes, it wasn't good. I don't remember precisely how I felt at the time, but I...I recall not liking some of it. We had money and jobs and freedom. We bought stuff and did stuff and people were always envious. Mitch loved that. People envying the illusion we created. When I let myself dwell on it, I can see that's what it was: an illusion. He never forgot my birthday, but he couldn't remember to stop at the dry cleaners. The big deal things that everyone talked about—no problem. The little things... hanging out in the kitchen while I put away the dishes, teaching me to shoot pool or keeping a dumb promise—that was always missing. Part of me feels stupid and selfish. He did so many great things, why should I care about doing the dishes together? If I wanted one, he'd have gotten me a housekeeper." She shut up then.

Her rigid stance, the way she hugged herself, and her too-tight control told him she needed to talk. He let her.

"We wanted a baby. I'm not sure why Mitchell did—probably because it fit our success story image. No. I'm being petty. Sorry."

"Why did you want a baby?"

"Because I love children."

Nolan sensed there was more. He waited.

"Because a baby would need me and love me for all the little reasons nobody can see. But I'm out of luck there too." Now, the tears came. A soft trickle, rolling across her cheek. "I have what they call *unexplained infertility*. There's no medical reason why I can't conceive. No one can tell me how to fix it." She hunched her shoulders. "Mitchell tried to fix it. We redecorated our condo. We bought a new Mercedes. He took me to Cancun. He booked the cruise home to extend our vacation because he was fixing it. But he couldn't fix me. Half of the time he didn't recognize me. And now, I can't recall the few precious moments I did have." She turned around again, agitated and sad. Very sad.

Nolan digested the information. She was as complicated as she was beautiful. He didn't have any words of comfort to give her. She wouldn't receive them anyway. He picked up the pool stick and offered it to her.

She took it on reflex. Positioning himself behind her, Nolan adjusted the stick properly in her hands. "You put your fingers like this... Hold the back a little higher."

"Like this?"

"Yes. You want to slide it through easy. Like this..."

His arms were around her, their fingers entwined as he guided her movements. Her tension ebbed away as she relaxed into him.

This was the comfort she needed.

CHAPTER 11

Angela brushed her teeth and spit. She looked at the mirror and asked herself, "Why am I awake? Nobody in their right mind gets up at five-thirty without a reason." Her reflection had no explanation, so Angela disregarded it. She'd take a walk, watch the sunrise or something whimsical like that. She didn't know why she was awake and chipper. Last night, she and Nolan drove to Key West, hunting donuts, and lingered at Mallory Square. Being at the edge of the continent was beautiful. Even at midnight.

"Wow."

Nolan's voice startled her. "Oh. Nolan. Good morning."

He colored. He watched her float down the steps with a faraway expression that was sexy as hell. Her distraction gave him time to access the amount of leg her shorts did not cover. That wow tumbled out without his permission. "Good morning. You're up early."

"I have no idea why." She completed her decent. "Are you coming or going?"

Staying right where I can see you. "I haven't taken off yet. Waiting on the coffee. Do you want a cup?"

"You bet I do."

They did coffee on the back porch and she helped him load his gear. As they were finishing up, Nolan realized he had a problem. He didn't want to go. Angela was standing there. Between her and his morning routine, he chose her. Unless… "Do you want to come with me?"

That sexy expression returned. "No, I won't intrude on your private time."

She wanted to intrude. That much was clear to him. He wanted her company. That was clear too. "Nonsense. I want you to come."

"Okay."

He offered her a hand. "I'm surprised. You usually say no to being in the water. Not that I'm complaining. This has all the makings of being a great day."

Her expression changed. The sexy had been replaced by something decidedly not sexy.

"You okay?"

"No." Angela climbed out. "I don't want to go."

"Angela?"

"See you later, Nolan."

"Angela." He called after her.

She waved him off and kept going.

"What the hell?"

■   ■   ■

Angela avoided Nolan for the rest of the morning. She spent time with Hilda until Hilda told her she was bad company and to go take a nap. With Nolan back in the house, she lingered at the dock, feeding breadcrumbs to the seagulls and avoiding him. She didn't know how to explain herself. She wanted to be with him—hang out, cruise the waves. But her husband drowned, she couldn't play in the water with another man. What kind of person was she? Mitchell died, and she wanted to go sailing with Nolan.

She heard the approaching footsteps and braced herself.

The silence was announcement enough. She didn't bother turning around. "You might want to leave me alone, Lexie. I'm not in the best of moods."

Lexie stared at her, unimpressed. She wasn't in the best of moods either. "Why are you always moping around?"

Angela's head popped up. She pinned the little snot with a glare. "You should talk. I've never seen you not moping."

"At least I'm not scared of the water."

Attitude or not, Angela wasn't about to let a nine-year-old push her buttons. "At least I know what I am scared of. Not like some people."

"I'm not scared of anything."

"Ppfffphh. You're scared of everything."

Lexie's buttons were already pushed. "You don't know me. You don't know anything about me."

"You are a scared little brat. Anybody can see that."

It was a shock to be talked to that way. "Why are you always so mean?"

Angela became attuned and with it, empathetic. Lexie was in pain. She softened her tone but remained firm. "What did you expect? You get what you give. When you come around people with your shitty little attitude, you're going to get a shitty attitude in return. Why should I put up with you? Honey, be grateful I'm not your momma. Your parents may allow you to get away with that nonsense, but don't bring it here. It doesn't work."

"This is my father's house. You can't act like that in my father's house"

"So do something about it."

Lexie stood there, unsure of how to respond. She rocked a bit, wavering between running off and, and… she didn't know what.

Angela read the emotion. Lexie's eyes filmed over. Her lower lip trembled. "Come here, Lexie." She said it with the kind of authority that did not allow defiance. The nine-year-old responded with obedience. It was a testimony to her distress that her feet carried her closer to Angela than she had ever come. Angela didn't waste the moment. She put both arms around the child and held her there. Lexie gave one half-hearted lurch in an attempt at escape, but Angela didn't budge. She held the child tighter.

Lexie's resolve crumbled. It was no match for a loving touch. She clung to Angela, desperate for the contact. She didn't cry, she wailed, unable to hold back the agony that had been her companion for months.

Angela held her tighter. When Lexie's sobbing reduced to a notch below hysterics, Angela said, "Didn't anybody teach you when you're sad, you're supposed to cry?" Her voice was maternal, soothing.

"Crying is for babies." Lexie ended her argument with a hiccup and more tears.

"Umm hmm," Angela said, "I cry all the time."

"You're a baby."

"Nope. I cry because sometimes life sucks. If I don't cry, I'll end up with a shitty attitude and then I can't get better."

"You have a shitty attitude." She was still crying, but her words were becoming less broken.

"Stop using swear words. Your dad will think I'm a bad influence."

"You are a bad influence."

"I am."

That one made Lexie snicker. She sobered quickly. "He won't care. He doesn't care about me anymore."

"Come on, Lexie. You're too smart for that. Your dad and mom getting divorced had nothing to do with you. That's what this is about, isn't it?"

Lexie gave a curt nod.

"You little attention hog." She caressed Lexie's hair. "They were dumb. Both of them. That's nothing new. People do dumb stuff all the time. They made a mess out of their old lives. When that happens, the only thing left to do is clean it up and start over again."

"They made a mess of me."

"Wrong again. If your parents stayed together, that would have made a mess of you."

"No. That's not right—"

"They weren't happy. The only happy person was you. And that's because you didn't realize how messed up they were, but you would have figured it out. You're sad now. Imagine how it would be if nobody was ever happy. Not him. Not her. Definitely not you, because they wouldn't be doing anything to fix their dumb mistakes."

To a child of Lexie's intellect, the argument made perfect sense. "Why do people have to be stupid?"

"No reason. Sometimes they just are. They don't usually mean it, but that doesn't change the fact that what they did was stupid. The trick," Angela stroked some blonde strands behind Lexie's ear and placed a feather-light kiss on her forehead, "is to get to another happy place since the last one got messed up."

"How do you do that?" Lexie wiped her face with the back of her hand.

"You get somebody to help you."

The child was silent for a while, contemplating. "Will you help me?" she asked.

"Yes, I will."

She focused on Angela, searching for something. "Then I'll help you. You have to go swimming." Before Angela could reply, Lexie continued. "You can't hate the water because of what happened. When people's lives get messed up," she repeated Angela's advice almost word for word. "The only thing left to do is clean it up and start all over again."

Angela was stunned. A nine-year-old stoled her words and used them to lecture her. She was annoyingly correct. "I don't have a swimsuit."

"Lame excuse." The turnaround did wonders for Lexie's broken spirit. "You have a car. We can go to the store right now. You can get a bikini if you think it will get you some attention."

Angela burst out laughing. "No, you didn't."

"Yes, I did."

This kid was something. *Why not?* "All right smarty. Let's go shopping."

"Let's go then."

"I have to change my top. Some bratty kid got snot all over me." She pulled the hem of her top down and made a face.

As opposed to being embarrassed, Lexie said. "It's an ugly shirt, anyway. While we're out, we'll get you some new clothes too."

"You should talk. I have half a mind to buy you a whole new wardrobe."

"Half a mind is all you got."

They bantered back and forth from the dock to the house. For the first time since they met, they enjoyed each other.

. . .

Nolan watched them from the kitchen window. He wasn't able to make out what they were saying, but he saw his daughter crying and Angela, of all people, comforting her. That was indication enough for him to stay out of it. When the giggling started, his heart swelled. He couldn't recall the last time he had heard that sound in his house. He became dumbstruck when Angela—who wasn't talking to him—announced she and Lexie were going shopping, for swimsuits no less. He nodded his assent and watched them leave wondering what the hell they talked about.

CHAPTER 12

"Get up! Get up, get up, get up!" Lexie bounced into Angela's room and onto her bed. "We've got things. Get up!"

Angela jerked awake. "Demon child! Get off of me."

Lexie, clad in a sunny orange and yellow swimsuit, plopped across Angela with no regard for the woman's comfort. "Com'on. You have to get up now."

"Why?" They spent the whole day shopping in Key West, buying swimsuits and an assortment of other things they had to have. They brought home a pizza for dinner and watched a movie of Lexie's choosing. That was yesterday. It wasn't eight a.m. yet. Yesterday was gone. As far as Angela was concerned, the friendship was over.

"We have to do this before anybody sees us. I can't keep them prisoners forever."

Angela sat up, purposely knocking Lexie off balance. "What are you talking about?"

"I made Dad go over to Mammaw's. I told them both to stay there until I tell them to leave. If we don't go down now, before Tank gets here, everybody will want to watch. So move it, slowpoke."

The workings of a nine-year-old. It made Angela well up with tears. Lexie had thrown herself into the task. She wanted to make it easier by keeping it private. Even at 7:50 in the morning, it registered as sweet. Angela had to respond. "Grrrr... It's too freaking early." She plopped a pillow on Lexie's face. "Did you give your dad a chance to make any coffee before you kicked him out, you little monster?"

Lexie batted the pillow back and hopped off the bed. "Yeah, and he's got a mountain of bacon. We can eat it on the way. I'll put some coffee in a thermos for you." Before she reached the door, she paused at the dresser to pick up her favorite bottle of Angela's perfume. "Wear the light-blue one piece." She pumped the spray once and inhaled.

"I can pick out my own swimsuit, thank you." The perfume was called *HisCinn*. It was Angela's favorite as well. She removed the expensive bottle from the child's fingers and gave her a squirt behind each of her ears.

Lexie's eyes lit up. She inhaled again.

Angela gave her a touch more on her wrist and showed her how to rub them together. "I'm wearing the green one."

"The blue one."

"You're a tyrant."

"I thought I was a monster."

"Same difference. Why the blue?"

Lexie debated the answer but decided to go with it. "'Cause how you look in the blue one is how I want my body to look when I grow up."

To Angela, that was as high as a compliment went. "The blue one it is."

.　.　.

Beneath the shade of the Willow Inlet, Angela looked out across the wide expanse of wet.

Lexie watched her watching it. "It's not going anywhere."

Angela held her foot out, preparing to stick her toe in.

Lexie nodded her head as if something had been said. "It's not cold."

"Yes, it is."

"Florida. It's not cold."

"It's still the ocean."

"It will be the ocean all day long." She gave Angela's fingers a tiny tug.

Not in a hundred years would Angela be able to explain how holding a child's hand gave her courage. Lexie thought all there was to facing fear was stepping into the water and wading out until you were completely wet.

Angela lost her will to resist. She wanted to please Lexie. She wanted Lexie to see her try. One deep breath and her foot went in. "Oh." It was cold. But she didn't get a chance to complain. Lexie stepped the exact moment she did. She had one foot in the water. Lexie had both in, waiting for her. In her own way, this nine-year-old stranger shared her burden. Angela repaid it the only way she could, with her other foot. One step. Two steps. Another. Another. And one more. Lexie was treading and she was crying, standing more than waist deep in the very ocean that had stolen her life.

Whether Lexie understood the source of Angela's tears was irrelevant. "It's not cold. You big baby." She splashed Angela in the face.

"OH! YOU!"

The game was on. Chasing, splashing, dunking. For more than an hour, the sounds of laughter and life filtered out from the Willow Inlet.

From the hidden shelter of the thick, viny trees, Nolan marveled.

. . .

"Eenee, meenee, desa-meenee. Ooh, ahh, al la-meenee. Otchie, kotchie, Liberace, I love you…"

"What?"

Lexie and Angela paused their hand game.

"What'd you say?"

They were finishing dessert on Hilda's porch. Rob and Nolan watched while Tank polished off his third bowl of ice cream and Hilda, Angela, and Lexie took turns discussing the various ways to smack one another's hands and sing chants about it. Currently, Lexie and Angela were racing to see who sung and moved the fastest. All the words were jumbled and made no sense. At least not to Nolan.

"Eenee, meenee, desa-meenee?" Lexie repeated.

"Yeah, that. What's that mean?"

"You're kidding, right?" Angela looked down her nose like he'd said something dumb.

Hilda gave his shoulder a shove. "Quit messing up the game. That will have to be a redo," she told the girls.

"It means," Tank licked his spoon, scraped it against his bowl and licked again. "Eenee, meenee, desa-meenee."

"Precisely." Ready to begin again, Angela nodded to Lexie.

They clapped their hands high and low and side to side while keeping rhythm with their song. "Take me-out-to-the ball game. Take me-out-to-the… Eenee, meenee, desa-meenee. Ooh, ahh, al la-meenee. Otchie, kotchie, Liberace, I love you. Mr. Boogie at the door. Bop-a-de-bop. He sure looks good. Bop-a-de-bop…"

Tank completed his comment. "It doesn't mean anything, 'cause girls say stupid things."

"The kid's a genius," Rob said.

Lexie won that round. Angela traded places with Hilda as it was the right of the champ to keep her spot. Angela's phone blared. "That's Deidra," she announced. "I better get this—if it's her. Give me that." She pried the bowl from Tank's fingers as he licked it (Hey, I wasn't done!) and took it inside to add to the dishwasher.

"Dei-dra," Rob called out after her. "Ask her if she wants an examination. Tell her I make house calls."

"Don't think I won't," she yelled back.

"The space goes two lumps together. I like the weather—Is he a womanizer?—bring back my love to me…" Lexie asked between verses of the current chant they were clapping to.

"What is the meaning, meaning, meaning—Without a doubt—That tells the story, story, story…" Hilda incorporated her answer in a sing-song manner.

"What's a womanizer?" Having run out of things to eat for the night, Tank made himself comfortable on Rob's lap.

"A man who knows what he wants," Rob said. He gave his attention to Nolan, who was half leaning out of his chair to follow Angela with his eyes. "Like Uncle Nolan. What's up with that?"

Hearing his name brought Nolan around with a jolt and a sheepish grin. "That's nothing. I just hope nothing's wrong."

"That ain't all you're hoping for. What'd she mean, if it's her?"

"Deidra has a glitch in her phone. It randomly dials Angela, even when it's locked or off."

"Maybe she should exchange it."

Nolan shook his head. "Angela likes it."

"You're becoming an expert on what Angela likes." That was all Rob had time to say. His cell phone rang. One quick glance. "Hospital. Mammaw?"

"...My heart goes criss, cross, apple sauce—of course—criss, cross, tomato sauce. Bom-barney-apple. Bom-barney-apple. Bom-barney-apple. Freeze." After a moment of frozen silence, Hilda and Lexie un-froze and Lexie declared herself the winner. Hilda allowed it and said, "Do want to sleep here with Tank and me?"

"Yep." Lexie had already decided.

"Go get a couple of sleeping bags. We can make a tent in the living room."

"Yeah!!!"

The response came in duplicate. Tank bounced off Rob's lap. Lexie jumped off the step.

"Come on, Dad." Lexie moved toward the house. You have to get the sleeping bags. I can't reach them. They're on the top shelf."

"Yes, ma'am." Nolan stood up to follow her. Lexie had been in a good mood for the last two days. He wanted to do his part to keep her that way. "Tell Angela I'll be right back."

"Something's up with that."

Nolan ignored his brother.

∎   ∎   ∎

"Hey, Deed!"

"You sound positively happy." The surprise was evident in Deidra's voice.

"I am happy. How are you doing?"

"Glad to hear it. But I have a question."

"Shoot."

"Do you have any intentions of ever coming home?"

That made Angela laugh. "According to Hilda, I am home."

"You may not have noticed, but it's not common for people to go off and live with strangers."

"You're a downer. They're not strangers. And I do have a job here. I help out."

"You have a job here too. A leave of absence is not, by definition, a permanent thing." Deidra took a deep breath. "I'm sorry. I'll stop being witchy. It's because I miss you. I'm worried. I want you home, but I also want you happy, which it sounds like you are. So I'm jealous. You're supposed to get happy by being with me, 'cause I'm awesome like that."

The ending had the desired effect. Angela snickered. "Well, Your Awesomeness, why don't you come down here to visit me? You can see for yourself how I'm doing and where I need to be."

"Umm. Yeah, right. Unlike you, I don't have a job down there and I don't live with strangers."

"They're not strangers. They own an inn. That's what people do. Come here and stay a while."

"I'm not people."

"Rob wouldn't mind seeing you."

"The doctor?"

"Uh-huh."

"Hot. Rich. Hot. Rich. The one who's looking after you for free?"

"That would be him."

"He wants to see me?"

"He wanted me to tell you he makes house calls."

"I should come down there."

Angela laughed outright. "Oh. You wouldn't come down here for me, but you'd come down here for him."

"I'm not dumb. A hot, rich doctor is worth a weekend."

"But I'm not?"

"How honest of an answer do I have to give?"

CHAPTER 13

Nolan grabbed two sleeping bags from the basement while Lexie put on her pajamas. They met in the hallway.

"Need anything else?"

"Nope. Mammaw's stocked up on junk food and batteries. We're good."

"I don't know if there's enough junk food in the world to hold Tank for long."

"Yeah. It's a good thing he's going to be my cousin. It's never going to be my job to feed him."

"You're funny." Nolan tugged her ponytail. "I like you like this."

"Me too. And speaking of that…" She tugged his shirttail, much like he had done her hair.

Nolan noted her wide eyes had gone serious. "What is it?"

Lexie studied him for a moment longer. "I think you and Mom were stupid." She huffed with the removal of that weight. "But, I'll try not to be mad at you all the time."

His eyes filmed over as he bent on one knee before her. "Thank you, honey. That's more than I have a right to ask of you. You're a better person than your mom and I put together." He hugged her to him, willing her to receive all the love she had been refusing. "You're the best of both of us."

She absorbed the love and returned the hug with equal affection. "Oh." She pulled back but kept her hands on his shoulders. "One more thing."

"What's that?" Whatever she wanted, he'd acquire.

"It's okay with me if you kiss Angela."

Nolan kept his smile in place. His chuckle was genuine, hiding his shock. "Where did that come from?"

"Sometimes when you're looking at Angela you want to kiss her. It's probably a good idea 'cause that's what she wants too."

"Did... Did you all talk about that or something?"

Lexie rolled her eyes. "I'm not dumb. I even know what happens when grown-ups say they're taking a nap together."

Nolan remembered all too well where that came from. A place he wasn't going to visit with his kid. "Umm. I'm glad you told me these things. I like it when we talk."

"Me too." Having said all she needed to say, Lexie led the way. It was time to get to the tent.

. . .

Nolan and Lexie returned to the Enn in time to see Rob swinging Angela around before planting a quick kiss on her cheek.

"He's a womanizer," Lexie informed her father and skipped up the steps into the house, presumably to locate Hilda and Tank.

Nolan didn't like that word connected to Angela. "What are we celebrating?"

Rob released Angela, yelled a loud good-night through the front door, and hurried down the steps past Nolan. "Angela is working her magic on her sister for me. I've got to get going." To Angela, he said, "Keep me updated."

"You'll know as soon as I do." Angela waved him off.

Nolan relaxed and then analyzed the emotion. *What the hell was up with him? Lexie's comment, no doubt.* "Are you about ready?"

"Ummhmm." Angela stuck her head inside the door and with slightly less volume than Rob used, she called out a 'good-night' and 'have fun' to the occupants inside.

The distance from the Enn to Nolan's steps gave Angela enough time to surmise he had something on his mind. "What's going on?"

"You did a very brave thing today. It took a lot of guts to get into the water."

Angela allowed herself a moment to reflect. It was a small thing, but she was proud of herself. "I can't believe I did it. Lexie is amazing." She meant it.

"She is. It seems like you two have been helping each other a bit. Not that I've been given any information to verify that."

She thought it was cute, the way he tilted his head when he probed. "What information would you like?" She tilted her head in imitation.

"I want to thank you. Whatever you're saying or doing to help Lexie get a grip on the divorce, please, keep doing it." He caught hold of her hand.

His approval was nice too. It always had been, but there was a difference in him tonight. She liked it. "We talk. No, I talk. She makes me do things, like buy swimsuits and get back into the water."

Yeah, he saw the swimsuit. Wouldn't mind seeing it again. That brought him full circle. "Have you and Lexie been talking about you and me, by chance?"

"You and I?" Why did that make her heart thud? "What would I be saying? To Lexie?"

"Nothing." He looked at the slender fingers resting in his palm. He liked them there. "She gave us permission to kiss."

"She what?" The absolute surprise on Angela's face was not feigned. Neither was the shiny glint in her eyes that revealed unmasked pleasure at the thought.

That was more than enough encouragement for Nolan. His brain had been fogged since Lexie's bombshell and there was only one way to clear it.

"She said we should do this." He stepped in and pulled her forward, touching his lips to hers. The initial contact was to him soft, sweet, and not enough. His free hand glided to her back to hold her to him while he deepened the kiss. Her sigh rippled through him. When her warm tongue slid across his, his body tightened.

It wasn't because he hadn't held a woman in two years, though that played a part. It was her. She felt so damned good in his arms, his body had to respond. His thoughts consisted of two words: Yes. More.

Angela's mind couldn't keep up with the thundering of her heart or the fire in her veins. She had never been held by anyone other than her husband. It didn't feel like this with Mitchell. She didn't remember how it felt with Mitchell, but it wasn't like this. That was certain. This was dangerous. Primeval. Forbidden. Hot.

She was a new widow; lonely, vulnerable, and in need of a man's touch. Nolan was almost a decade beyond her twenty-eight years. He had a failed marriage and a child. He was a bartender. Technically, he still lived with his mother. Not to mention, his southern-white ancestors would pop out of their graves over the interracial thing.

None of that mattered. Not while his mouth moved over hers so deliciously. She wanted the heat and the friction. She wanted to be in his arms. She wanted his tongue dueling with hers. She wanted her pulse racing and her breath gone. She wanted Nolan.

It was the sound that separated them, not a voluntary act. They were startled to find Lexie, half in shadow, rolling her foot across a downed coconut, watching them with a wide-eyed frown.

"Why are you doing that?" She fixed her gaze on Angela.

Angela surmised by the set features Lexie expected to disbelieve what she heard. She had no intention of talking down to the child. "Because it's fun."

The child's leeriness became surprise.

"From what I understand, it was your idea."

Her surprise became pleasant. "Yeah, but I didn't mean out in the yard where the whole world can see you."

"You're kind of short to be the whole world. What are you doing outside, anyway?"

"I forgot Ollie." She skipped past the grownups, headed toward the house.

Angela turned to Nolan. His eyes were possessive and focused on her. Her heart leapt with anticipation. It took a moment to find her voice. Her mouth was still tingling with the taste of him. "Ollie?"

"Her stuffed elephant."

Three words. That's all he said. Three words. Unrelated to her emotions, yet she felt every letter, every syllable like warm water trickling across her spine. His voice was sinful. His mouth was sinful. He stared at her possessively.

Lexie was back with the scruffy grey elephant tucked under her arm. "Night, Daddy." She stood on her tiptoes to kiss his cheek.

He leaned down. "Night, sweetheart."

"Kiss Ollie." She held the toy up for his affection.

"Night, Angela."

"Good night, squirt."

"Kiss Ollie."

Angela kissed Ollie and then kissed Lexie on the top of her head. "Sweet dreams."

Lexie hugged her and grinned. "I'm done. Now you can go back to kissing each other." She didn't look back.

Angela laughed. She glanced up, expecting to share her amusement with Nolan. She had his attention, but he wasn't smiling. He was probing her with his eyes. He was drinking her in, tasting her in his mind. He mesmerized her.

"Should we talk?"

"Pro-probably. I guess." That was the best she could do.

Nolan reached for her as if he would kiss her again, but he held off. For a long time, neither of them spoke. It became too much for Angela. "Are you going to say anything?"

"Do I need to apologize?"

She shook her head no.

"It will happen again."

There was surety in his words that made her uneasy. She glanced away. "Look. Mitchell's not here—"

Her head snapped back with the mention of her late husband's name. Her expression clouded with guilt. She hadn't been thinking of Mitchell.

"I'm not saying it to hurt you, but it's the truth. I'm divorced. It's not the same, but in some ways, it is. What I had is gone. It's not coming back. I haven't been with anybody since Jackie left because I don't take relationships lightly. Can you understand that?"

She didn't understand her feelings, but she wanted to share them anyway. "I didn't date in high school. I met Mitch early in college. I've never been with anyone else."

Damn. "I understand. I'll respect your memories and your need to go slow. When we get to where we'll have to make a decision, we'll do it together. Is that agreeable to you?"

He didn't ask anything of her, yet. Which was good. "I can handle slow."

"Good. Because I need to kiss you again." He didn't give her time to react.

She didn't want the time; she wanted him.

■　■　■

It took a lot to go to bed alone. But true to his promise to go slow, Nolan contented himself with her kisses. There would be time for more. Sooner rather than later, he hoped. He just needed to work on his eight-step program. Her bedroom door was eight steps away from his.

■　■　■

It was hard for Angela to sleep. Everything was awkward and new. It was amazing to feel new. Nolan did that to her. He made her giddy, like a teenager. Dwelling on the whispers and the make-out session. Wondering what would come of it or if anyone would notice. Wondering too, what it would be like to be with him.

CHAPTER 14

Kasey Kay was an artist; a genius in all its forms. It wasn't pride, although she had that in triplicate. It was truth. Her instincts were unequaled, and every idea she had was great. Like now.

Her fingers were in every big story in the lower eastern corner of the US. She didn't sleep with pertinent people to *not* get information. How would she maintain her persona of the bimbo who slept with people to get information? Not everybody—people who mattered. An air traffic controller, a coastguard petty officer, a detective or two... or three, a few busy businessmen, and a handful of politicians—Republican and Democrat, because unlike the rest of the country, *she* was bipartisan. She had the body and the attitude for it. People thought her services were for sale, so she sold her services. Win-win all around. Like now.

No other freelance reporter in the southern quarter had her combination of intellect and cleavage. No other reporter had her sources because they didn't blow an air traffic controller, or bang a coastguard petty officer.

It was simple to contact Mitchell Pointe's family and intriguing to tap into the undertone Mrs. Pointe—the elder—put out concerning her daughter-in-law. Kasey sharpened her nails and packed an overnight bag. Angela Pointe's presence in the Keys was suspicious. Kasey Kay loved hunting down suspicious leads. Because she was an artist.

Turning into the drive, Kasey caught sight of two kids running through the yard. She practically purred. Kids were easy. She fluffed her hair from habit and popped out of her car. "Hey guys," she called out.

Tank and Lexie halted their game to observe the approaching stranger.

"I'm looking for two things. The Eellek Enn and Ms. Angela Pointe. Am I in the right place?"

"Yep." Tank pointed. "The Enn is right here. We spell it with an E instead of an I because Mammaw likes it that way."

"I'll remember that. And Ms. Pointe?"

"She's my aunt."

"She is not." Lexie made a face at Tank's stupidity. "Not yet, anyway."

"She will be."

Ignoring him, Lexie cast a suspicious eye on the stranger. "Who are you? What do you want Angela for?"

Kasey decided the girl was the leader. *Mistrustful little critter.* Better be careful. "I'm a reporter. Angela's accident was big news. People are interested in her. If she agrees, I'll write a story about her."

Lexie considered.

"Can you get her or someone?"

"I'll go get Mammaw."

"Thanks." As soon as the girl departed, Kasey focused on the boy. "You said Angela is going to be your aunt? How's that?"

"She loves my uncle Nolan. She should marry him. He's not really my uncle. Not yet," he said before Lexie came back and protested. "But he will be because I'm going to live here forever."

"You should."

"I used to live at the foster home but I didn't like it there. I like it here. Angela used to live in a foster home too, but not the same one as me."

"Is Angela going to live here forever with you?" She pointed to the Enn.

"She lives at Uncle Nolan's with Lexie." He pointed to the house across the yard. "I live in the big house down the road with my new dad." He swung his finger in the other direction. "Mammaw lives here. But I thought she was going to live at jail. She got caught stealing a motorcycle from my daddy's garage. She didn't get in trouble for stealing 'cause it's her bike. She got in trouble for driving it. She doesn't have a license. My dad has a bike too. We ride all the time."

"Awesome. What's your name?"

"Tank."

"Tank. Do you like Angela?"

"I love Angela. Everybody does." Tank frowned. "Wait. Are you redlining?" Lexie told him about that. "Angela can live wherever she wants."

Kasey was quick to soothe. She reached into her purse and came out with a pack of chewing gum. "She certainly can. Your uncle loves having her there, right?" She offered him a piece.

Tank accepted. "Yeah. They kiss all the time. Can I have one for Lexie?"

"Sure."

The front door opened. Lexie followed a hippie outside. "Can I help you?"

"Hi," Kasey stepped forward, offering a hand. "I'm hoping to rent a room for the night."

"Come on in. We've got plenty of space."

Kasey loved being an artist.

■   ■

In her room, Kasey looked over her notes. Collecting information from Hilda Woods had been easier than getting it from Tank. The locals at the Summer Shack filled her in too. The only thing left was to tackle the elusive Mrs. Pointe and her lover. Kasey didn't doubt they were lovers. Even now, while the grandmother babysat, they were off on a boat ride somewhere. Or some kind of ride. Given the fact that Angela had been in a shipwreck, Kasey doubted the boat was supplying the thrill.

MITCHELL

CHAPTER 15

Nothing made sense. Mitchell opened first one eye and then the other. He couldn't identify his surroundings. He was moving. The motion made him ill. A boat. A creepy little boat. Unless he was hallucinating, he wasn't alone. There was a man, crying, from the sound of it. A woman—probably the man's wife—complained about something. Who the hell were these people? Where was Angela? *Angela*. Everything came back. Raw anguish tore from his soul. Angela was gone. They were stranded. He was dying, and he couldn't wait. Angela was gone. His baby. He couldn't think past it.

It had been the longest dark. Horrific to contemplate. Impossible to endure. The dinghy was for fishing and crabbing, not saving lives. It was meant to remain tied to the yacht and had no anchor. Nate secured it to their wrecked vessel, but daylight showed the railing had come loose. They were adrift. Nate blamed himself and gave in to his despair.

Keira stared off into the vast blue nothingness. She was proactive and optimistic by nature. But there was no bright side. That they were alive was good news only if they didn't suffer a slow, painful, death. Death. It was there but she refused to see its face; their faces. Captain Shoemaker. Buzz Millyo, a crewman on his second run with the company. And Roger, first mate, engineer, mechanic, everything guy. It wasn't often the *Siren's Fire* sailed without Roger. Those guys ran the ship while she and Nate took care of their passengers. Nate cooked, served, and kept them satisfied, while she saw to their comfort and entertainment. Keira was the only female traveling in Captain Shoemaker's crew this week. She was glad. Mona, her counterpart, was newly engaged. Sitting in the middle of the ocean, waiting to die was not something an engaged person should do.

Too disturbed by her thought process, Keira changed her focus. Nate sobbed; Mr. Pointe sobbed. It drove her crazy. She wanted to sob. She understood Nate freaking out—a reasonable thing to do. Mr. Pointe was in shock, grieving for his wife. It was natural, but it didn't help their situation at all. Hell, she was the girl. If anyone cried, it should be her. She was a sensitive person and wired for it. They were infringing on her tear-rights. Acknowledging she had the most water experience and seniority, she was the captain. She had to hold it together. But still.

Diversion. "Hey Nate-Nate, pull out the survival kit. Let's see what we got so we can figure out what we're going to do. Mr. Pointe, have you ever fished?"

Mitchell turned toward the sound. Conversation. Words. Anything was better than where his mind was. He nodded. "I can fish. Call me Mitchell."

She smiled, encouraged to see them move on her say-so.

Her encouragement lasted less than ten minutes. The content of their survival kit was less than meager. Besides the unhelpful whistle, there was a first aid kit—missing most of its medications—some fishing line and a couple of hooks, a dozen MRE's, a box of waterproof matches, a package of water purifiers, and a poncho. Everything else that should have been in there was not. "Where is the flare gun? Where is the chocolate?" She shook out the folds in the poncho. "Where is the radio? The GPS?"

"Damned hoodlum vandals," Nate muttered. Somebody used a sharpie to scribble 'Die Losers' on the backside of the box.

"We don't even have a utility knife." For the first time since their nightmare began, Keira lost hope.

"No sense in worrying about something you can't change." Mitchell didn't know what he said. But Keira was a nice girl; he needed to say something. He pulled himself up from his slumped position and put a hand on the oars. "Should I row us somewhere?"

Keira tried to sound upbeat. It was the least she could offer for his attempt at encouragement. "That would be great, Mr. Pointe, but my navigating skills are minute at best."

"Mitchell."

"Sorry. Mitchell. I'm guessing we're not far from La Habana. But do we risk going south? There is a lot of ocean that way. Any of the other three directions improves our chances for land, but without provisions or an anchor, would we last long enough to get there? I don't want to tell you to do something that will make matters worse."

"We're in the middle of the ocean, Keira. I don't see a worst."

"Gulf."

"Gulf. Ocean. It's all cold, wet and deep," Nate said. "Make it easy on yourself, Mitchell. Go with the tide for a bit. I'll take over when you get tired."

Mitchell looked to Keira for confirmation. She nodded and he put the oars in the water. "I guess anything is a plan."

Now that he was talking, Nate had some questions for Keira. "Should we eat something? Try to fish?"

"I thought about that. One MRE a day will hold us for four days. They'll be looking for us, but we should halve it to be safe."

"Half a pack it is." Nate stood up with his back to Keira. "Turn your head. I've got to take a leak."

Oddly enough, the mundaneness of an everyday function gave them a sense of comfort. It was the only normal they had.

. . .

"Somebody talk." Nate flipped over. They alternated between rowing the dingy and letting it float wherever for two and a half days. They took turns using the poncho for protection against scorching heat during the day. At night, they slept in shifts; two huddled together in the tiny bow, sharing body heat, while the watcher used the poncho for a cover. They ate little and conserved their energy. The silence was maddening.

"And say what?" Keira cleared her dry throat.

"I don't know. You got a life story?"

"You already know my story."

"Mitchell doesn't."

"Mitchell doesn't care."

"Yes, he does."

"He's asleep."

"I'm not asleep," Mitchell said without moving. He hadn't moved in hours. "I'd like to hear your story."

"I don't have a story."

"You do." Nate flipped again. "Quit stalling. I ain't got all day."

They all chuckled.

"Why don't you tell your story?" Keira whined.

"We'll get to it, I'm sure. Quit stalling."

"Ppfffh." Keira shifted into a more comfortable position. "Let me see. I'm an only child. My mother is a wannabe marine biologist. My dad sells pineapples and coconuts to tourists. I used to work on a cruise ship until about a year or so ago. I signed on with Captain Shoemaker and I've been on the *Siren's Fire* ever since."

"You're right," Nate said. "You don't have a story. Where's the drama? Where's the suspense? How many times have you been married? Are you a secret agent? Entertain me."

"Put the poncho over your head, Nate-Nate. The sun is baking your brain."

"It's not my fault your storytelling skills need work."

"Oh, yeah? What's your story? And make it interesting."

Nate imitated Keira's 'ppfffh.' "I used to see Sharee, my wife, once or twice a month because she works in Tallassee and I don't. We thought we could do it. We couldn't. Now we're getting divorced. It's costing me a lot. My life used to suck. That is, until night before last. Now, I can't remember one day that would qualify as bad."

It was quiet then. All three of them focused on the sad reality of their circumstance.

Mitchell recalled their attention. "After all that about Keira's storytelling, you crashed and burned, Nate. That was pitiful." He still hadn't moved, but humor could be detected in his tone.

"I have to agree with him, Nate," Keira said. "Your life has left me underwhelmed."

"My life has left me underwhelmed. Your turn, Mitch."

Mitchell's face split into a huge grin. "Can't. It would be too cruel. You'd die from envy. The excitement is too much for a person to take in all at once."

"Envy. That's what I choose to die from," Nate said.

"I vote for envy." Keira nudged Mitchell with her toe. "Bring on the envy."

"All right suckers." Mitchell opened his eyes and then closed them again. "You asked for it. I met Angie at college. I tricked her into going out with me."

"How'd you do that?" Keira asked.

"I saw her at a party that had gotten wild. The next day, I showed up at her dorm pretending we had a date. She was too embarrassed to say she didn't remember. We'd been dating for two months before she found out."

"Slick." Nate sat up, rocking the boat when he moved. His dreads were everywhere.

"She never dated anyone else but me. We have great careers—"

"What do you do?"

"I'm an actuary. She works for a company that designs uniforms for athletes."

"What's an actuary?"

Keira laughed. "I'm glad you asked, Nate-Nate. Because I didn't want to be the dumb one."

"An actuary is someone who determines the risk involved in a company decision. Good money. Great money. We spent most of our time acquiring shit and having terrific sex. Life doesn't get any better than that." Mitchell stopped speaking. His life was over. He started to heave, although with only half an MRE in his stomach, there was not enough in him to come up. Anguish came up with misery and destitution of spirit; his soul bled over his loss. He was lost and he had lost everything.

Keira reacted instinctively. Putting both arms around Mitchell, she pulled him to her. "You're okay, Mitchell. You're okay. It may not be the worst. You're okay…"

Nate rowed the boat while Keira consoled Mitchell. It took a while. Afterward, when he could speak, he told them more about Angela. About her childhood. About her job. About her sister. About her favorite foods. Every detail that popped into his head spilled out of his mouth. He had to talk about her, keep her in the forefront of his consciousness. She was his sanity. Without Angela, he had none. Without Angela… Mitchell wasn't anything without Angela.

The rise and fall of the waves lulled them while the gentle slap of the oars echoed across the water and in their thoughts. Mitchell was asleep with his head on Keira's lap, worn out from his worry. Nate rowed steadily. His need for activity rather than a destination prompted his vigor. Keira leaned against the side of the boat, her hand playing in Mitchell's hair. The coarse texture made her fingers tingle.

"I guess your new line of work is babysitting." Nate indicated Mitchell with a nod of his head.

Keira studied her charge. "He needs it. We all do. At least Sharee is safe."

"Is she? News is hard to come by out here."

"You know what I mean."

He glanced around at the nothingness.

"Quiet, huh?"

"That's what's bugging me," he said. "Is it me, or what? We've been out here for almost three days too many. I haven't seen, heard, or smelled an airplane. Are they not looking for us?"

"Yes, they're looking for us. They have to be."

"They don't have to be."

"What's that mean?"

"By now they have a headcount. There were more people of color than not. If they found the white people, they don't *have* to be looking for us."

She didn't want to acknowledge that reality. "Don't freak out on me, Nate."

"Why not? We don't have a refrigerator drifting out here with us. Ain't no pizza places delivering. What we do have won't last forever. I can't handle another night freezing my ass off while we're floating around waiting to die."

"It hasn't been that bad." Keira stopped to assess the incredulous look he shot her. "Yes, it's terrible," she amended. "But we're alive. We have had some food and water. It hasn't rained on us, thank God. It's not one person sitting out here alone. In the scheme of things, we've been damned lucky so far."

"How lucky will we be in a week?"

"I'll tell you in seven days."

He snorted, enjoying her sassiness. "I'm being a dick. I'm sorry."

"Yes you are, but I'm not sorry. You can be in any mood you want. Just don't quit on me. I won't make it without you, Nate-Nate."

"Yeah, who else will bitch and complain and keep you optimistic?"

"Exactly."

Nate rowed for a while longer and pulled the oars in. It was getting dark. "Should we wake up Sleeping Beauty?"

"Naw, I'll keep watch."

Nate stood up and stretched before he worked his way to the bow. "I'll be asleep in a minute. It will be a good time for you to take a major dump."

"Ha ha. I haven't eaten enough for a major anything. So there."

They caught on early that having to relieve herself in their presence was an embarrassment to Keira. She preferred her body to only function at night, if at all. It had become a source of entertainment for Nate and Mitchell. They teased her at every possible opportunity.

"What would she do if I waited until she started and then sat up and yelled?" Mitch asked, startling Keira. His head was still on her lap and his eyes were closed, but he was awake.

"She'd shit herself." Nate laughed. "But at least she'd be in position for it."

Keira gave Mitchell a mock shove. "Oh, you two are very funny. Don't you have anything better to do than pick on my bathroom habits?"

"No." The men said together.

"Find something better to do and go do it with your heads turned. I have to pee and I can't hold it." She scooted away from them.

Nate settled himself in for a rest and Mitchell turned his back to her.

"Ohmigod! Look!"

"You really want us to do that?" Mitchell asked.

"Payback?" Nate kept his eyes closed.

"LOOK! LOOK!"

Mitchell turned around. Nate sat up straight. Keira pointed to something a long way off but distinguishable. They saw the tops of a clump of leafy green trees.

Not willing to stop for anything, they took turns rowing and after hours with nothing but moonlight and determination they finally reached the shore. Keira cried. She got her crew to safety. Regardless of what became of them, they didn't drown.

Too tired for anything other than to rejoice that they were on land, they pulled the boat inland. Then, the three of them nestled together, exhausted. For the remainder of the night, they slept without anyone keeping watch.

CHAPTER 16

CLANG! CLANG! CLANG!

Mitchell and Keira jerked awake, startled by the unidentifiable, deafening noise. Nate banged a cowbell with a stirring spoon. "Wake up! Wake up! Wake up! You're missing breakfast!" He had the happy attitude of a well-fed morning person.

Mitchell tuned in to the most important word. "Breakfast. You found some food?"

"Ha ha." Nate's eyes were aglow with a secret he was bursting to share. "Food, lodging, food. No phone, but it's solar-powered, and the TV gets two and a half channels."

"We found civilization?" Keira jumped up, gloriously overwhelmed with the news.

"I wouldn't go that far," Nate said. "But the bathroom works. I tried it just for you." He grinned.

"Food," Mitchell repeated the most important word.

"Lots of it. And seeing as I am the cook, I handled that situation. Now, don't piss me off by ruining my mega-meal because I might have been on fifths and sixths waiting for you to wake up naturally."

That was more than enough encouragement. Mitchell and Keira followed Nate down a clear path no one noticed last night. Less than four hundred yards away was a cozy beach house with three bedrooms, one bath, a great room, back deck, and screened-in front porch.

"Does anybody live here?" Keira spoke in a whisper.

"Not that I've met." Nate held the door open for them and they were overcome with the aroma of freshly brewed coffee. "I've been here since daylight. I looked around. The chicken population is out of control. The garden hasn't been tended to in a while, but everything inside is clean and in order. The front door was shut tight, but not locked."

The house morphed into paradise when they saw the spread Nate laid for them. He had made about fifty pancakes to go with the dozen or more fresh eggs he collected. The deep freezer proved to be a gold mine, offering bacon, sausage, tortillas, and the ham he was defrosting.

Mitchell and Keira raced to the table.

"Eat slow and all that stuff." Nate took a seat with them.

"Did you?" Mitchell said with his fork halfway to his already full mouth.

"Hell no." They laughed as Nate reached for a plate.

For anyone who wanted to be there, the island was a lush paradise. Twenty years prior, the house was state of the art. Ten years ago, it would have been a great romantic getaway. Now, it appeared as if the owner had more important places to be. There was a boat dock, void of any seaworthy vessels, and a storage unit they treasure-hunted the key for. Inside they found an archaic dirt-bike with a saddlebag containing two or three handfuls of pesos. Besides the tree frogs and the society of chickens living in their backyard, there was no other notable life on the island.

The black and white television was made sometime in the mid-seventies. Instead of a remote, it came with a wire coat hanger for an antenna. The stations were in Spanish. The half channel was cheesy soap operas.

Still, for Keira and Nate, not much dampened the euphoric atmosphere of no longer being stuck on the ocean. Mitchell was uplifted for a while. Having his belly full and a shower every day made things hopeful. But night would come. Going to sleep in a real bed was bliss for the others, but it was torture for him. It was impossible to sleep in a bed without Angela. It was impossible to sleep without Angela. It was impossible to sleep. He couldn't turn off his brain.

With nothing to distract him from his depression, his conversations became less frequent and more monotone. His days became more days, and his interest in life waned.

. . .

The waves crashed against the rocks. There were a lot of rocks. It was amazing, they avoided them, landing in the dead of night as they did. Mitchel wished they would have crashed. Or drowned. Drowning was more preferable than living with the knowledge Angela was gone. Nothing was worse than that. People—his family, colleagues, frat brothers—they already thought he drowned. He wished he could make their grieving worthwhile. But not Angela—she didn't grieve. She was gone and he wanted to go with her.

"If you're looking for a rescue ship, I'll take it, but I have to be honest, it's not my preferred mode of transportation." Nate picked up a stone and flung it.

Mitchell turned toward the sound. "We're on an island. If we get rescued, I'm betting a sea vessel of some sort will be involved."

"Damn. I may have to stay stranded then." Nate flung another stone. "You can send me supplies every month and I'll be good. Do you want to talk about it?"

"Your supplies? You're not getting any."

"Your wife. Or your losses. Any of the crappy shit you're going through."

Mitchell went back to watching the rocks. It was a long while before he said, "I lost my wife and it's crappy as shit."

"It is crappy as shit, but maybe she's okay. Maybe she got rescued."

"Did we get rescued? We were the ones waiting in the boat."

Nate nodded once.

A tear raced down the side of Mitchell's jaw. One tear, lonely like him. "I miss her, man."

"Of course, you do. I miss her. And that's just based on your description." Nate hurled stones as he talked, making them skip across the waves. "I lost a good friend."

Mitchell snorted, amused in spite of himself.

"What are we going to do about missing your wife? Ha." A smooth pebble took four hops before being swallowed by the foam.

Motivated by Nate's display, Mitchell grabbed a handful of pebbles. "What do we do about that?" He launched them one by one in rapid succession.

Not to be outdone, Nate countered with a volley of the tiny missiles. "We throw rocks. That's what we do."

. . .

"Guess what I found?" Keira stepped onto the porch swinging a bottle of rum and two glasses.

Mitchell looked up but did not comment.

"Three cases of it in my closet. This proves I'm right and Nate-Nate's wrong. We're on a Caribbean Island. He keeps calling it Gilligan's." The quirky comment made Mitchell smile. Encouraged, Keira sat near him and offered him the bottle to open. "Nate took one to his room. Didn't give me the impression he wanted to share."

Mitchell had gone back to not commenting. He unscrewed the top and poured them each a generous amount.

Keira took a sip.

Mitchell took a gulp.

They both choked and spit, then laughed.

"Wow," Keira said. "I'd say go light, but that doesn't help."

Mitchell rubbed the sting out of his eyes. "Can't say that I've ever tasted anything like it."

"Can't imagine anybody doing it a second time." Keira took another sip. "This stuff is awful."

"It tastes like moonshine or some equivalent." Mitchell took a second gulp. When his breathing caught up, he refilled their glasses.

They sat in silence for a while, letting alcohol warm them.

"It's funny the things you miss," Mitchell said, "but they don't seem important so you don't realize you miss them. Like drinking."

"Drinking is important to some people."

"Not me. Although, it is now. " He drank some more and made a face. "Wow. This shit burned a hole in my throat." He chased it with a second swig. "Know what I miss?"

She expected him to say Angela. Instead of asking, she refilled their glasses.

"Routines."

"Routines?"

"Yeah. Wake up. Go to work. Go to the gym. Doctor's appointment at two. Traffic jam at four fifteen. Routines. The everyday stuff that makes up your life."

"I miss mine," Keira said. "Things that belong to me. My pillow. My jersey sheets, my ratty slippers. A sense of identity. I'm not myself because I don't recognize a thing about me. Does that make any sense?" She touched her forehead. The rum was the strongest she'd ever had.

"Yes. One day you're living your life, and the next, nothing is the same. Like one of those find-the-hidden-object puzzles. Where is Mitch's car? Where is Mitch's desk? Where is Mitch's wif—" He didn't finish the thought. "Where is Mitch? Anybody seen Mitch?" His eyes filmed over, but not from the alcohol.

Slightly dizzy, but full of compassion, Keira leaned over and embraced him. "The good news is, all you need is patience. Every single object in the puzzle gets found. I promise."

Their faces were only a few inches apart. Keira noticed his eyes were very light for being brown. She thought they were more like a shade of gold. That was fascinating. Likewise, Mitchell studied her deep chocolate orbs. It was an interesting combination: the rum and her. His body stirred. For once, he wasn't numb.

Keira smiled and pulled back. "Nate had the right idea. You should be close to a bed when you're drinking this junk. I'm beyond a buzz."

"You should get some sleep."

"You might be right." She stood up and swayed. "Correction, you are right." She moved toward the door.

"Keira."

She paused.

"Thanks. You keep my shit together."

"You. Me. Nate. We make a good team."

"We do." He looked out at the night, for the first time that evening, seeing the night and not his ghosts.

"We do." She went inside.

CHAPTER 17

They were on Gilligan's Island for ten, eleven, twelve... they lost track of their days. This was the first rain. It came down soft and steady, tapping a gentle rhythm against the windows. Helped along by the rum, Nate and Keira slept protected and soothed.

Mitchell paced. Sleep wouldn't come. Peace wouldn't come. Nothing would come. That scared him. The nothingness. He was frozen in his grief. "I miss you, Angie." He clasped his hands together and prayed to her. "I don't want to be by myself. I don't want... anything." As soon as he realized he was praying, he stopped. He didn't want to pray. He didn't want to hope. He didn't want to be by himself.

Mitchell left his room without a plan. He stood in the hallway and considered the closed doors. He had to wake someone. If he didn't, he was certain he wouldn't make it through the night.

He opened Nate's door. The rum bottle beside his bed was empty. Nate's snores were so loud, Mitchell didn't bother trying.

He slipped into Keira's room, closed the door, and leaned against it. She was a beautiful, nice girl. After Nate, he had to strain to hear her quiet, even breathing. He sank to the floor, content with her company. As long as he wasn't alone, she didn't have to be awake.

. . .

Mitchell awoke with a start. When had he fallen asleep? What woke him?

"Mitch?" Keira's sleepy voice cut through the darkness. "What are you doing on the floor?"

"I must have dozed off. I didn't mean to bug you."

"Come on over." She sat up and wiped the sleep from her eyes. The cloud-covered moon offered no light, and the room did not have a bedside lamp. Neither was necessary. Their nights on the water were darker, would always be darker. She felt the bed sink under his weight and his thigh touching hers. "What's going on?"

His lips trembled. He couldn't answer. Keira's nearness had a thawing effect on his emotions. A tear he didn't understand rolled down his cheek.

She didn't see it, but she knew. The slight hitch when he drew breath. The shaky vibration of his exhale. She responded with a caress to his cheek before drawing him into her embrace. She rocked him, rubbed his back, and offered him her peace.

Mitchell let her lead his head to her shoulder. He needed the comfort she offered. She pulled him in close, and he wrapped his arms around her waist. For a long minute, he allowed himself the freedom to grieve. Sharing the burden with Keira made it lighter. Her warm body pressed against his. She was soft. He breathed her in, thankful she was there. She kissed his cheek. He burrowed into the hollow at the base of her neck. He closed his eyes and placed a feather-light kiss of gratitude on the satiny skin above her pulse. He did it again. And a third time, because nothing felt better.

Her head tilted back, offering him better access. She pressed against him. Mitchell's tongue darted out. He licked her neck, nipping the underside of her jaw and nibbling on her ear. A throaty moan rippled through her. She turned her head and his lips found hers.

There was no hesitation, no caution, only need. He took the lead, pulling them down to the mattress. Their legs entwined as he raised her nightgown, his fingers seeking.

She arched into his roaming hands, her body craving his touch as badly as he wanted to touch her. He was hard and tight. She was soft and yielding, promising him ecstasy, offering him fulfillment and forgetfulness. Foreplay was not a luxury they wanted to indulge overmuch. The urgency was upon them and resistance was non-existent. Desire had crowded out debate. They were consumed by frantic need, hunger, and a driving force to sate it.

Afterward, they made love. Slowly. Carefully. Aware. Giving and taking. Learning pleasure with each other.

.   .   .

The cloud cover finally disbanded. Pale grey light filtered in through the half-opened curtains in Keira's room. She lay sleeping with her head on Mitchell's chest. Her hair splayed across him like a silken sheet.

He held her against him, fingering the dark strands. He hadn't shut his eyes, not yet. His mind was too full. He hadn't been with another woman in over seven years. Not since he and Angela started dating exclusively. But, he admitted, if he were a cheating man, Keira would be the one. He wasn't a cheating man. He was a widower. Angela drowned and he didn't. The whole world had gone crazy and Keira was the only thing that made sense. Somehow in all this insanity, God must have some plan in mind. It couldn't be a coincidence in his darkest hour, the worst days of his life, he would meet somebody truly special.

CHAPTER 18

Ohmigod. How did this happen? Keira got out of the bed and reached for her nightgown. She pulled her head through and noticed Mitchell watching her.

"Good morning."

"Oh. Uh. Hi. Good morning." She eased the gown downward and smoothed the folds. "This is... awkward."

"Is it?" Mitchell's expression hadn't changed.

She couldn't read his mind. "Look. I'm...sorry. I didn't mean for this happened, but you don't have to feel bad or anything. I'm not like that."

"What would I have to feel bad about?"

She frowned. He wasn't making it easy. "Some sort of plan or intention is usually involved when people do this kind of thing. All I'm saying is that I wasn't stalking you or being weird. I know what you're going through."

He huffed. "Stalking me? I came into your room."

She stopped wringing her hands and smoothed her gown again. "Yeah, you did. I guess we can blame it on the rum. Even so, you don't have to worry. I won't get weird or anything."

"Keira. It's early. Whatever this is, we'll figure it out. Right now, I wish you'd come back to bed."

. ■ ■

Nate was watching the half-channel soaps when Mitchell and Keira came down the steps. "Brunch is on the table. It's cold since it started as breakfast."

Perceiving a chill, Keira went into the kitchen. Mitchell stayed. He sat on the sofa. He didn't say anything, but watched Nate.

"Kind of scary, but I almost understand it." He pointed to the screen. She's married to that guy there, but she's having an affair with this guy who might be her husband's long lost brother or father or something. Either way, he's getting ready to do something dirty."

Is he doing that on purpose?

A few silent seconds passed before Nate looked over. "What?"

"I slept with Keira."

"And you feel the need to give me a report? Should I give a damn?"

"Do you?"

"Nope."

"Are you going to be okay with it?"

"Would it matter?"

"It might," Mitchell said. "No, it won't, but I want you to feel like your opinion counts."

Nate chuckled. "Naw, I don't like it. You should leave."

Mitchell chuckled with him.

"There's another Gillian's Island down the road," Nate said. "Why don't you head on over there?"

"I have a sucky sense of direction on the water."

"Then I guess we'll make do with the present arrangements."

They didn't say any more for a while.

Thinking the conversation over, Mitchell stood up to leave.

"Hey, Mitch." Nate turned. "I'm getting a divorce because Sharee and I lived separate lives. I had an affair. Biggest mistake of my life. This adventure fixed me. When we get back home, I'm going to persuade her to take me back. I planned to prove myself by not going after the hot babe we're stranded with, even if she is the only woman on the planet at the moment. You're doing me a favor."

"Happy to be of service."

"Keep the sound bites and special effects to a minimum—I am across the hall—and we'll be good."

"I'll do my best."

Nate nodded.

"Are you sure? I don't want things to get weird."

Nate shook his head. "You need her more than I do."

Mitchell did not comment.

"Hey, Keira!" Nate surprised him by yelling.

They heared her hurried footfalls as she rushed into the room. "What? What's wrong?"

"Damn, girl, all night and you still have that kind of energy. Somebody ain't doing something right. I wondered if you would make me a plate while you were in there. I'd get it myself, but this one coming on is my favorite."

She blew air between her lips. "You almost gave me a heart attack."

"That's 'cause you ain't living right. It's been almost two weeks since you had a job." He returned his focus to the television. "At least now, when somebody asks you about your life story, you'll have something interesting to say."

Keira waved her hand at him, and then returned to the kitchen, presumably to get him some food. Nate was fine. Everything was fine.

Mitchell followed her out. For the first time in days, he felt like he might make it.

．　■　■　●　　■

Time on the island stretched, but they all had their way of coping. Every morning, Keira walked to the edge of the beach searching for seashells and rescue ships. Nate jogged the seven-mile circumference of the island. If there was anything new to be noted, he would discover it. Mitchell hung out on the widow's walk. Miles and miles of ocean for him to observe, all of it empty.

Still, their way of coping worked.

Nate—running up behind Keira—saw and scared off the snake she hadn't realized was there. From his perch, Mitchell saw the exact moment Nate fell down. Tangled in vines, he lost his footing, turned his ankle and would have had aggravated it more if he had had to make his way home unaided. Keira found a nest of Cuban crocodiles. Together, they made the hen yard and garden functional. Together, they made a life, and they coped.

. . .

An old board game made game night a new family tradition. Not that any of them knew how to play. Neither did they understand the instructions, as they were printed in Spanish with no other translations. They had fun with it anyway, making up their own rules as they thought of them.

Nate rolled the dice, moved his blue game piece twice the number of spaces rolled, and landed on a green square.

"Ha!" Keira raked in all the play money in the pot. "Can you land on green again?"

"Only if you land on a red. I'm almost broke."

"Get a loan."

Mitchell shook his head. "The bank is closed until you get something better than those non-matching bird pictures you had last time."

"The bank is closed because you're an embezzler." He gave the dice to Mitchell. "Land on red and see how fast the bank opens for you."

"The bank better open for me," Mitch said. "I've got three of a kind." He laid down three cards with pictures of pink-nosed bunnies and snatched up the dice to complete his turn.

"Scary how nice this is." Keira laid down two ducks and a rooster, then helped herself to some of his money.

"It's nice to you. You're kicking our asses," Mitch said.

"Yeah, you are," Nate agreed.

"Yeah, I am." Keira plucked one more bill from his pile. "But that's not what I'm talking about. I mean, playing a game. Hanging out. Like we're living a normal life. I didn't get to do a lot of stuff when I was younger. When we get back home, I'm reliving my childhood. You two can be my girlfriends."

"If you want me to be your girlfriend, you'll have to loan me some money," Nate said. "One more go and I'm out."

"I will if you let me win."

"Deal."

She gave him the money she had taken from Mitchell.

"You're too gullible for me to be your girlfriend." Mitchell rolled the dice, doubled the points, and landed on a green square. He eyeballed Keira's outstretched hand, moved his piece backward half the paces and landed on a yellow space.

"That's mine too." She wiggled her fingers.

Mitch handed her more money and the dice.

"How come you didn't do this when you were a kid?" Nate dealt a fresh round of cards.

"Only child. Not a lot of girlfriends."

"You?" Mitchell's forehead crinkled at the revelation. "You're bubbly enough to have a hundred girls. Aren't you the type who shops every other week?"

"That's because I'm a woman. You don't need friends for that." She laid down her bet.

"That doesn't explain why you didn't grow up with a collection of gigglers." Nate matched her.

Mitchell matched and raised. Keira had a full house: three cats, two dogs. She rolled the dice, landed on a yellow, and collected the pot again. "I don't have a lot of girlfriends because of cleavage envy. Woman will judge you by your boobs in a heartbeat. It's usually not favorable."

Nate knocked his game piece over. He was out. "Unless you want to loan me some more money, I can't be your girlfriend after all. It's your cleavage. I envy it."

"I envy her bra." Mitch said.

"Yeah, well, my bras are expensive. When we get home, you'll need to exchange all the money I've taken from you for some real dough."

"And then I'll be your girlfriend and you can give me a real loan," Nate added.

It was nice, Mitchell thought, playing games, doing nothing. When they got home, he'd buy Keira all the bras her enviable cleavage could handle.

And anything else she wanted. He wouldn't loan Nate anything; he'd give it to him.

It was also nice, Mitchell thought, being part of a family. Having Nate and Keira saved his life. He wasn't letting either of them go. They had become the family he never got with Angela.

CHAPTER 19

BAM! BAM! BAM! *"Policía! Abren!"* (Police! Open up!)

Mitchell's first thought was Nate had the television up too loud. He pulled Keira against him and put her pillow over his face.

BAM! BAM! BAM!

"What is it?" Keira muttered, half asleep.

"Nate."

Almost as soon as he said their friend's name, Nate called from the hallway. "YO! What the hell are ya'll doing in there?"

Keira sat up, alert.

There was a slam and a crash as the front door was kicked open.

Mitchell was up and moving so fast that he was only a few steps behind Nate when he stopped midway down the stairs.

"Levantarse las manos! Manos arriba!" ("Get your hands up! Hands up!") A gun brandishing officer of the law yelled at them.

Keira peeked down.

The officer spoke again. *"No se mueva!"* ("Don't move!")

The room was overrun with cops with more coming. All held weapons at the ready. None of the castaways spoke Spanish, but it wasn't necessary. Guns were a universal language. They raised their hands slowly.

"Bajan los pasos lentamente. Lentamente! Allí." ("Come down the steps slowly. Slowly! Over there.") He used the barrel of his gun to beckon them in the desired direction.

"What the shit is going on?" Nate asked.

"We're saved. That's what." Grinning, Keira followed the men down.

"No hablar hasta que le digo." ("No talking until I tell you to.") The lead officer was forceful. He gave them each a scowling head to toe look-over. Keira tugged at her nightshirt, wanting to stretch it.

"Por qué en casa de Santiago? ¿Quién eres? ¿Hablas español?" ("Why are you in Santiago's home? Who are you? Do you speak Spanish?")

"Suenan como los estadounidenses." ("They sound like Americans.") A second gun-wielding police officer said, *"¿Hablas inglés?"* ("Do you speak English?")

The word registered, prompting Keira to attempt communication. "English! *Sí!* We're Americans. We've been shipwrecked." She talked with her hands, imitating waves attacking a boat.

It didn't matter that they couldn't understand her. She was a beautiful woman in a short, thin nightshirt. She would have held their attention no matter what she said.

"Shipwrecked." She imitated swimming. *"Siren's Fire.* Sunk." She plugged her nose and went down with the ship.

"Incendio de la Sirena!" (*"Siren's Fire!"*) A third officer came to the forefront. *"Sí. Lo sé. Es el barco que se hundió en el Golfo."* ("Yes. I know it. It's the yacht that sunk in the Gulf.") He explained to the officer in charge. Focusing on Keira, he said, *"Incendio de la Sirena. Sí. Barco."* (*"Siren's Fire.* Yes. Boat.") He mimicked her imitation of a boat.

"Sí! Yes!" Keira answered. She repeated the gesture. "Thank you! Thank you. You saved us!" Unable to contain her glee, she threw herself at the officer, embracing him with her joy.

For one intense moment, the police weren't sure of her intentions; they returned to high alert. But, realized soon enough, she meant no harm.

Carefully, Mitchell and Nate lowered their arms.

When Keira freed him, the communicating officer explained further. *"Creo que estos son sobrevivientes del Incendio de la Sirena, un barco que se hundió hace unos meses. Había una mujer que sobrevivió. Su nombre era..."* ("I think these are survivors from the *Siren's Fire,* a vessel that sunk a few months ago. There was a woman who survived. Her name was...") He paused, attempting to recall. *"¿Pointe? Sra. Pointe?"* ("Pointe? Mrs. Pointe?")

Mitchell arched his eyebrows. "Mitchell Pointe." He pointed to himself.

"Mitchell Pointe!" The officer repeated.

"Mitchell Pointe," Mitchell repeated. "Nathaniel Dovey, Keira Brigham-Hoffman." He made the introductions, placing a protective arm about Keira and taking a step forward to shield her. In his opinion, they'd seen enough.

The officer nodded but remained less concerned with the others. *"Mitchell Pointe. Creo que fue su esposa quien fue rescatada."* ("Mitchell Pointe. I believe it was your wife who was rescued.") The lack of comprehension prompted him to reach for Keira's hand. He touched her ring finger and said, *"Esposa."* ("Wife.")

That was easy for Mitchell to comprehend. "Yeah, she's my wife." He pulled Keira closer, tucking her securely beneath his shoulder. "Bunch of vultures."

"Law is corrupt," Nate said. "Do they expect to get paid for rescuing us?"

Keira leaned around Mitchell. "I am not taking one for the team."

Nate patted her on the head. "If that's our way home, then yes, you will."

"You'll be okay," Mitchell agreed. "I'll buy you flowers when we get back."

"Oh. Well, I guess you better get roses. There's like ten or twelve men here?"

"Nate will help you."

"I'll get you a pillow."

"Gee thanks. Both of you."

■ ■ ■

The Cuban police had their own conversation.

"Creo que ella es su esposa." ("I think she's his wife.")

"Ella debía ser la esposa de alguien. Esa dama es magnífica." ("She ought to be somebody's wife. That lady is gorgeous.")

"Voy casarse con ella." ("I'll marry her.")

The communicating officer insisted, *"La mujer que se encontró fue nombrada Pointe."* ("The woman who was found was named Pointe.")

"Tal vez fue su hermana." ("Maybe she was his sister.")

"Tal vez." ("Maybe.")

The commanding officer spoke up. *"De cualquier manera, no importa. Él descubrirá tarde o temprano. Asegúrese de que Santiago no ha estado aquí. Conseguirme uno que habla inglés. Averiguar si saben algo. Si no lo hacen, les enviar inicio."* ("Either way, it doesn't matter. He'll find out sooner or later. Make sure Santiago has not been here. Get me someone who can speak English. Find out if they know anything. If they don't, send them home.")

The police split up and scattered about, searching for something beyond the trio's understanding. They sat side by side on the sofa, content to remain out of the way until it was time to leave.

"What made them come here?" Keira asked.

"For whatever reason," Nate hunched his shoulders. "I am happy they came. I love you guys and all, but it's time for this vacation to be over."

"Amen to that, Nate-Nate."

Mitchell had withdrawn into himself, overwhelmed by his thoughts. Being suddenly rescued had a ton of connotations. The implication that Keira was his wife took his mind to Angela and his guilt for surviving when she didn't. The sadness sent his heart back to Keira. His savior. Why shouldn't she be his wife?

"Hey?" Her voice called him to the present. "Are you with us?"

He slid into the conversation. "I'm hoping they're not looking for the rum."

"Yeah," Nate chuckled, "Not only is that shit ten ways to illegal, we drank the evidence."

"I want to take it with us. I'm getting kind of used to it."

That was an amusing thought; nobody was used to it.

ANGELA

CHAPTER 20

"Don't you want to get that?" Nolan said when Angela's phone rang for the second time in fifteen minutes. "Might be important."

"Nope." Angela shut the device off. "I already told you. An unknown number is an unimportant number. At least tonight."

"The first one was unknown. That one was Deidra."

"Or her elbow. I'll find out in the morning."

They cuddled on the back bench of the speedboat, eating popcorn and watching the stars. There were only a billion visible.

"I imagine this is what it was like being at a drive-in movie." Angela popped a kernel into Nolan's mouth.

"There may have been a screen somewhere and perhaps a movie of some sort was involved."

"This is better." She offered him another kernel from her fingers.

"This is better." He opened his mouth to receive her gift. He closed his lips on her finger and sucked the butter.

She pushed her finger further in.

He indulged her a moment before exploring the rest of her hand. He nipped and kissing her wrist, her arm, her shoulder.

She slumped against him with a sigh and closed her eyes, giving in to the craving.

It wasn't a surprise to either of them, this moment. It had to come. They had days to dwell on it, to fan it. The desire had been building from the beginning. The conversation, the looks, and the touches were all leading toward this intensity. This smoldering heat was spiraling out of control. Nolan claimed her lips and neither of them wanted control. His heart galloped as he pulled back only to return again and again. The scratch of her nails trailing across his pecs, the silk of her thigh under his palm... It had to happen. But he needed to be sure. "Is it time?" He spoke against her throat and licked her pulse while he waited for her answer.

Is it time? No...yes. "What's time? Day, week," she could hardly talk around the sensations, "month, year... What's the difference?" Was any of it going to bring Mitch back? Was prolonging her need for Nolan going to change it?

"It's all eternity when you've been waiting." He slid his tongue between her teeth, his fingers beneath her bikini and his heart into her hands.

She felt the rush of heat, the aching need he created with his touch. She moaned and clung to him, riding the wave of passion.

Long minutes passed while they lingered in foreplay, but not too long that Nolan lost sight of his objective. He wanted to make love to Angela, not screw her. That would come later. Tonight, he would take her to bed. He would worship her body long and slow. He would use the whole night to make her his.

Carried by the thought of anticipation, he released her. Her lips were kiss-swollen, her eyes glossed over. The glow on her skin gave him a sense of pride—possessive pride. He did that to her.

"Let's go home." He pulled her with him to the driver's seat. Angela sat on his lap and steered the watercraft for him. Nolan kept control of the foot pedals, but his hands were otherwise occupied.

Nolan marveled at how easily dreams came true. Last night, he dreamt of her breasts. Now, those luscious globes were in his hands. Her curvy ass drove him to distraction. It was marvelous. He pressed his face into her back and branded her.

She wiggled, trying to get closer, trying to get away, trying to get more of him. He liked the way she moved. Undulating and bouncing, the sounds of her pleasure carried on the salty air. This woman was made for loving in all its forms.

Nolan made quick work of docking the boat. He assisted Angela in climbing onto the pier. Here, he asked one final time, "Are you sure you're ready for this?"

She stepped in close, fitting herself snug against him. "I'm sure of you. I'm sure I want this. I'm sure I won't have any regrets. Any of that count?"

"All of it." He held her to him, unable to keep his hands off her. Long minutes and several kisses later, Nolan said, "If you're certain, then go ahead. I'll tell Mom to keep Lexie there tonight." He kissed her once more, then released her. If they didn't move now, he was going to take her right there. That wouldn't be right, but in a minute his brain was going to disintegrate and it wouldn't matter.

"Okay." Her voice had taken on a husky, inviting quality. "If she's awake, tell Lexie I said, 'Go to sleep, alien.' Quote me."

They held each other as they walked. The touching was glorious.

"You want me to quote you insulting my daughter?"

"Precisely."

"If she insults you back?"

"We'll know all is right in her world tonight."

Nolan nuzzled her hair and caressed her ass. "All *is* right in the world tonight."

She rested her head against his shoulder and let him guide her. It was such a lovely thing to do. "It will be better once we're sure Lexie's okay too. I have to check on her. She's my buddy."

Nolan smiled. Those easy words made him feel complete. "Are the insults some sort of code?"

"Yes, they are. For her, being a wiseass is a shield. If I like her when she's bratty then I'll like her when she's not. I won't let her down when she's afraid or vulnerable. Also, it's fun to have an adult playing her kind of game." Angela snickered.

"Sounds like you've got it under control. I will pass on the snark and leave the rest to you." Nolan stopped her at the fork between the houses. Pressing his erection against her and letting his hands do what they pleased, it was a minute before he said, "Are you sure?"

"Shhh." She stopped him with a hot, needy kiss. "I'm going to get ready for bed." She kissed him again. "Yours."

He groaned and sucked on her tongue. "I'll be back in five minutes."

.   .   .

Hilda assigned Kasey a lovely room at the back of the house, away from the television and those gathered around it. Tapping away on her keyboard, engrossed in her notes, it was a small wonder she heard them. Soft murmurings wafted up through her open window: husky whispers followed by inaudible sounds, the kind of sounds lovers make.

The nosy reporter hurried to the window. There they were. Oh yeah, they are all over each other, going at it like rabbits. It had to be less than fifty yards to the nearest bed, but it didn't look as if they were going to make it. She reached for her camera.

When she thought it was about to become porn, Mrs. Pointe and her lover separated. She went toward their house, but he came to the Enn. Kasey stuck her feet into her shoes and snatched up her pocket recorder. She would snag an interview with Mr. Hot-and-bothered. Distracted people let things slip.

.   .   .

Angela got in and out of the shower in no time, too keyed up to measure out lotions and creams or dwell overmuch on scents. She wanted to feel soft and smell good. She didn't care which bottle or jar accomplished it as long as she was ready when he got there. She chose a long, satin, midnight-purple nightgown with a neckline that plunged to her waist and a split that left her thigh exposed. She twisted left and right. Every angle offered a peek-a-boo glimpse of flesh. The lace panties underneath were the same midnight-purple, but see-through. There was no point in having them on other than to give Nolan something to do. She had never worn this nightgown for Mitch. She had so many and he had his favorites. She was glad. She didn't want memories and sentiment. Not tonight.

She ran the brush through her hair but let it hang free. A touch of lipstick and she was ready. Still, she was nervous. Going into his bedroom crossed a non-returnable boundary. She didn't want to return. Her future was on the other side. Catching her reflection in his mirror, she wondered about the woman she saw. Widowed for only a few months and giving herself to another man. Why not? No amount of dwelling or grieving would bring Mitch back. Moving on didn't diminish her love for him. Emotions she vaguely recalled. Here and there some feelings had returned. But they were distant and elusive, triggered by Nolan, not Mitchell. What was she supposed to do about it? Mitchell was a man of action. He wouldn't want her languishing over something they couldn't change. Hadn't that been the problem before? Her inability to move on after learning she was infertile. Their last months together were miserable because she was stuck.

Now, she was moving. She had help. She had Nolan. It was a new, different love with its own focus and passions. With Nolan, she was recovering from both her losses. Lexie was already the daughter of her heart. Should she not accept a gift because abstract people had opinions? It wasn't rushed. A heart can only take so much grief. Life had to be lived, regardless of timing. Love had to be given. Because she had it to give.

The grandfather clock downstairs chimed. It had been more than fifteen minutes. Was Lexie still awake? She pondered what excuse he'd come up with. It was doubtful Lexie would buy any. That girl was too smart for anyone's good. Angela removed herself from Nolan's room, just in case he didn't return alone.

She noted her phone beside her bed, where she tossed it and thought about giving Deidra a quick call. She didn't want to talk, but she was giddy with excitement. It was the type of thing girls giggled about. She'd call her later, when she had something to report. Maybe Deidra called her to report something interesting about a guy. *Hmmm*, Angela thought. *That would be funny.* The front door opened and Angela stopped caring.

Nolan took the steps slow and steady. She was in his bedroom, in his bed. Waiting. His heart thundered, and he struggled to take a breath. He was at the top of the stairwell when she surprised him by coming out of her room. His eyes filmed over. She was so damned beautiful. He wanted to take her. He wanted to have her right there in the hall and then he wanted to grab her and run.

"Nolan?" The intensity of his gaze melted her. Angela had never experienced the kind of heat coming off him. She sucked in her breath, heady with want of him.

"Mitch is alive. It's on the news. They were rescued."

THUNK.

Angela's legs shot out from beneath her. She landed on her bottom as if she had been struck by a forceful blow. She had been struck by a forceful blow. She stared at Nolan with wide, horrified eyes. Mitchell was alive. *What did that mean? How did that happen? What was she supposed to do? She was falling in love with Nolan. They were about to make love. Mitch wouldn't like that. Was he okay? What kind of wife was she?*

Nolan was there in a flash, helping her to her feet. Her entire body trembled, but he didn't notice beyond his own shaking. He brushed a light kiss against her temple. "Get dressed. I'll make us some coffee." He beat a hasty retreat down the stairwell.

.   .   .

Jeans, sweatshirt, socks, shoes—she covered every inch of skin except her hands and face before she walked into the kitchen and sat down. He placed a steaming mug in front of her. She inhaled the rich brew and waited.

Nolan leaned against the counter. "You just missed the update." He used his mug to point to the small television he had on. "They were stranded on an island near La Habana. It belonged to some drug lord who's on the run. The police thought he may have run there and investigated. They didn't have any communication, but they don't appear to be any worse for wear."

She spoke her first word. "They?"

"Three of them. Mitchell and two crew members. They were taken to a hospital to observe them overnight. They're flying them home tomorrow."

Three sips of coffee. Mitchell was alive. "I guess that's what Deidra was calling about."

"She left a message on the house phone. She's catching the first flight down. When you call her back, tell her, Mom will leave the door unlocked."

Angela nodded. She'd wait up for Deidra; there was no way she'd be able to sleep. She wanted to ask about them, her and Nolan. But what was the question? She was a married woman, not a widow in the process of falling in love.

"Angela." Nolan had something to say. He was afraid if he didn't say it now, there wouldn't be another opportunity. "I can't take back what's already occurred. I wouldn't. But, I realize, you can't make a relationship work when three people are involved. So, I won't interfere. But I will always be here. Don't forget that."

The television interrupted him with a live update of the rescue of two crew-members and a passenger from the ill-fated yacht, the *Siren's Fire*.

They watched in silence as the happy trio disembarked from the coastguard vessel amid cheers and waves from a small crowd who gathered to greet them.

MITCHELL

CHAPTER 21

"That's a serious role reversal." Mitchell's voice carried across the hospital room. Keira closed the door.

She giggled at the reference. At the beach house, he always came to her room. "I doubt you'd be able to find my room. It's down the hall and around two or three corners, hidden in some nook." She scooted him over with her hip and sat on the bed.

"At least you speak English." He sat up, clicking on the light.

"Well, we're not in the U.S., Sparky. They don't have to care if we understand. At least they're nice… to me, anyway."

"They are. I think they're updating us. A doctor told me somebody's kitten won a baseball game." He reached for her. Kisses had been constant. He didn't mean to miss any. She allowed the liberty, sought it. When he was done, he leaned back to take her in. Her eyes were bright. Her grin was mischievous. "You're in a good mood. Getting rescued must agree with you."

"It does. It's been a great night, but that's just icing on the cake." She rubbed his chest.

"Icing? What's better than going home?"

She grinned. It was so good.

"Spill." He gave her a nudge.

"It might not be the same for you. I get that. Regardless, this is perfect for me."

"Okay. What you're talking about?"

"Mitchell, I'm three weeks pregnant. We're having a baby."

Mitch sat up with a jolt. Keira was sitting there, looking more beautiful than any woman had a right to. Pregnant. With his child! "A baby," He whispered the words. "Are you sure?"

She nodded. "I was so surprised when they told me; I had them test me twice to be sure I understood. I had no idea."

"A baby." He reached for her again, hugging her as his heart slowed down. "You're right. This is better than being rescued. Marry me?"

"Mitch?" His reaction was better than she hoped, but marriage was beyond her scope.

"You have to marry me." He said it again and kissed her. "Obviously, it's not the way you would have wanted it, but we'd have gotten there, anyway. We've been through a lifetime together. I'm not doing the real world without you."

Her eyes widened. His surprise was as big as hers.

"A baby. Keira. What we have is good. My baby deserves that. Not one weekend here, one weekend there, while we waste time."

If she hadn't spent endless days on an island trying not to die, she may have been offended. As it stood, she didn't have time for pettiness. They had real life to get to. "People will say it was because of the island."

"I don't give a shit. I had the most beautiful woman in the world all to myself on an island. I knocked her up so I could keep her. I'm a genius. People will be jealous."

He made her laugh. "I want romance."

"You can have it. We can do whatever you want. I'll take you anywhere you want to go. But I'm not getting back on a boat. You can forget that."

She laughed harder. "Agreed. What happens when I'm fat and ugly and the attraction wears off?"

"The attraction is not going anywhere. That's why I want you to have a ring to prove it. And, for your information, my baby won't make you fat. If she does, consider it an honor."

"Your baby? An honor? She? What is this?"

"An honor my baby enhanced you." He nibbled the corner of her mouth and caressed her stomach. "Mine. That's my baby. Be happy I let you share. She, he, them. It doesn't matter."

"Them? Are you crazy?" Joy brought her to the brink of tears.

"Yes, I am. I want a lot of kids. And, just so we're clear, I was already falling in love."

She kissed him and let the tears come.

. . .

It was a small plane, but spacious and classy. While the copilot manned the controls, the pilot reviewed their itinerary. "Your families have been gathered. There will be an informal reception and some private time. Then you'll have to give a few interviews; tell the world your story."

"I'll have plain orange juice," Keira told the stewardess when she offered them a tray of mimosas.

"After that, will they leave us alone?" Mitchell asked.

"I hope not." Nate helped himself to his mimosa and Keira's too. "I like attention."

"You can have my share," Keira said. "I hate it."

"Pardon me." The stewardess returned with Keira's drink. "Captain, you're needed in the cockpit."

"Excuse me." He departed.

Left to themselves, they made jokes and toasted their rescue. In a quiet moment, Mitchell turned to Nate. "Are you planning to return to bar tending?"

"If I can find a place on land. It's what I'm trained for. Sharee will be happy about that."

"I have a thought I'd like you to kick around."

"What's that?"

"I would like for you to come to DC. My condo has four bedrooms. I want to hire you as my temporary assistant. You can see what I do, first hand. If you like it, I'll train you and help you prepare for the tests so you can go professional. If not, then I'll help you do something else."

Nate closed, opened and reclosed his mouth. "You would do that for me?"

"I'd do that and more. It's not just for you. I'm doing it for me. Call it fear of freedom, island attachment, I don't care. I don't like not having you near. You're one of two people I trust with my life. If there is a way I can help you with yours, I will."

As far as surprises went, it was a good one. None of them liked the thought of separation. A cheesy grin split Nate's face. "Yeah. Wow. Why not? I'll think about it, but really, why not?"

"Why not?" Mitch raised his glass for a toast.

"So what are you getting?" Nate asked Keira.

"Ohhh, I got the gold." She did a little dance in her seat.

"She got the gold," Mitch repeated. "She'll get the gold as soon as we can go get it. What are your thoughts on being the best man?"

"Married? You two are getting married?" Uncertainty filled Nate's tone.

"ASAP." Mitch reached for Keira, pulling her onto his lap.

"Is it because of the island? What will happen when we hit reality?"

"It's because this is the way it should be. Marriage is the least of what I owe her. We won't let reality mess up a good thing. That's why we're keeping the team together."

Nate finished his mimosa. He started working his way through Keira's. "Can't say I am surprised. It didn't take you two weeks to get her undressed. Slow is not your middle name."

Keira hit him; Mitchell laughed.

"This has been some morning," Nate continued. "We should get rescued more often."

The stewardess returned with fresh glasses. "Is there anything else I can get for you?" Her service was without a smile, but they didn't notice.

"One last thing," Mitchell remained focused on his friends.

"You want to go on a cruise?" Nate failed at being innocent.

"You'll be waiting a long time for that one."

"What's left?"

"I'm wondering how you would feel about being a godfather?"

"Wha—"

Keira repeated her chair dance and rubbed her belly. "I told you, Nate-Nate. I got the gold."

"Congratulations! As I said, slow is not your middle name."

They raised their drinks for another toast. The clink of glass ignited a unified memory. They shared a toast before the accident. They stayed together because they started together. That first toast was also to Mitchell's future with children.

CHAPTER 22

THE POINTES

Kasey left before Angela knew she was there. Kasey didn't interview Nolan; it wasn't necessary. She had the pictures. Standing in the shadows watching him as he watched the news, learning his lover was an adulteress. His expression told her more than his pitiful words would ever convey. She had a story. A big one. The kind that wrecked people's lives. Kasey Kay was an artist.

.　.　.

Deidra led Angela to a chair at the far side of the room. "Breathe. You look peaked. Do you want a drink?"

"I don't know what I want." Angela's mind replayed the hours before they arrived at the airport in Key West. How she and Nolan walked and talked like zombies, stiff and formal. The inappropriateness of their behavior was an embarrassment. He knew what she felt like. She knew his taste. Neither of them knew how to make it go away. The memories would not stop. The more she concentrated on Mitchell, the harder it was to ignore thoughts of Nolan. Until finally, it was a relief to be in the car, to have Deidra drive her away.

They weren't three minutes down the road before Deidra tapped her nails against the steering wheel. "Did you sleep with him?"

"No."

"You both acted like you slept together."

"We didn't."

Deidra stopped tapping and waited.

"We were getting ready to when we found out."

"Oh. That explains why you weren't comfortable. That's too close for comfort."

"Tell me about it. This is weird."

"He's pretty damn hot. I'll say that."

"Telling me doesn't help."

"It's not intended to be a help. It's a statement of the obvious. An attempt to cheer you up."

"That's the problem. I'm so guilty, I can't cheer up. I'm afraid when I see Mitch the first thing I'll do is confess while he was suffering, I made plans to get laid."

"No, you're not. That is the last thing that is going to come out of your mouth. Your husband wants to reunite with you. Not do a Jerry Springer rerun. Give him that. Nolan will come up, if and when he should, at the appropriate time. Not before. While you're kicking yourself, you might want to recall that almost means no, it didn't happen. You thought he was dead. You didn't do anything wrong, Ange."

"You're right. You're right. I need to get myself together and focus on what's important. Mitchell is alive. Mitchell is alive! My baby."

"That's better. Mitch is back. Keep that in front of you."

It worked until the reporters found her. They questioned her about how she felt, what she thought, what she did, and how she had coped since the search was stopped. They wanted information she didn't want to share.

Things got worse when she saw Mitchell's parents. Before the accident, they made her feel guilty because she was infertile. During the early days of her recovery, she avoided talking to them because they made her feel guilty for surviving. Then she avoided talking to them because she was in Florida, crushing on another man. She couldn't avoid them here.

A small reprieve came when she met the families of the other survivors. She was happy to speak with the stewardess's parents and the cook's wife, mother, and brother. In her short time aboard the *Siren's Fire*, she had met and liked them both. There was consolation in noting the cook's wife, Sharee, seemed as out of place and uncomfortable as she did. This reunion being on public display was overwhelming.

They announced the plane's impending arrival. Soon, they would lead the families out to ground level for the world to watch them reunite. *Was Nolan watching?*

•   •   •

There was a hushed excitement both inside and out when the plane touched ground. In a few minutes, the horrifying ordeal that changed lives would be over.

"Wow! All of these people are here to see us." Nate had never known anything like it. "We're famous. Who's going to play me in the movie?"

"Miley Cyrus." Keira leaned over him to peer out of the window. "Whoa. That is a lot of people."

"Who knew a shipwreck is the fastest way to stardom?" Mitch saw what they saw and was glad he had gotten his hair cut. Showing up unkempt would not have worked. "It's not that many, mostly reporters."

"No, it's—" Nate stopped talking. He pressed his face against the glass.

"What?"

"What?"

"Hot damn." Nate flashed them a smile that was larger than his face. "That's Sharee. She came here to see me."

"Aw, Nate-Nate," Keira gushed. She put her arms around him. "That's got to mean something good."

"It means she wants to be in the movie too," Mitchell teased, "as Billy Ray Cyrus."

There was no time for a response. The pilot collected them. Mitchell helped Keira to her feet. Nate stayed at the window for one happy moment, watching his wife.

CHAPTER 23

Keira was first out of the plane. The cheers and applause were deafening. It made her so nervous she kept her eyes downward, lest she stumble. Mitchell came a step behind. He was calm, expressionless, as if he had everything under control. His life was back in order. He did have everything under control. Nate emerged grinning and waving—all celebrity.

Led by a small welcoming committee, they made their way across the concrete. It bothered Mitch that Keira had yet to hold her head up. This was a proud moment; she ought to bask in it. Cameras flashed, people waved, news crews called for attention. Mitchell clasped his hand to hers, brushed a kiss across her knuckles and waved.

"What'd you do that for?" Nate came up on Keira's other side. Still grinning, he clasped and kissed her other hand.

"Because I can," Mitchell said.

"What's Sharee going to say about you holding my hand?" Keira teased. The double support and Mitchell's open display did as he intended. She became more confident with each step.

"Sharee ain't your problem," Nate said. His smile was still in place, but there was an edge to his tone. "Don't do anything else stupid, okay."

They didn't know what they missed, but Nate's unwillingness to speak while being escorted was obvious. They had to trust him. Mitchell, however, would not relinquish Keira's hand. Neither did Nate.

Behind the castaways, the pilot, copilot and stewardess ventured forth, unnoticed.

Before they reached the spectators, reporters converged on the trio. The horde was too big for the escort to hold back. Cameras focused. Lights flashed. Microphones were thrust forward. Questions were hurled at them from every direction. The reporters pushed forward. The escort pushed back. More security arrived and the news crews were forced to move back. Then they were there, in front of a roped-off section containing a tiny group of people. For the first time in agonizing weeks, the survivors saw their families.

"Holy Shit! Angela!" Mitchell forgot everything. Angela was alive! He sprinted the last few yards separating them. Reaching her, he hugged her, crying her name over and over again; he cradled her, kissed her, touched her, and held her. Angela was alive! His life. His love. Angela was alive! His wife was here. "Angela, baby. Baby. Oh God. Angela." His tears were real and full of gratitude. Angela was alive. His wife was alive.

The weight of her relief caused Angela to sag against Mitchell. She caressed his cheek, taking him in. He returned from the grave. He came back to her. They were together again. She cried with him, for him, and for herself. She heard his voice and the echo of his heartbeat. Mitchell held her. In his arms, she was home.

. . .

Nolan left the room. He wanted to watch, to see for himself. But he couldn't take any more. It wounded him, and he felt selfish for it. A husband reunited with his wife. What did that have to do with him? They had been separated for months. Of course, they were supposed to hug and kiss. The world was supposed to see it and be happy for them. He wanted to be happy for them, but he wasn't the world. He couldn't watch.

Hilda, Rob, Lexie, and even Tank stayed silent in his wake.

Keira swallowed the lump in her throat. She refused to react. Her mother and father were there. They mattered. They hadn't seen her in weeks, months. They needed to be assured she was safe. Right now, she needed her family more than anything.

Likewise, Nate gave and got affection. Mitchell and Keira were momentarily forgotten. Sharee came to meet him. She forgave him. He would get a happy ending.

Mitchell's parents, Deidra, Nate's mother, and his brother, Rubin, were all included as the happiness spilled over.

Thirty minutes later, with their families huddled around them, the public was treated to the first thoughts and words of the castaways.

"How does it feel to finally be back home?"

Nate answered that one. "About like you would expect. Great."

"How many days were you lost at sea?"

Again, Nate answered. "Three or four." He turned to the others for confirmation.

"Three," Keira confirmed.

"Too many to be sitting in a rowboat," Mitchell said. "But at least we had one. Keira was our captain. She saved our lives." He wanted to say something encouraging to her, not just about her.

"Initially, were there other survivors with you?"

"No."

"No."

"No." Keira said, "We couldn't find the others." She gave Angela a small tentative smile.

"Can you tell us about the island you were stranded on?"

"Land with some trees and water all around it." Nate kept a straight face.

Over the chuckles, Keira said, "It wasn't something we expected, that's for sure. A house with food, and a bathroom; it's not usually how a person gets shipwrecked. We were thankful."

"Did you meet with Fuentes Santiago or any of his associates?"

"No."

"No."

"No, we had no idea whose house we were in." Mitchell added, "We were banking on somebody eventually coming home."

"Yes, we were."

"We were."

"The outside world mourned your death while you were safe at a vacation home. Any comment on that?"

Nate hunched his shoulders and frowned. "We found shelter, not a hotel. We didn't have access to a phone or the internet."

The next question was for Mitchell. "Mr. Pointe, what was your initial reaction to learning Mrs. Pointe had also survived?"

"You saw it. No one told me Angela was here." All irritation forgotten, Mitchell grinned at Angela. "It was a detail that should not have been overlooked, but all things considered, it was the best surprise ever."

"Mr. Dovey. Before the accident, you and Mrs. Dovey experienced some difficulties. Is that behind you now?"

"When you've been missing and you should be dead, but you get to come back, you stop having marital issues. What you have instead is proper perspective and real appreciation."

"Miss Brigham-Hoffman, was being stranded with two married men a different experience than you would have expected from two single guys?"

Keira erupted in a fit of nervous laughter. "I assure you, I was more concerned with getting rescued than who left their socks on the floor. It took all three of us to survive. We thought Angela—Mrs. Pointe—had perished. We wanted to get Nate back to Mrs. Dovey. It required us to live in the present. Food, water, and shelter were the main things. That came before memory lane and baby pic...tures." She fought to keep her smile in place. She hadn't meant to say it. She hadn't meant to go there. But the word slipped out. It was hanging in the air for her and Mitchell to breathe around.

"Miss Brigham-Hoffman." Kasey Kay stepped forward, haughty and self-satisfied to an extreme. "I have information from an *exclusive* source. Would you tell us if you are pregnant and which of your married companions is the father?"

CHAPTER 24

The silence. The horrified shock in Keira's eyes. The sharp look that passed between the trio. It was confirmation enough. Cameras flashed twice as fast, eager to capture the moment. Questions were rapidly fired as if an admission had been given.

The first poignant response came not from the castaways, but from Sharee, Nate's wife. She snatched her hand from his and ran from the platform.

"Sharee!" Nate called once. When she didn't turn around, he steeled his features but remained where he stood.

"Go get her, Nate," Keira whispered under the crowd noise. "Don't let her think that."

"She didn't wait to find out." With that, Nate clasped Keira's hand and said aloud, "I'm the baby's father."

Mitchell watched his wife. She was tense, but he had no words of comfort to give her. He hated her finding out like this. Sharee left the podium and Angela leaned into him, visibly relieved. He took a deep breath when Nate's confessed. Keira didn't deny it. He was off the hook. Angela could be spared. Nobody needed to know.

But he could not.

He would not.

Keira carried his child. She and the baby were his responsibility. Nate was noble, but it wasn't his responsibility. Not for anything would he intentionally see Angela hurt, but hiding from the truth was wrong.

He squeezed Angela's hand then released it. He took a step in front of both Keira and Nate. "That's not true. Nate is trying to protect my marriage. The truth of the matter is he was unequivocally faithful to his wife. I thought I was a widower. Keira is carrying my child."

The room spun. Angela got nauseous. She wanted to follow Sharee. She wanted to run, hide, and not hear what Mitchell said. That he cheated was the second blow. Another woman was going to have his baby—something she couldn't do. Compounding everything was the knowledge her humiliation was being viewed by millions in real time on national TV.

She didn't run. Partially, because she had to maintain her last shred of dignity. Mostly because Deidra held to her with a vice-like grip. It was a show of solidarity and anticipation of Angela's reaction.

Mitchell had more to say. "I realize we're news, and reporters love to break a story and be the first with the latest gossip. However," He pointed at Kasey Kay. "This is wrong. It's a blatant disrespect of privacy. We've just returned today. My wife was in that accident too. She spent these last couple of months thinking I died. You do this to her in front of the world. Thanks to you, instead of the happy reunion we all deserve, Nate's wife is gone. Keira is not some whore or a home-wrecker. We thought Angela was dead. We were planning to get married. We," he waved his hand at the people beside him, "haven't had a chance to talk about it, but you were happy to fuck up our lives for the sake of a scoop. You, lady, are what's wrong with America." He turned his back on the reporters and halted. Angela and Keira were looking at him. One with admiration, the other with repulsion. What the hell was he supposed to do now?

Still holding Keira's hand, Nate took the lead. "Get your wife," he said as he ushered Keira away.

Mitchell reached for Angela. She stiffened, resisting his touch, but he would not let go. With him on one side and Deidra on the other, they led Angela away.

As soon as they were away from the cameras, Angela pulled away from him.

"Baby, I'm so sorry." Mitchell reached for her again. "I'm sorry."

She slapped his hand away. "You stay away from me."

"No," He shook his head and tried to reach for her one more time. "We need to talk. We'll get it worked out. I promise. Honey, please—"

"I'm not your damn honey. Leave me alone." She turned her back on him, missing his shattered expression. Her tears were at the surface. "Don't let him follow me," she told Deidra and walked away.

Mitchell tried anyway. "Angela! Don't do this. We need to talk. I just got you back."

Flanked by his parents, Deidra cut him off. "Mitch. Give her a minute. She needs ten seconds to breathe."

His mother stepped in to embrace him. "It will be all right Mitchell. You handled that beautifully. I am so proud of you."

"Yeah," Deidra rolled her eyes. "Congratulations."

.　.　.

"Nolan." Hilda's voice came across the yard. She found him readying his speedboat.

"I don't want to talk, Mom."

"Good. Because I didn't come out here to listen to you. I came out here to tell you—"

"I don't want to hear it. I want to be left alone."

"Nolan, shut up. I'm not trying to interrupt your pity party. Angela's in trouble."

He had been focusing on his tasks, attempting to tune her out. But when she said that name, he snapped to attention. "What trouble?"

"On television, in front of everybody, she found out her husband got that girl pregnant and they're planning to get married."

.　.　.

Hiding in a restroom, banging her head against the wall between the stalls, the last thing Angela expected was Nolan's ringtone. *Oh no. No, no, no.* She wasn't going to answer it. She couldn't talk to him. She couldn't face him. She denied the phone all the way to her ear. "I guess you saw it?"

"Is it all right for me to call you?"

"Why not? It's not like you got me pregnant or anything."

"Where are you?"

"I'm hiding in the restroom, where else?" That was the end of her courage. She crumbled on the floor and wailed.

"Angela… Angela… Angela, talk to me…" He said it every few seconds, waiting for her to calm down. "Angela… Calm down… Angela…"

Eventually, it sunk in.

"Angela…"

"Y-yes?"

"I'm on my way. I'll be there in twenty minutes."

"No. No, d-don't come. That's g-going to-to add to t-the mess."

"I don't give a damn about the mess. I'm already in the car. I'm coming for you. Do you understand?"

It was a relief. Nolan had been taking care of her since he saved her life. He was dependable. That hadn't changed. "Thank you."

"If you can, meet me somewhere. If not, I'll come in and find you."

"Thank you."

■   ■   ■

It was difficult dodging reporters while searching every corner and cranny of the airport. Deidra did it twice. Tired of the hunt, she reached for her cell phone and found she had a message from Nolan waiting. *This is going to be a bad idea.* She opened the text.

Angela is with me. In case you're looking.

"Even worse," she muttered as she typed. **Is she okay?**

A few minutes later, she got his reply. **She will be.**

On my way.

CHAPTER 25

Angela's relief at seeing the Enn was almost as great as when she threw herself into Nolan's arms at the airport. He rescued her and brought her to the only safe place she knew. He brought her home.

Her intention to go straight to her room at Nolan's was thwarted by Lexie. The child charged down the steps and threw herself into Angela's surprised arms. She kissed her cheek and laid her head on Angela's shoulder. She didn't have any words. She didn't need any words. Her comfort, freely given, said it all.

It was the softest comfort Angela had ever known. Lexie was a lifeline. Angela held her tight and swayed as a fresh wave of sobs rocked her body. She wasn't aware of Nolan guiding her into the Enn or leading her to the living room. She sank into the sofa cushions still holding Lexie, who didn't want to be freed anyway. Nolan sat beside her and gathered them both close. Hilda brought her a cup of tea laced with brandy.

The silence stretched for such a while that Angela wondered if Lexie had fallen asleep. She glanced down to see the child watching her with wide, sad eyes. She touched the small face, wishing she could remove the sadness.

"Are you going to be okay?"

Angela offered her a brave smile. "I will be, sweetie. You're helping me."

"I told you I would."

"You did. You've kept your word."

"I don't even know what's going on, but I'll keep helping you."

Nolan leaned forward. "Would you help us by giving us some time alone to talk?"

Lexie looked from one adult to the other. She told Angela, "I won't go too far. Call me if you need me."

Angela nodded and released the child. Lexie scooted off her lap and headed out. She turned in the hall to face them. "If you want, we can swim tomorrow."

"That's exactly what I want," Angela said.

Hilda got up from her chair. "Lexie, do you want to help me with dinner? That will give these two plenty of time to talk."

"Okay. We'll be in the kitchen." Lexie announced and went that way.

Hilda paused in the hallway too. "Angie, honey, I know it's going to take a while, but try to let it go. It wasn't anything personal against you. Life happens. Shit happens. Anything can happen. You're home now. Stay home and let it go."

Nolan wrapped both arms around Angela and they listened to his mother's footsteps fading down the hall. They didn't talk on the drive. Angela cried and Nolan let her. It had been a good idea. She slumped against him, cried out and dry.

"Don't you wish you would have left me on that jet ski?"

"No. That was the beginning of the best part of my life."

He made her smile. She didn't know how he did that. "All this drama."

"None of it was your doing."

"Nolan, have you ever witnessed anything so screwy?"

"Men get women pregnant all the time." She stiffened but he held her in place. "That isn't the worst that might have come from this. I realize you're going through hell, and I'm trying to keep it in perspective. But I have to admit, there is a part of me that isn't sad at all."

She smiled a little more, glad to be with him. "I am so confused. I don't know what to do or how to react."

"React to this." He put her palm on his chest, over his heart. "Do something with this." He kissed her. It was a hard kiss, meant to be possessive. He meant to make her his. "That's all you need to worry about." He kissed her again, this time soft and gentle. "Give yourself a break." He spoke without breaking contact with her mouth. "Don't think about anything but this." He pushed his tongue inside.

He took her mind away from her hurt, numbed her to the pain. Her body responded to the attention, the adoration. Nolan's arms were strong and safe.

Angela was still cocooned in Nolan's embrace when Deidra arrived. Deidra took in the scene and scowled.

"Here, have a seat." Hilda nudged her further into the room. "Dinner will be ready shortly. In the meantime, you can tell us what's going on."

Deidra did sit down, but she did not relax. "I'm not sure we'll be staying. This is such a mess, Ange. How are you?"

"About how you would expect." Angela tucked into Nolan's side.

His arm was around her shoulder; he held her tighter.

Deidra rolled her eyes at the display. "I told them I would try to bring you back."

"I'm not going back there." Angela shook her head and pushed further into Nolan's space.

"Mitchell can come here if he wants to talk," Nolan said. "If that's what you want."

"You would allow that?" The idea had not occurred to Angela.

"Whatever it takes to get through this."

"And the rest of them?" Deidra cocked her head in Nolan's direction. "Can they come too?"

"This is an inn," Hilda said. "I'll take money from almost anybody."

"Are you kidding?" Angela leaned forward. "Why would I want to see the rest of them? I'm not certain I want to see him."

"Because at the moment, they're a package deal." Deidra shifted forward too. "There is a real concern about post-traumatic stress, especially with these new developments. The girl being pregnant and you and Mrs. Dovey taking off. The doctors from the insurance company have already noted Mitch and the other two behave like Siamese triplets. They've deemed those three can't be separated yet. The first thing they did was hand them cell phones to keep tabs on one another. Everybody and their families are being put up in a hotel—away from the media—for the next couple of days. Mitch is beside himself trying to find you. They won't leave his side. So if he has to come here, you better make room for them all. With their families—a handful of people who would like to go home, but can't. And, do you really want to introduce Nolan to Mitch's mother?"

"Ugh." Angela's face scrunched at the mention of her mother-in-law. "Has she said anything to you?"

"To me? No. She was happy to meet the girl though. I don't want to make you sad, but I can't help it. That woman gets on my nerves."

"Mine too." Angela wanted to sound brave and unaffected instead of broken and insignificant.

"I'll deal with her for you." Hilda's attempt at humor had the right effect. "Drama Queens are my speciality."

"It is," Nolan added.

Angela snickered at the thought. Nolan's mother and Mitchell's mother were polar opposites. And Hilda wasn't one to be messed with.

Deidra kept them on point. "You have to talk to him, Ange."

"Why? And why now? I can't handle this right now."

Immediately, Nolan pulled her back against him, offering her his comfort.

"Because two days ago, you thought he was dead. He was on some island thinking you were dead. Besides the fact that six different hells have broken loose, you need to see your husband. He needs to see you. You don't have to deal with anything. That's up to y'all. But, you do have to see him. If you don't welcome him home, it will be like you wanted him to be gone."

"I did welcome him home. I was at the airport, saying *welcome home* when he told me he was involved with another woman."

With his free hand, Nolan stroked her shoulder.

She leaned into his caress.

"He didn't tell you that." Deidra shook her head. "I'm on your side in this, but you can't blame the announcement on Mitch. He didn't have any control over the timing. It would have been the same thing if I started talking about Nolan." She'd been trying not to notice the way Nolan touched her sister, but it was becoming hard to ignore.

The subtle reminder was enough to make Angela stiffen and put some space between her body and Nolan's. "That's different. Besides, you couldn't be that callous."

"It won't be different to Mitchell. You're right. I'm not that callous, but the media is. Don't punish Mitchell for that."

CHAPTER 26

At the sound of the knock, Mitchell huffed. He wanted to be alone. No, he didn't want to be alone. But he wanted his wife, not company. He opened the door and his mood lightened. Keira wasn't company. "You all settled?" He opened the door wide enough for her to duck under his arm.

"Somebody bought me clothes and had them in the room when I got there. No settling required. I'm supposed to be resting, so you haven't seen me." Keira glanced around the two-room suite. "Yours is nice." She walked into the other room and made herself comfortable on his bed.

"I've seen you." Mitch locked the door and followed her. He stretched out beside her.

"No, you haven't."

"Who's looking?"

"My parents won't let me out of their sight."

"Yeah, well, look at what happened the last time you went off by yourself."

They shared a smile before Keira got serious. "How's it going?"

"Shitty."

"Have you talked to her yet?"

The shake of his head was small, dejected. "I tried to call her four times. She doesn't want to talk."

"She'll come around."

He flipped on his back and dragged her against his chest.

"She must be devastated."

"It's not easy for any of us. We can't get anything figured out as long as she keeps hiding from it."

Idly, her finger traced circles across his chest. "Put yourself in her place, Mitch. What if the first thing you learned after kissing her hello was that she was three weeks pregnant and planning to get remarried?"

"I'd listen to her. Give her a chance to explain."

"Mitch."

"What?"

"Please."

"What?"

"Explain? What's incomprehensible about it? It's not hard to figure out what happened."

"Yeah, but it's not like some one-night-stand cheating. This thing needs to be looked at and understood properly."

She didn't answer. Instead, she leaned on her elbow, looking down at him.

Her eyes reminded him of chocolate. Chocolate shouldn't be sad. "What are you thinking?"

"I'm not getting an abortion."

"What?" He frowned. "No, you aren't. Don't even talk like that."

Her brow smoothed as her tension evaporated. "I realize we had plans, but I want you to know I'll be okay. I mean, you have to stay with your wife and get things worked out. Don't worry about the baby. I'll take care of it."

"Shut up. I will take care of my baby. I'll take care of you too." He put his arms around her, bringing her face close to his. "I'm not going to let you down, Keira."

"Mitchell. You are a married man."

"Yes, I am."

"So what? You're going to keep us both? You want me to be your mistress?"

He gave an exhausted sigh. "What do you want me to say? I don't know how any of this is supposed to work. Regardless, I can tell you this. I wasn't lying about my feelings and they don't turn on and off. They're there. You and the baby are a part of my life now. I don't know how the pieces fit, but I will make them fit." Because he was tired and lonely, and it was a terrible first day home, and Angela walked out on him, and Keira was there in his arms, needing him to give her some measure of security, needing him, he kissed her. Long and deep and slow, because he needed her.

Keira let him kiss her, let him have her, because he needed her.

.   .   .

"This is so not a good idea," Deidra said from the back seat of Nolan's car. "You shouldn't be here."

"I'm as invested in this as anybody." Nolan caught sight of her in the rearview mirror. "Better to deal with it all at once."

"Yes. And, then a big no. At best, it will weaken her case. At worst, it's going to come off as petty retaliation."

"It is what it is," Nolan said. "Doesn't matter how they see it. Regardless, I'm not sending her into the lion's den unprotected."

"What am I? Non-existent?"

"You're her sister, not the man who has a stake in the outcome. Besides, I'm not sending you back into the lion's den unprotected either."

She turned toward the front passenger seat. "He's a nice guy, Angela."

"Yes, he is. He doesn't deserve this." Angela had been quiet on the ride to the hotel. Her head was full of pain and fear. This thing with Mitchell was hurtful and confusing to an extreme. But facing it with Nolan was comforting, and humiliating. She was flashing her boyfriend in her husband's face. Her husband who was only one day out of the grave. Of course, she hadn't expected to meet his pregnant fiancée, either. "You don't deserve this, Nolan. You shouldn't be here."

"Why not? You're here."

"I probably shouldn't be here, either."

"I guess it's too late now," Deidra said as they came upon the hotel parking lot. "We're all here."

.   .   .

Mitchell dried himself vigorously. Sex with Keira had energized him. She returned to her room to take a nap in earnest, but he was hungry. Luckily, he had a plan. Find Nate, eat a lot, and ignore his problems. He was contemplating his genius when the phone rang.

"Mitchell Pointe."

"Mr. Pointe. This is the lobby. You asked to be notified of your wife's arrival. She's here now, sir. They're on their way up to your room."

Mitch's brain froze, but he managed to stammer out a thank you. Angela was here; on her way up to his room. He searched the closet. A moderate but complete wardrobe had been supplied for him—Angela, too. He threw on the first pair of jeans his hands touched. He followed it with a T-shirt and was searching for socks when he noticed the bed. It looked like it had been slept in—not the kind that produces rest. As fast as possible, he smoothed the covers and punched the pillows in place.

The knock came.

CHAPTER 27

It wasn't Angela.

"Still can't sleep. Wanna eat?" Keira's relaxed face beamed at him.

Nate was beside her. "Which room is your parents'?" He waved a finger at some of the doors in question. "The families are gathering downstairs. The food at the hotel restaurant is supposed to be good. We'll see."

"Angela's on her way up."

Keira gasped.

Nate didn't need any more information than that. "Where are your parents? We'll take them with us and you can give us an update later. Come on, Keira."

They didn't get to turn around before the elevator opened. Angela, Deidra, and a man they didn't recognize stepped out.

The pause was long and awkward, like a showdown nobody wanted to have.

"Angela." Mitchell stepped further into the hall and stopped. There was accusation in his wife's eyes.

Angela knew. She didn't have the ability to articulate it, but her spirit raged. Beyond a doubt, she was betrayed.

Nolan broke the trance. He came forward. "I'm Nolan Woods. Welcome home." He offered his hand first to Nate, then Keira, and finally Mitchell. There was tension in that last shake.

"Nolan." Nate took control of the situation. "May I call you Nolan?"

"Please do."

"Good. Nolan, would you and Miss... Jefferies... It is Jefferies, isn't it?" He asked.

"Deidra's fine," she said.

"Deidra." He gave her an appraising glance. "We were about to get dinner. You're more than welcome to join us." He nodded toward Mitchell. "They need the time."

Rather than answer, Nolan turned to Angela. "Your call. We'll do whatever you want."

Angela looked from Mitchell to Keira, to Nate, to Keira, to Mitchell. "I want some dinner." There was a bite in her tone. "We should have some dinner and get to know each other since we're all so intimately involved."

Keira flinched as if the venom was aimed at her.

Most of it was.

"Let me get my shoes." Mitchell left them staring.

. . .

The restaurant had an unrecognizable theme. Painted in shades of green and cream and orange, no two walls were the same. Antiques, sporting memorabilia, famous advertisements, whatever junk was available became part of the décor. The floors were carpeted and tiled, hardwood and brick and linoleum—something different at every section of tables or booths. The music was loud, the staff louder. The smell of lemon zest, cinnamon, and not so subtle hints of chili powder wafted through the air. It was sensory overload. Nevertheless, it was clean and the portions were huge.

Other than being the man who rescued Angela, and a friend, nothing was said of Nolan's presence between Angela and Deidra. There seemed to be an atmosphere of reservation surrounding the lone white man at the table. It was assumed he was there to offer moral support. Mitchell thanked Nolan for his wife's life, but they did not interact.

As for the rest of the party, the conversation varied from relaxed to strained, depending upon who chatted with whom.

"We never expected the possibility of a grandchild," Nicolette, Mitchell's mother, said to Keira.

Across the table, Latoya Dovey, Nate's mother, talked at the same time. "Of course, you were grieving, Angela, but, were you able to get out there and experience single life? It's more fun than people let on."

"I hope you will consider coming to Washington," Nicolette said. "There is so much culture and education for a child."

"You should spend some time in Florida," Latoya talked louder. "Sunshine and orange juice... with a little vodka in it can make you forget the rest of the world."

"She's already aware of that." This time, Mitchell's mother spoke to Nate's mom. "She vacationed here while Mitchell was missing."

"Vacationing?" Deidra raised her voice. "The medical term is recuperating. Her doctor deemed it best for her to be away from the stress that lives in DC."

"No matter how hard you try," Nicolette looked down her nose at Deidra. "There are some things you can't heal from."

■　■　■

As the dessert orders were being taken, Angela pointed to a caramel brownie. "Lexie would love that. We'll have to take her a piece."

"She has excellent taste," Latoya said. "Who is she, may I ask?"

"She's my daughter," Nolan said.

"She is phenomenal," Angela said.

"Quite a little personality," Deidra added.

"She's nine. Smart as anything." This was the most animated Angela had been all evening.

"Oh," Nate's mother quipped, "a child everyone can love."

"I'm not getting dessert." Deidra struggled not to laugh as she changed the topic. "But if either of you is getting that," she touched the menu between Nolan and Angela, "I want a bite."

Nicolette jumped at her chance. "Nolan, I've been trying to figure it out. How involved are you exactly? What I mean is," she said over Angela's attempt to respond, "you rescued Angela weeks ago. Hopefully, she hasn't made you responsible for her. You appear to be one of the few people who can get along with Deidra. It makes me wonder. This can't be a comfortable atmosphere for a singular Caucasian. Why do it? Are you on your way to a future relationship that qualifies you to be among us?" She frowned at Deidra.

Nolan counted the number of zingers Mitchell's mother directed at Angela. He didn't like it. Neither did he like Mitchell's ineffectual attempts to stop it. He didn't like her. "Under the circumstances, I'm surprised my race is a pertinent topic. I don't mind being the white guy in the group. Perhaps my history played some part in me owning a boat. This time, it worked in Angela's favor. You can skip the race-baiting, this isn't a social discourse." He didn't blink. "As far as a relationship, I'm looking at the present and the future."

Stinging from the reprimand, Nicolette said, "I confess I am having a hard time visualizing you with Deidra. You two are not what I would call typical."

"Sure we are. My relationship with Deidra is purely platonic. Our connection is Angela."

Deidra choked. She covered her mouth and reached for her wine. Angela gaped at him. The rest of the table went quiet.

"What?" He looked from one woman to the other. "No reason for me to lie."

"I'm afraid I don't understand." Nicolette sat up straight.

"I do," Latoya snickered. "At least I hope I do. Go-head, girl." She pointed to Angela. "You've been living, haven't you?"

"Mom," Nate said, "would you stay out of this?"

"I'm just saying. This girl is real. She ain't nothing like that damn Sharee or... some other people you made friends with. That should be acknowledged."

"If it's all the same to you," Mitchell said, dismissing the mothers and turning to Nolan, "What do you mean by 'connection to Angela?'" The analytical part of his brain calculated. If she forgave, he'd forgive; easy answer. Another part, a more animalistic part responded to the threat.

Angela put her hand on Nolan's arm, a silent plea for him to use caution.

Mitchell saw it and was instantly agitated.

Watching the play of emotions across his face agitated Angela. "I'm not pregnant, if that's what you're wondering."

"As if it were possible," Mitchell's mother muttered.

"What I mean," Nolan said to Mitchell, "is *after* you were confirmed dead, Angela and I began to build a relationship. I'm already in love with her. But, as she's still married, how this all works out affects me personally." He turned to look at the elder Mrs. Pointe. "I have more of a right to be here than you. Your son doesn't force you to respect his wife, but I am going to insist you refrain from making harpy-ish comments to or about the woman I love or her sister. There is enough drama here without you being the center of attention."

If his mother was offended, Mitchell didn't notice. He was all about Angela. "Just like that? You haven't talked to me, but you're going to drop a bomb on me like that in front of everybody?" He wasn't sure he believed it.

"It wasn't on the news."

That she didn't deny or flinch was a blow to him. Also, she was right. But still… "Here you are, all high and mighty and pissed off, meanwhile you've been doing the same thing."

"Wrong again." She didn't elaborate.

"Wrong about what?" He needed her to elaborate.

"How about this." Deidra got up from the table. "Mitchell, I'm going to go to your room and chill. You, you, you and you," she pointed to Nolan, Angela, Mitchell, and Keira, "go somewhere by yourselves and hash this out. The rest of you," she looked around the table, "should give them some privacy."

"Good idea." Mitchell tossed her his room key. "But you and I need to talk first," he said to Angela.

"We can't talk until everything is out in the open. That's going to take all four of us."

"Fine." He looked to Keira. "Can we use your room?"

"Yes." She retrieved her key.

"Wait," Keira's dad said. "I don't want her upset. I don't want her involved in your issues."

"Too late for that," Latoya threw back the last of her wine. "She is the issue."

"One of them," Keira snapped. She loved Nate, but his mother was not her favorite person.

CHAPTER 28

They began with uneasy silence and let it grow until it became unbearable. Nolan and Mitchell waited each other out, neither man willing to reveal or concede anything. Keira and Angela weren't waiting on each other; they were waiting on Mitchell.

Keira had the least amount of patience. "I am so sorry things turned out like this. It wasn't supposed to be this way."

Angela rolled her eyes. "How was it supposed to be? In your perfect world, I'm not here and you and Mitchell can play fairytale and live happily ever after? Would you like me to leave?"

"Whether you leave or not is your business. I said I was sorry. It would be nice to work this out like sensible adults."

Angela turned to Nolan. "I hate it when people talk like that—it's privilege. You're only acceptable if you behave the way they decide is appropiate." Now she focused on Keira. "I'm sure your apology is sincere, but it doesn't mean anything to me. Whatever your definition of sensible is, decide if getting impregnated by a married man was a *sensible* way to behave."

Mitchell finally spoke. "Is it sensible to be married with a boyfriend?"

"A: I was under the belief I was a widow and B: I'm not the one suggesting how other people should behave."

"I was under the belief I was a widower. We all have some level of responsibility for this situation. The media and lack of time and preparation made everything worse, but we can't change that now. So, how do we move forward? What do we do about it?"

Nobody had an answer for him. Keira waited on him, but he'd already given her all the assurance he could. It was Angela's turn. "Let's start with you," he said to his wife. "What do you need? What can I say or do to help you get through this?"

Somewhere in the rhythm of his syllables, Angela heard the echo of the man who had once loved and cherished her, who had been her husband for four years. More importantly, her heart received and remembered. "What is there to say?"

Mitchell knew Angela better than anyone. She'd bristle a bit, but her heart wasn't hard. She'd get through it. He'd get her through it. "Can we at least agree we've all screwed up here?" he cut a glance toward Nolan. "Not intentionally," he said when his gaze touched Keira. "But, this is about us all."

"All right," Angela said. "So what? We screwed up. We made a royal mess of this situation. What's the point? What are our lessons? Regardless of the circumstances," she aimed her finger at Nolan first. "Don't get involved with a married woman." Next Keira. "Don't sleep with a married man." And then Mitch. "Keep your penis to yourself." Finally, she pointed to herself. "And me? What's my lesson? What did I do wrong? Don't fall overboard? Don't get rescued? Don't trust the coastguard? Don't attempt to pick up the pieces of my shattered life? 'Cause as far as I can tell, that's the list of my crimes. That's the lesson I'm getting out of this!" Her voice raised an octave with each declaration until she ran out of breath.

"Oh, knock it the hell off!" Keira yelled loud enough to shock Angela into temporary silence. "We get it. Poor woebegone you. Yeah, yeah, yeah. You might be telling the truth, but at this moment, it doesn't mean jack shit. Especially not to me. You want a pity party? That's too bad, 'cause we're fresh out. You can whine all day about what you didn't do, but nothing is going to change because you're so much better than the rest of us. That married woman Nolan shouldn't have been involved with, have you met her?" Keira kept going even when Angela tried to speak. "You don't need to waste my evening picking out everybody's flaws, I'm pregnant. I don't have time to relive the past. I have a future to worry about." She touched her belly. "My baby. Nolan's little girl. If you want to dwell on who's innocent, start with them."

"Waste *your* evening? I don't need you here. If you have a problem with my *whining,* excuse yourself and go attach to some other married man."

"Hey! Hey, hey. Whoa." Mitchell stood between them. "Nix the catfight." He caught a glare from each of them. He turned to Keira, "You, chill. The baby doesn't need that." The possessive concern in his tone and the way his eyes lingered made Angela glare all the harder. "You both are right; you are. But we need to not get sidetracked. We need to move on."

"No. We need to stop." Nolan said his first words since coming to Keira's suite. He stood up too. He had seen the death of something in Angela's countenance. Productive communication was not going to happen, at least not right now. "We need a break. Angela, would you walk with me, please?"

"Whoa, whoa, whoa." Hearing his wife's name fall from another man's lips in that compelling manner was not something Mitchell would tolerate. He pointed to Angela. "That's my wife. Do I need to make that clear to you?"

Nolan looked at him with something close to pity. "I know precisely who she is. I also know she's too upset for this bullshit. Perhaps you missed it. These ladies have escalated and need a break. As uncomfortable as it must be to your pride to see Angela walk out of here with me, you can't tend to them both. It seems inappropriate for me to whisk Keira away. However, it's your choice."

Mitchell took a step forward with his fists balled.

Simultaneously, the women moved. Keira grabbed Mitchell's arm. Angela got in front of Nolan. It wasn't necessary. Nolan stopped him with one sentence. "Yes, I'm sure that will be beneficial."

Mitchell saw a red haze. Everything was fucked up. Everything! There wasn't one single thing about this whole situation that wasn't. Angela was his wife. His. But how can the baby not be everybody's first priority? Woods needed his ass handed to him. He wasn't being the voice of reason. Woods was setting him up for failure. Calling a halt and all but telling him to pick a girl. Fuck that! Fuck that bastard. It wasn't up to him. It was up to Angela. He patted Keira's hand to let her know he was back to calm. "Angela."

Angela noted his hand on Keira's. "I don't have anything to say to you right now." She turned to Nolan, ready to give him a dose of her anger as well. "I don't need anybody's permission to leave. I can go when and where I want."

Nolan's expression was unreadable. "I didn't ask anybody but you."

She almost smiled. Almost.

He caught it anyway, prompting her to roll her eyes at him before walking out. Likewise, Nolan did not acknowledge the others as he left. No point in Angela being mad at him.

Instead of going toward the elevators as he assumed, Angela surprised him by taking the stairs. She ended up in an out of the way alcove on the next floor.

They sat close, but not touching. They wanted to touch but nobody defined the rules; nothing seemed acceptable.

"I hate this."

"Yeah, it sucks."

"Does this make any kind of sense to you, Nolan? I mean, what are we doing?"

"It makes perfect sense."

"To you."

"To you too. Nobody has to like it for it to be understandable. This is a billboard moment for 'shit happens.'"

"Would you lose it, for once?"

"Pardon me?"

"I wish you'd go nuts, get angry, curse, stomp, not always be so damned composed. You make me feel like I'm having a tantrum."

Viper fast, he grabbed her by the shoulders and locked his grip. "Look at me." His tone was cool and soft, but his eyes were electric. His temples pulsed and he clenched his jaw as if he were holding back an eruption. "I am angry," he said it slow. "I want to curse and stomp. But I don't want to have a tantrum. I want to kill your damned husband. I wished he would have stayed on that island and never came back. I want to grab you and Lexie and get the hell out of here. I want to go somewhere where none of this matters and we can pick up where we left off." For a long moment, he didn't say anything. He focused his heat and intensity on her and she took it. She felt him. He had somehow gotten inside of her. It was sexual, on the verge of becoming explosive. His breathing came in heavy puffs. "But I don't get to do that. I don't get to take you away. I don't get to curse or stomp or whine. I don't get to be angry. At least not where anybody can see it. Because you're not mine. I don't have any rights here."

He pulled her in close and held her there. His whiskers tickled her bottom lip, made it tingle with yearning. She wanted to cry from the desire.

"You're not mine." He released her. He had to. Otherwise, it would cease to matter. He would take her and make her his, regardless that she already had a husband.

Angela worked to get her breathing under control. "Careful what you wish for." She mumbled. "This is nuts," she added.

He used the time to get his own breathing under control. "What'd you expect?"

"I never expected this. That's for sure."

Nolan put a hand on her shoulder. This time his touch was gentle. "What do you want to happen, Angela?"

She didn't have an answer.

"What he did. What you thought." The dim backlighting in the alcove highlighted the silver wisps at his temple. "The only thing that matters is what are you going to do now?"

Angela studied the place where their bodies met. He had strong calloused fingers that were used to hard work. She let her eyes travel up his arm, past his shoulder to settle on his face. His deep-set eyes were more violet than blue—a true testimony of his personal storm.

CHAPTER 29

"Well, that was productive." Keira locked the door behind Nolan.

"Yeah," Mitchell said. "We obviously can't do a foursome. It will have to be the three of us."

"Which three would that be, exactly?" She folded her arms.

"Right," he scoffed. "The only three that matter. Woods is trying to get his dick in, but that ain't happening."

"I guess we don't have to wonder why your wife is so venomous toward me."

"What?"

"Listen to yourself. I'm supposed to matter. She's supposed to accept me in the picture. But you get to dismiss him like he's nothing."

"He is nothing."

"Not to her. And, recognizing he and I have the same status, I'll end up as nothing too."

"Never." Mitchell pulled her to him because holding Keira was always right. "You have a place and a part in this. A very important part." He rubbed her stomach. "Two parts. Woods is trying to get on the inside. It's not the same thing."

Contrary to soothing her as he thought, she took an offended step back. "And yet, you want to convince Angela that it's exactly the same thing. That our discrepancies offset."

"You're twisting—"

"Enough, Mitchell. Enough for the night. This was annoying and I'm tired. Here's what we're going to do. I'm going to bed. In the morning, I'm going home. I want to be in my own house. I want to get my head around this without the drama." She went to the door and opened it. "The three of *you* can figure out what's what and you can let me know. Good night."

Mitchell jerked. It was a blow… and a way out, temporarily. He could handle this one woman at a time. Angela was his wife; she ought to come first. "I'm going to agree only," he followed her to the door, "*only*, because my baby will never, ever be in the center of an argument between you and I. Never." He leaned down and kissed his baby. "You rest easy. Daddy loves you." Then he straightened and caught Keira with a second kiss. "You rest easy too. Let me know when you get there and I'll call you as soon as I can. Fair?"

No, it wasn't fair, but it was the best she was going to get. "Ummhmm. Good night Mitchell." She kissed him.

. . .

"We should go home."

"Home?" Angela repeated. She didn't know where she lived.

"Yep." Nolan nodded. "This day has been too long. We're not fixing anything tonight."

"What will it mean if I go home with you?" She whispered the question. "Would I be walking out on my marriage? Would it mean I didn't try?"

He shook his head. "No, that's not what it means."

"I have to be sure because I'm tired and confused, and I really want to go home with you and not do this anymore."

She was broken and needy and he wanted to rescue her. He wanted to hold her and love her and make her forget. He would take her home—their home—and make her forget. "You're going to get your wish. It's what I want, too."

She kissed his cheek. That was safe. That was her way of saying she wanted to do more.

Nolan savored it. It wasn't enough. He retrieved his cell and dialed Deidra. It made him frown when his call went straight to her voicemail.

"She must be sleeping. No," he said when Angela tried to get up. "I'll get her. You sit here until I get back. "We'll be out of here in ten minutes, max."

"What about Mitchell? I have to tell him we're leaving."

"We'll tell them on our way out. Just sit there and rest."

She nodded. The world had been too heavy; she didn't have the energy to do any more than that.

"I'll be right back." Nolan brushed his lips across her forehead.

He watched her from where he waited in front of the elevators. There were two and neither one was moving very fast. He jammed the button, willing the cars to arrive quicker. The light over the door on the left lit up first. The one on the right was a moment behind. Nolan stepped into the first car as the second set of doors opened to receive passengers.

Mitchell looked out. There was no one waiting to get in, but Angela was in the alcove, wide-eyed, and alone. He stepped out.

"Hi," he said when he was near enough to speak.

"Hello."

"I was coming to find you. I thought you'd be in my room with Deidra. Lucky I saw you here."

"I guess so."

"Where's your boy?"

"Nolan is on his way up to get Deidra. You just missed him." She pointed to the elevators.

Mitchell nodded. This was as ideal as this screwed up scenario was going to get. He wasn't going to waste his opportunity. "Keira's leaving in the morning."

Angela had been mentally preparing herself to tell him she was going home with Nolan. His declaration changed her focus. "What?"

"You and I haven't been properly reunited yet. How are we supposed to figure anything out like this?"

She didn't know.

He knelt in front of her. "Would you consider having him leave us for a while? So you and I can talk as a husband and wife without interference?"

Angela responded to him, the part of herself she thought dead. She didn't recognize it anymore. "I can't do that, Mitchell."

"Why not?" He kept his tone even.

"I told Nolan I wanted to leave. We're going back to the Enn."

No way in hell was she leaving him again. "We have a room here. You and I. They even supplied you with a wardrobe. You're supposed to stay here with me."

"Do they have rooms and clothes for Nolan and Deidra? I can't ask them to stay here."

He wasn't meaning for them to stay. "Angela, this is our marriage, our life. May I please have ten minutes of your time? Why would you want him to stay? I promise you, you're not going to get lonely."

"I might. Besides, I don't want to spend the night with you and your girlfriend and your boyfriend and their parents and your parents and nobody who gives a damn about me." Her eyes glossed over.

He immediately regretted his sarcasm. "I'm sorry. I am. How about this? I'll go with you to this Enn or whatever. They can stay. I'll be the one that's outnumbered. Whatever it takes to get this right."

"Whatever it takes? How is this ever going to be right?"

"Don't say that, honey."

"Why not?"

"Because it means you've forgotten how much I love you. If you forget that, I might as well go back to that island. Or better yet, drown."

She didn't answer. She didn't want to tell him she had forgotten how much he loved her. Literally.

CHAPTER 30

Nolan tapped on Mitchell's room door. He wanted to get out of there ASAP and hoped it wouldn't be too difficult to get Deidra moving.

Deidra yanked the door open with an amazing amount of energy. "Oh. Nolan. It's you. Where's Angela?"

"She's downstairs waiting. You ready to go?"

"We're leaving?" He only got to nod once before she replied. "Thank God. Let me get my purse."

He followed her into the suite, glancing around, unimpressed. "You're wound up. What's the matter?"

"Nolan, I want to kill someone. Mitchell." She grabbed her bag as if it had somehow offended her.

"Okay."

"Guess what the bastard did?"

"Came back and interrupted my life."

"That too."

"What happened?"

"He slept with Keira."

"That's not news. She's pregnant."

"Today."

"What?"

"I doubt he would have given me his room key if he remembered he left their dirty sex towels on the bathroom floor. Or if he realized that whore's hair is all over his pillows. Nolan, he's still involved with her. There's no excuse. This is an affair."

Nolan's mind raced. The sheer joy of the revelation bubbled up inside of him. He fought hard not to smile. "That bastard."

Deidra read the play of emotions on his face. "This is serious. What's this going to do to Angela?"

Hearing Angela's name put it in perspective. "Let's go before I get arrested for doing something to the bastard."

They were met in the hall by Angela and Mitchell getting out of the elevator. Presumably, Mitchell was telling her something amusing. Her smile was natural. It faltered when she came under Nolan's scrutiny. "Umm, there's a slight change in plans... that is if it's okay with you?"

Mitchell had been anticipating Nolan's reaction. He whipped his head around to Angela. "How'd it get to be up to him?"

"Because it's his place, that's how." As uncomfortable as she was, she wasn't about to be bullied by either of them. "Nolan, Mitchell wants to come home with us. To see if we can hold a conversation away from the circus." She squared her shoulders. "I'd like to try."

She wanted to bring her husband to his house. Nolan supposed he should at least be grateful she asked. But he wasn't grateful. He was annoyed and becoming more so by the minute. "Is Keira coming too?"

"No."

"No."

Although they answered at the same time, Mitchell continued the explanation. "She's going home. She's giving Angela and me some space. It's a good idea. We need it."

His subtle hint wasn't. But Nolan was all about directness. "I hope you're not looking for space at my house." He walked past them. He didn't care what anybody else did, but he was going home.

"I'll get my things." Mitchell left the girls in the hall.

"Your quietness is a dead giveaway," Angela started. "I'll listen to anything you tell me, but let me say something, first. Please."

Deidra nodded. Her turn would come.

"He is my husband. That didn't go away. Earlier today, I said screw it. You made me come here. Now, I'm dealing with it. I owe him an opportunity to say or do whatever. I owe myself an opportunity to decide for myself. Without any negatives thrown at me. Not the news, not Keira. I need to get beyond the numbness and see what I think. Is that terrible?"

No. It wasn't. Angela's day had been a cesspool. It would be terrible for Deidra to throw a hand-grenade at her tonight. A few hours wouldn't make a difference. If Angela responded the way Deidra expected, they could use Nolan's boat to dump Mitchell's body out to sea, where all this trouble began. *Fitting.* "Tomorrow, after you've had some time to see what you think, I'll tell you what I think. Deal?"

"Deal." Angela embraced her big sister. "Thanks, Deed. Why is it you always end up taking care of me?"

"It's my job."

"I'd never make it through anything without you." They hugged again. "Will you wait for Mitch? I want to get Lexie a caramel brownie. She'll never forgive me if I don't."

Twenty-three hours, Deidra amended. If she had to be around Mitchell, it was going to eat some clock. "Ummhmm. Go get her some sugar. I'm sure Hilda will love you for it."

"I better get one for Tank too, or Lexie won't get any." Angela walked away.

Deidra watched, noting the change in Angela's mood. It happened at dinner. The subject of Lexie seemed to make things better for Angela. *Good information.*

She was still talking, obviously to herself. "Probably should get him two. No, that's just encouraging a bad habit…"

.　　■　　.

Mitchell opened up the door with his head bowed. It was as if he had to work up the nerve to re-enter the hallway. Seeing Deidra scowl at him didn't help. "Where's Angela?"

"Downstairs." Deidra folded her arms across her breasts.

"Did you say anything to her?"

That he did not deny, ignore, or insult her intelligence was crucial. "Not yet. Emphasis on yet."

"Thank you."

"Don't thank me. She's had a hard day."

"It's not what you think, Deed."

"I think it's a married man having sex with another woman. Is it that?"

Mitchell sighed. "Angela isn't the only one who's had a hard day. This is complicated and crazy and I need to process it. So thank you for not making it worse."

"Don't expect me to feel sorry for you. Better or worse is your department." *Within twenty-two hours. Guaranteed.*

• • •

Nolan sent his mother and brother a quick text. He wanted them prepared. He was leaning against the car when Angela came around with a carry-out bag. "Dessert for the kids."

He put away his phone but didn't say anything.

"I got a whole pie. That way, Hilda and Rob can have some too."

This time there was no movement to accompany his silence.

"Say something."

"What are you doing? And what is there for me to say about it?"

"I realize this is uncomfortable for you—"

"Uncomfortable? That's one way to look at it. Yes, it's uncomfortable."

"You could tell me that even though this is awkward, you understand why I need to do it."

"Why do you need to do it?"

Angela took her time. Everything she told Deidra was true, but there was more. "He is my husband..." The comment lingered. "This has all been thrust on me. On us. I don't like it. Any of it. I'm tired of having everything put on me. I want the upper hand. I'm sorry if that's selfish. I don't want to make things any harder for you. But I can't do this crap anymore." She pointed to the hotel behind them. "I have to fight on my turf."

Her turf? Eellek was still her home? It sounded like she said that. His heart thundered. If that's what she meant, then the world was going to right itself. The sooner Mitchell came and went the better. "You're not going to lose on your own turf. I promise you that."

She heard it, the abiding assurance in his tone. With Nolan, she would always be safe. "I don't know how this will play out. But I trust you. That count?"

"Always." They didn't shift or move or come any closer, but his eyes told her he wanted to.

She wanted him to.

The scene appeared cordial, not romantic, when Mitchell and Deidra arrived. Coming up on the passenger side, Mitchell held the front door open for Deidra. She ignored it and climbed in the back, intentionally not sliding over for him to join her. Being on the opposite side of the car made Angela the candidate for the seat behind the driver. She got in and plopped her take-out bag between her and her sister. Nolan got in and popped the trunk. Mitchell was given no choice but to ride shotgun. He stored his suitcase and mentally braced himself.

CHAPTER 31

Nolan caught Deidra's eye in his rearview mirror. She responded to his unvoiced question with a negative shake of her head. He set his face to stone and drove.

"Have you talked to Mario or Vin lately?" Mitchell half turned in his seat to see his wife.

"No." Angela hadn't spoken to her own colleagues. Why would she want to talk to his? Their friends were supportive in the beginning, but other than Deidra, she never wanted support. She wanted to be left alone.

"Did anyone tell you what's been done with my office? My clients?"

"No."

"Where is the Mercedes?"

"In the garage."

"Have you taken it out, driven it around some?"

"No."

"Talked to Bertram?"

"No."

"Given the circumstance, I figured you'd want to be in touch with our lawyer."

"I have his number."

"I guess you haven't looked at our portfolio either?"

"No. I haven't." Angela closed her eyes, dissuading further discussion.

Mitchell realized if he wanted conversation it would have to be with either Deidra or Nolan. He stared out of the window.

Hilda was in the yard when they parked. She had a flashlight searching for something along the ground. She waved hello, but continued her search. When they disembarked and came near she said, "Angela, dear, I had a handful of your bangles and dropped them, right along here, somewhere. I got most of them, but I need you to tell me how many more I'm looking for."

"Alrighty." Angela wondered why Hilda had her bangles, but it wasn't a cause for concern. Anything was possible with Nolan's mother. "Hilda, I'd like you to meet my husband, Mitchell. Mitch, this Nolan's mom, Hilda."

"Good evening."

"Pleasure to meet you, Mitchell. I've got a room ready for you, second floor, last door on the left. Right next to Angela's. It's across from the one I got for the girlfriend in case she popped up. You all can play musical beds until you get your sleeping arrangements sorted."

Having nothing to say to that, Mitchell left it at, "Thank you."

"Deidra, honey, I put you on the third floor. If I were you, I'd want the space."

"Hilda, you are a darling. All I want right now is space." With that, Deidra gave her hostess a mock salute and headed for the house.

Hilda talked on, "Rob's got the kids up at the eyesore. When they conk out he'll bring them down and meet you at the Shack."

"Good." Nolan made a beeline toward the Summer Shack.

Angela had been quiet. Her mind was still stumbling over Hilda's casual comment about her room. She didn't have a room at the Enn.

"Why don't you go on up and get settled in, Mitchell. Angela, here," Hilda held out her arm. A neat stack of bracelets covered her wrist. "Count these. Tell me what's missing."

As soon as Mitchell was away, Angela confirmed her suspicion. "You switched my room?"

Hilda held her hands up in surrender. "Nolan's idea. Not mine. He said it wouldn't be right for you and him to sleep in the same house with Mitchell hanging out next door. Pfff. You can sleep wherever you want."

"Nolan said that?"

"You sound surprised. He's always going to have your best interest at heart. Where's the hussy? Did you slap her?"

"Going home with her momma where she belongs. I'd like to slap her, but she's pregnant."

"I didn't say slap her in the belly."

Angela chuckled. "Oh, Hilda. What am I going to do?"

"Anything you want."

"What do I want?" She counted the bangles.

"To go back to DC and pick up your marriage. It's what I'd do."

"You would?" That sounded easy and wrong.

"Either that or I'd count my blessings and cut my loses. I'd stay here and start a new life with a man I loved."

That sounded easy and wrong too. "Looks like you got them all."

"Are you sure?" Hilda swished the light back and forth. When you wear them, it seems like four or five times as many."

Angela pushed the loops on her wrist. "Yeah. They're cheap anyway. It's no loss. I've got to get this inside." She held up her carry-out bag.

"What have you got?" Hilda read the name of the hotel restaurant.

"Dessert. I thought Lexie would like it. It's good. You might want to get a piece before Tank sees it."

"I'm all about dessert." Hilda clicked the flashlight off and led the way inside.

"Just pick, huh? I wish it were that easy."

"It is. Once you get out of your feelings and start thinking logically. Work it out or move on. Win-win. Best of all, it's all up to you."

Angela handed Hilda the bag and trudged up the stairs. She didn't want it to be up to her.

.   .   .

Mitchell was in *her* room. She watched him touching her things and remembering. She waited until he felt her presence and glanced up before entering.

"Either your method of organization has changed or somebody took your stuff. This isn't your room."

His perception was impressive. She wondered what other things he hadn't forgotten. "It was the room Hilda gave me when I first came down. I've never actually slept here. It will be interesting," she said.

"Do I need to ask where you've been sleeping?" He sat on her bed and leaned forward, elbows on his thighs.

"Guest room at Nolan's. It's across the yard." She pointed out of the window.

"Why would you sleep in the man's house when there is a perfectly good and respectable place for you to stay?" He wasn't aggressive, but there was a note of accusation in his tone.

"When I woke up from the accident, I was a guest in his house. I'm safe there." She stood in front of the dresser, arranging things.

"That makes sense." Mitchell wanted to talk, not argue.

. ■ ■

"I hope you don't mind." Deidra was in the kitchen making a cup of tea when Hilda joined her.

"Not at all. Grab me a cup too. I'll get the good stuff and we'll do a little taste test on this pie thingy."

Deidra didn't know what the 'good stuff' was, but she retrieved a second teacup.

Hilda went to a cabinet and returned with a bottle of E&J Brandy. "It's been opened, but there's still plenty to share."

"You are… an answer to prayer. You're like, perfection." Deidra kissed her fingertips, the Italian way.

"Living my life, you learn a thing or two about dealing with shit." Hilda poured a healthy dollop into each of their teacups.

"This is some shit, Hilda. You don't know the half of it."

"That's why you're getting ready to tell me. And this bottle is going to be here the whole time."

They helped themselves to the pie and let the E&J do its magic.

After the retelling, they moved on to thoughts and opinions. "Define irony," Deidra said. "I can remember Mitchell and Angela watching that Tom Hanks movie, *Castaway*. Did you see it?"

"Yes, I did. Did they like it?"

"Angela thought the husband should have stepped back for a while, to give them time to see if what they had was still there. Mitch," she remembered with a scowl, "said no way. He thought Helen Hunt belonged with the guy she was with. He didn't think the new guy should have to step aside and change his life just because Tom Hanks came back. I wonder what they'd say now."

Hilda snorted. "That's easy. I can tell you, Mitchell doesn't give a shit about the new guy and if I were you, I wouldn't mention that movie to either of them."

The back door opened. Lexie and Tank pushed past Rob as they raced into the kitchen.

Tank caught sight of the food and for him, all activity stopped. "Oooh. What's that?"

"Hi, Tank. Say hello to Miss Deidra." Hilda reached for the knife.

"Hi, Miss Deidra." Tank didn't look at her. He measured the slice Hilda cut for him.

"Hi, Miss Deidra. Where's Angela?" Lexie double checked the kitchen.

"She's upstairs, but she needs a minute. She's talking—" Hilda shut up. Lexie ran down the hall.

"Hi, Miss Deidra." Rob grinned.

"Hello, Dr. Woods."

"Rob. Please."

"Rob. Would you like some dessert?" Deidra pointed to the brownie pie.

"I would. I want everything." He pointed to the E&J.

"Yeah, well, that's going to have to wait, isn't it?" Hilda grabbed her bottle. "Get your butt over to the shack. Nolan needs you."

Rob gave Deidra a dramatic bow. "Ahhh. Sibling duty calls. You understand."

She moved her braids out of her way. "I do. Hence the E&J."

"Please, please, please, may I have a rain check?" He pressed his palms together in a prayerful salute.

Deidra's face lit up. He was too cute. He was a doctor. He was a too-cute doctor. *Raincheck? Yeah.* "Absolutely."

"Can I have some more cake?" Tank licked the last bit off his fork.

Only Deidra seemed impressed with his speed of consumption.

CHAPTER 32

"Can I move my things in here?"

"Pardon me?"

"Angela, we're married. I haven't been with my wife in months. I feel stupid for having to ask. But I'm asking."

She flung her arms out. "This day has been hella crazy. Are you trying to claim some kind of one-upmanship because we're at Nolan's house? I'm telling you now, I can't deal with it."

"No." He was calm, tired. "I'm not horny. Not at all." He wouldn't look at her. "When you walked out on me today, I lost it. I thought that was it. I came back and you didn't care. So I lost it. I turned to Keira—"

Angela turned away.

He held his hand up, halting her progress. Still, he did not look at her. "Yes, I slept with her, but then you came back, and I knew I shouldn't have. I should have had more faith in you. I don't ever want to do that shit again. That's why I'm here. I want my life to begin. Tonight. With you. It's not about sex. It's about love. Angela, I love you."

She didn't respond.

"Did you see the headlines?"

She shook her head. "I've had enough news for one day."

"No, you haven't." He opened the browser on his phone, clicked the appropriate article, and handed the device over to her.

Angela took it, looked at the picture, and resisted the urge to turn it off. She glanced up to see Mitchell studying her face, anticipating her reaction. She didn't give him one.

The headline began: **Save your sympathy. This would-be widow doesn't need it.**

There was a picture of Angela pressing herself tightly against Nolan. His hands and her bikini bottom were blocked out of the picture. The article went on to say:

For those of us who watched the reunion of <u>Mitchell and Angela Pointe</u>, the turn of events was confusing, to say the least. What began with us believing Angela Pointe was the only survivor of the _Siren's Fire_ shipwreck took us to a romantic high when we learned her husband, Mitchell Pointe, and two others, <u>Keira Brigham-Hoffman</u> and <u>Nathaniel Dovey</u> were alive. We thought we would witness the blissful meeting of long lost loved ones. What we got was a drama with a cunning plot twist. Turns out,

Related: <u>Fooling around on Fantasy Island</u>

Mr. Pointe hadn't been missing his wife much at all. The world was stunned to discover, while she was mourning, Angela Pointe had been jilted and replaced. Mitchell Pointe is currently in a relationship with Ms. Brigham-Hoffman. The couple is expecting their first child.

It was as if the bottom dropped out of our fairytale expectations. But wait. Now, we learn the bottom didn't drop out.

Related: <u>Is it cheating if you're dead?</u>

It wasn't that kind of a ride. Folks, we're on a roller coaster. It appears Mrs. Pointe found solace in the arms of her rescuer, <u>Nolan Woods</u> of Stock Island, Lower Keys FL. The photos shown are of the two of them, the eve of her husband's return. So we, the innocent bystanders are left with a dilemma. How

Related: <u>Mourning or Moaning, a Widow's choice</u>

should we handle this tug-of-war with our emotions? More importantly, what are we witnessing: A happy reunion, the traumas of a shipwreck, or a couple of non-discreet indiscretions? What exactly is the Pointe?

"I guess you made the news after all," Mitchell said when she handed him back his phone. "This wasn't photoshopped, but it doesn't matter."

Her eyes widened but she didn't comment.

"It can't matter. Nothing that happened before I got off that plane matters."

"You said it."

The thin line of her lips told him he made a mistake. Better not to acknowledge it. "So where does this leave us?"

The room was quiet while he waited. While she waited. He waited for her to speak. She waited for the world to stop spinning. Or to go away. Anything would be better than the waiting.

Soft thunder rumbled up the steps. "Angela!" Lexie yelled.

A distraction was definitely better than the waiting. "In here, sweetheart." Ignoring Mitchell completely, Angela opened her arms wide. Lexie threw herself into Angela and the two embraced as if it had been years. In all the chaos, Lexie was the only person who made sense. "Did you get some dessert?"

"No. I came to find you."

"Make sure you get some because I bought it mostly for you."

"Tank's in the kitchen. It's probably too late. Are you sleeping here?"

"I am."

"Mammaw said that was stupid."

"It was your dad's idea."

"Grown-ups do stupid things sometimes."

"You're the smartest person I've ever met. A lot of adults don't undertand that yet."

Angela was engrossed with the child. It didn't sit well with Mitchell. He didn't like the exclusion. "You must be Lexie," he interrupted. "Hi, Lexie." Just as quickly, he dismissed the child and claimed Angela's attention. "Apparently, you have other matters to attend to, so I'll excuse myself. I understand there is a bar within the vicinity. I'm going to go find it."

Lexie answered. "Straight down the road. You can't miss it 'cause it's got the only flashing sign on the peninsula. If you go the wrong way, don't worry, the ocean will turn you around."

"It wouldn't be the first time. Thanks, kid. I'll talk to you later." The last part was for his wife. He left the room.

CHAPTER 33

They called it a bar but it was a pub by definition. Mitchell wanted a bar. He wanted smoke and noise and too many people for him to be recognized. What he got was about a dozen patrons, a big screen TV flashing his face every forty-five minutes, and Woods. He saw the bastard leaning on the working side of the counter, talking to a couple of good ol' boys. If Mitchell didn't need a drink, he'd skip the encounter altogether.

The generic ring from his pre-paid cell phone startled him. Only Nate and Keira had his number. And Angela. But he doubted Angela would call him.

"Is this a good time?" It was Nate.

There's nothing like an ally. "The best. I'm getting ready to have a drink. You can have one with me."

"Things going that well, huh?"

"It's better than having your cruise interrupted by a whale. But not by much."

"Umm. Make mine a double."

Mitchell entered the Summer Shack, made eye contact with Nolan, and chose a table on the opposite side of the room. He traded information with Nate while he waited to be served.

A big man disengaged from Nolan's huddle and approached Mitchell. "What can I get for you?"

"A shot of Jack. No, make it a double." He spoke into the phone. "What do you want?"

"Get me a beer," Nate said.

"And a Corona," Mitchell told the waiter.

"Where's Angela?" The waiter asked.

Mitchell stared at him, stunned by the man's audacity.

The waiter frowned. "I'm a friend of Angela's. I'm checking on her wellbeing."

"Don't concern yourself with her wellbeing. In fact, other than filling my order, you don't need to concern yourself with anything over here. Capisce?"

Joey, the waiter, replied, "I don't give a shit about your hero status or whatever they labeled you with. Around here, you ain't got no status. Don't forget that." He walked away.

"Did you hear that?" Mitchell talked to Nate.

"What did you expect? You are at the bottom of the food chain."

"I expected to be on my way to DC by now. These people live on the Keys because nobody wants them on the mainland."

. . .

"He's charming," Joey said when he went behind the bar. "You want me to lace his drink?"

"No," Nolan said. "If he gets sick, he won't go away."

"I'm not going to treat him." Rob, on the stool in front of them declared.

"Naw," Joey said. "He won't need a doctor when I'm done."

. . .

Mitchell enjoyed his phone conversation too much for Nolan's liking. He supposed the jackass came here to call Keira. Nolan didn't have anything against Keira. He liked her. He hoped she and Mitchell would go somewhere and live happily ever after. However, he didn't like the pain this situation caused Angela. He didn't like Mitchell and Keira not being upfront about their relationship. And, he didn't like the bastard running his game in Angela's house. The house, the Enn, the Shack, it was all Angela's.

"I'll take it." Nolan relieved Joey of Mitchell's order.

"That's not going to be a good idea." Rob's tone held no conviction.

"It's a great idea." Grabbing his own beer, Nolan headed over to confront his enemy.

.　.　.

"I'll call you back." Mitchell disconnected. "This table is occupied."

Nolan sat down. "Why don't you take it up with the owner? Or, better yet, see if you can find somebody who gives a damn."

"Seriously, man. Angela ain't here. We don't need to pretend. Go on back to your crew."

Nolan took a sip of his beer. "Do I come across as someone who's playing with you?"

Mitchell threw back his shot, then reached for his beer. "If I get into a fight with you, over my wife, trash your bar, break your tables, the whole nine yards, the only thing anybody will say is that poor shipwrecked guy is under a lot of stress, having to put up with that asshole who's mad because he didn't get a chance to fuck the guy's wife. What are they going to say about you?"

"Same thing they always say. Nolan Woods doesn't put up with other people's shit. You can cut yours short."

"I only caught part of the conversation," Rob joined them with a full bottle of Jack and extra glasses. "But I heard the part about a fight. You don't want to do that, bro."

"Bro?" Mitchell repeated back to the man he had yet to meet.

Rob raised his hands in surrender. "I mean that in the appropriate sense. I'm Angela's doctor and angling for Deidra's attention. If I get my way, you'll be my brother by marriage." He poured himself a shot. "Or you." He toasted Nolan and drank it down. "Depending on how things work out for Angela."

"I'm already your brother," Nolan said.

"But not by marriage. By the way, did somebody explain to you about the amnesia?"

"Amnesia?" Mitchell huffed. "You into poorly written romance novels or something?"

"No," Rob refilled his glass. "I'm into advanced medicine and science. Angela's trauma has blocked some of her emotions. That's why she was here. A place where emotions registered."

"Or get taken advantage of." Mitchell glared at Nolan.

"Anyway," Rob pulled his attention back. "Don't go the *fight* route. There's more to this than hormones. Drink up. It's on the house." He pushed the bottle over.

Mitchell did help himself. "Deidra's not interested, Doc. Neither am I. You can leave the bottle, but take your brother and go away."

"You trying to claim that one too?" It was Joey. He took the fourth chair, switching it around, he straddled it. "How many women do you need?"

"You must be bored in this town," Mitchell said. "Not one of the three of you have anything to do with me or my personal business, but here you sit, worried about what I'm doing." He faced off with Nolan. "You have something to get off your chest. Why don't you say it and lose the intimidation tactics? I'm not impressed."

"Fair enough." Nolan pushed himself out of his chair. "I had every intention of backing off and being respectful. But the fact that you're still sleeping with Keira tells me you don't give a shit about your marriage vows. That being the case, I don't give a shit about them either. Say or do whatever you want, but your marriage is over."

"Respectful? Fair? Ha." Mitchell pulled the article he saved and slid the phone across the table. Nolan picked it up and Mitch was rewarded with a momentary glimpse of unveiled guilt. "All you are is a piece of shit asshole, on the prowl for some black ass—"

Joey raised his eyebrows. "Race card? Really? That's where you're going?"

"No. That's where we are. You're a stupid mo-fo if you claim race ain't involved. If white people hopped off that plane, they would have been afforded some privacy and respect. You three amigos helped yourselves to my space—uninvited—because you think you're unstoppable. But I'm not here for your wants, so fuck off." To Nolan, he said, "The game changed before you got any further than a handful. Respectful?" He sneered. "Naw, you want to finish the job. Do you have any woman of color on this strip? Or is Angela exotic?"

Nolan's blue-eyed gaze pierced Mitchell. "Angela and I talk about race all the time. We talk about a lot of things. But, I don't need to do race with you. You're not that important." He shoved the phone back across the table. "This is another reason your marriage is over. My intentions—whatever they may be—didn't change because you came back."

CHAPTER 34

Mitchell didn't plan it; He just let it happen. Angela was his wife; she belonged with him. That's all there was to it. They had a good life; a great marriage. They needed get back to that. There wasn't going to be another option. He let himself into her, *their* room. He undressed, got into their bed, and pulled her close. There wasn't going to be another option. He woke her with a kiss. Several kisses. It had been a lifetime since he held his wife. She was dead, but now she was back. She was his, would always be his. There wasn't going to be another option.

Angela lay in a restless sleep. Her mind wouldn't quit. The whole world thought she was a whore. Images of oceans and babies filled her with sadness and loss. It was dark, Nolan was distant, and no child would ever love her. She cheated on her husband, but she hadn't meant to. The ocean drowned her and Nolan was lost. She couldn't see Mitch, but he was with her. If she clung to him, he'd save her…

The passion was in progress when she became coherent. Mitchell, her Mitchell. Attentive, giving, focusing on her as only he knew how. It had been so long. She suffered so much. He knew where to touch her, how to hold her. Every caress, each stroke, this pleasure, just for her; she remembered it, she remembered him. He was her husband; it was his duty, his right. He'll save her and make it right…

■   ■   ■

Nolan started his boat and hoped the noise startled Mitchell awake. In truth his engine was quiet, but anything to make the bastard uncomfortable was a good idea. He wanted him up and gone. If he left at dawn, he'd beat the traffic. Nolan was certain Mitchell was leaving. His marriage was not his top priority. The man didn't have a marriage, anyway. Angela deserved better—so much better. Not that he, Nolan, was better... Yes, he was. No, he didn't have the money Pointe had, nor was he young or black, or any of the things she may have found appealing about her husband. But, he was stable. He was dependable. He would never cheat on her—not under any circumstances. Never. He would love her and take care of her. He didn't care if they couldn't have children. They had Lexie and Tank. They'd adopt if she wanted. He'd help her deal with it; the infertility and all her problems. He wouldn't try patching it up with a vacation. He would never put himself first. That's why she would get a divorce and marry him. Angela would stay in Florida and never leave him.

Jackie left him. He never talked about it. He didn't like to think about it. The pain was devastating. He had done all a husband was supposed to do and more. He'd given her a home, security, time, and attention. He supported everything she wanted to do. But the problem lay therein. Jackie was uncommitted. Jumping from interest to waning interest, she thought she deserved everything but was satisfied with nothing. She wanted a house; she wanted to travel. She wanted kids; she wanted a career. She wanted to escape and not be responsible for anything. That Nolan had allowed it put her on a path to discover his limits. What wouldn't he accept? Drugs and adultery. It should have been a no-brainer. That didn't make it hurt any less.

Angela made it hurt less. She was leaving that asshole and staying with him. She would give her life and her love to him, explicitly. He wished Angela had been there when Jackie left to buffer the pain and love him through it. He would do that for her: love her through Mitchell's betrayal.

The sun pushed over the horizon. Nolan closed his eyes and breathed in the salt air. Finally. The day was official. Mitchell Pointe would leave and his life could begin.

Angela opened her eyes and hated the guilt. She shouldn't feel guilty for sleeping with her husband. But she did. It was the Enn, yes, but was still Nolan's house. She was Nolan's girlfriend. But, she dirtied his sheets with another guy... Not another guy. Her husband. The only person she was supposed to be sleeping with was Mitchell.

Her back was to him, but she felt him awaken. His arm tightened around her and he pulled her close.

"Did you do this to taunt Nolan?"

Mitchell sighed. Gently he turned her over, so they were facing one another. "Good morning, Angela."

"Did you?"

"I did it because you're my wife and I love you. I swear, there is nobody in this room but us."

She believed him. "What happens now?"

"We make love again. No distractions. No coercions. Just a husband and wife, reforming their bonds. After that, we get out of bed. We get dressed. We say thank you and good-bye. We go home and return to our lives. That's what happens."

In that moment, nothing seemed easier.

Nothing was harder. Angela watched Nolan bring his boat in, knowing she didn't want to leave him. But she waited to tell him good-bye. She chose to walk away from the temptation, from the potential, from the beginning of true love.

Nolan watched her watching him. He knew. He knew when he saw the rigid way she held herself, the lack of warmth in her smile. She wasn't smiling inside. She was dreading. He felt her betrayal down to his bones. This was worse than Jackie. Worse because he dared to hope. He wanted to hate her, but couldn't see the point. It would be a lie. He wanted to tell her Mitchell slept with Keira not twenty-four hours ago. There was no point in that either. Angela would be devastated and humiliated, but she wouldn't thank him for the information. She would see it as a desperate attempt to trash her decision to remain with her husband. It *would* be a desperate attempt to trash her decision. And, that's what it was: her decision, her choice. She didn't chose him.

He tied the boat and stepped onto the dock.

"Nolan."

"Don't say it, Angela."

"I have to."

"Why? I don't need to hear it. And, whether I want to admit it or not, I get it. He's your husband. Enough said."

She came forward, touching him. "Not enough said. I have to say thank you. I have to say there is a part of me that is dying over this because I love you. I didn't lie about that. I have to say I'm choosing to make my marriage work but it's not without regret. I'm so sorry for doing this to you. Three days ago, I didn't know I was going to hurt you. I would never have guessed I'd be leaving. If I had a clue, I might have done something different. Maybe." She hunched her shoulders. "I don't know." She raised her trembling hand to touch his face. "I believed you when you said you loved me."

"What's not to believe? I do love you."

"I wouldn't be the woman you love if I threw away my marriage for selfish reasons. I think of you as my own personal happiness. It doesn't get any more selfish than that."

He couldn't take anymore—the touch of her hand, the feel of her so close, knowing it was the last time he would get to see her. Knowing he was the loser.

She came willingly into his embrace. He felt her sob and the warm moisture of her tears. His own eyes filmed over. He wanted to kiss her, hold her, make her stay. But he didn't. With superhuman strength, he released her. "If you change your mind, I'll be waiting."

"Don't." She shook her head against the pain, against the temptation. "Nolan, don't say that."

He offered her a sad, crooked smile. "You're not the only one to make decisions, Angela. That one will be mine."

Deidra didn't go home with them. She said she thought it was better to give them the time.

Mitchell agreed.

Angela guessed there was more.

Deidra added, she owed Rob a drink and dessert.

Rob agreed, enthusiastically.

Angela sensed there was still something more, but Deidra remained closed.

. . .

"You *will* keep in touch."

"I will, Hilda, I promise." Angela hugged her tight and kissed her cheek.

The older woman's voice did not lose an iota of its sternness. "You *will* also make arrangements for a visit." Not waiting for Angela to answer, she said to Mitchell, "This doesn't have anything to do with Nolan. I," she pointed to herself, "have a relationship with Angela and I," she pointed to herself again, "intend to keep it."

"I understand." Mitchell didn't care what she wanted, but there was no reason to be rude about it.

Angela leaned down to hug Lexie. "Everything I told you stands."

"We'll see." Lexie did not take the news of her leaving well at all. That she was still talking to Angela was a testimony of how strong a bond they developed.

"Put it to the test. Go ahead, pick a date."

"Halloween."

"Halloween it is." Angela grinned as she stood. "Mitch, Lexie and I have a date on Halloween. Do you have any objections?"

Other than it isn't going to happen, no. "Sounds like fun. Are you coming to DC, Lexie?" Mitchell didn't have a problem with Nolan's kid, other than she was Nolan's kid. She had gumption. He kind of liked her. But Nolan was not going to be a fixture in his life. The sooner Woods's family realized it, the happier he would be.

"If my mom lets me." Lexie pouted.

"She will," Hilda said. "I'll see to that."

"If she doesn't, I know how to get to California." Angela tapped Lexie's nose. She wondered what she would do when she found the bottle of *HisCinn,* the perfume Angela left on her bed next to Ollie.

"Either way. It's going to happen, kiddo." Hilda told her.

Angela kissed Tank and promised to send him a big bag of candy on the condition he didn't drive Hilda crazy. She thanked Rob and made him promise to look after Deidra.

He said he would.

She made him promise to behave.

He said, of course he would.

Nobody bought it.

They waved from the Enn's massive porch as Mitchell maneuvered Angela's car out of the driveway. It had been a long time since that rainy night of her arrival.

CHAPTER 35

They'd been home a week when Mitchell first attempted to broach the subject.

Angela broke down into hysterics.

Two days later, he tried again. She locked herself into the bathroom and cried for three hours.

Four more days passed before he mentioned it again. She concluded he didn't love her and should have left her in Florida. She also perfected her aim by throwing things at his head.

Keira and the baby were not topics Angela was ready to discuss. However, her lack of cooperation did not make it go away. Mitchell couldn't concentrate on anything else. He had a responsibility. The last thing he intended to be was a deadbeat dad.

A dad. Mitchell Pointe was going to be a dad. Twice over. Soon.

.   .   .

Angela filed her nails, inspected the contents of her purse, and checked her lipstick. She played a game on her phone, texted Deidra, and checked her hair. She thumbed through a magazine, bit her nails, and checked the time.

"Relax." Mitchell captured her anxious fingers and held them. "You're going to give yourself a heart attack."

"I can't help it. I'm so nervous."

"Don't be." He kissed the back of her hand. "This is good."

She took a deep breath. "Yes. You're right. This *is* good. It's exciting." She granted him a breathtaking smile. "Mitchell, we're going to have a baby."

"Yes, we are." He would do anything for that smile. He had done everything for that smile. It was his flamboyant money flashing that earned them a fast appointment with the adoption agency. It was his not taking no for an answer that had them sitting in the waiting room waiting to hear about the possible matches Mr. Mercer, their host, found for them.

"Thank you." She was excited, and scared, and appreciative.

"I told you things would work out for us." He was smug and satisfied.

"Mr. and Mrs. Pointe." Mr. Mercer appeared before them. "This way, please."

Angela squealed as Mitchell helped her to her feet. She clung to him as they entered Mr. Mercer's private office.

"Please." He pointed to the side by side wing chairs stationed in front of his white oak desk. When all three were seated he said, "We have a problem."

The Pointes clasped hands.

"You'll have to forgive me. I did not immediately recognize you or I would have spared you the wait." He didn't give them time to respond. "You both have been through quite a dramatic experience with the boating accident."

"We've seen doctors." Mitchell was brusque.

"I've no doubt."

"Then you'll have no doubt we wouldn't be here if we weren't capable of caring for a child."

"Your capabilities aren't in question, Mr. Pointe. It's your family structure. Your situation is complicated, to say the least. The extramarital relationship and the natural child you are expecting make it impossible for us to place a baby in that environment. I am sorry, but at the present time, you do not have a stable home."

Angela left the meeting stunned.

She walked out of the second agency in tears.

After four agencies, Angela was done. She grudgingly respected the priorities of the people who would not be swayed by Mitchell's money. She despaired that her body didn't function right. For what his actions cost, she hated Mitchell.

What could he say? *No, Deidra can't bring Lexie up for the weekend.* Yeah, because Deidra was prone to following his orders. Another time, he would have laughed at the thought. Mitchell didn't laugh. It wasn't funny and he was out of ideas.

The child's presence was a relief. Not that he saw her. But the haunted shadows faded from Angela's countenance. She used full sentences when she talked to him; she remembered he was a person. Granted, the gist of her conversation was limited to information concerning her plans with Lexie and her time at Deidra's. But anything was better than nothing.

Angela was at Deidra's now. She would be there for another day and a half. Mitchell was lonely, but grateful for the peace. He didn't like these feelings of failure. He didn't like being the cause of so much anguish. He didn't like not talking to Nate. He didn't like being away from Keira.

Angela was out of the house, entertaining her boyfriend's child. There was no reason he couldn't call and check on his. Mitchell was lonely.

CHAPTER 36

"I'll get it." Angela wiped her dishwater hands on the way to the front door.

"Good afternoon, ma'am." The FedEx guy said. "I have a package I need you to sign for."

"Sure." She signed and accepted a large envelope. "Thank you."

"Have a good day."

"You too." She closed the door and inspected the address.

"Who is it?" Mitchell, twenty-five minutes home from the office and fresh from his shower, strode down the hall in sweats, chest bare, with his towel tossed over his shoulder. His mood improved from earlier. Angela had been on the phone with Lexie again. The days after the child's visit had been good, but that relationship was getting old.

"FedEx. Why are we getting priority mail from a real estate agent?" She flipped the envelope over to open it.

Mitchell removed it from her fingers. "Sweetheart, we need to talk."

"That doesn't sound good." She let him lead her to the couch. "Are we moving?"

"No. We're not moving." He made his tone light. "Not until you say so." He brushed his lips across the back of her hand. When they sat down, he pulled her against him.

"You're making me nervous. Unless you've got other things on your mind." She rubbed herself against him.

She still gave herself to him. Even after the adoption failure. It was a marvel, to both of them.

"Always." He nipped her neck once before separating himself. "But we do have to talk."

"So talk. What's with the realtor?" She tapped the envelope.

"I bought a condo. It's two floors down."

Her brow crinkled. "You did what? What do we need another condo for? In the same building?" As soon as she said it, she knew. The color drained from her face. Her body went stiff and icy cold. Something in her died.

Mitchell didn't hold back. "Before we got back, I asked them to come and live with me. Because I thought you were gone and I didn't want to be alone. I told Nate I would hire him as my assistant. I'm going to train him to do what I do."

She didn't talk. She didn't move.

"Angie."

"Th-Them?"

"Well, yes. Of course. The baby is my responsibility. I'm going to take it seriously."

She knew that. She put all her energy into blocking it. She certainly didn't want to talk about it. "Live here?"

"That's why I bought the condo. I'm doing it for you. For us. I'm sure you don't want them living here. But, they've got to live somewhere. The baby's got to have a decent home."

"Here."

Somewhere in the course of the conversation, they separated. They sat a sofa cushion apart. Stiff. Formal.

"This is my baby, Angela. I am going to raise my child. I want you to be a part of that. The only way to do it is to have everyone involved in the same place, on the same page."

"On the same page? You spent money, *our* money, so your mistress can live next door. I learned out about this deal from the mailman and you say we're on the same page. What page are you on?"

"I tried to talk to you. Over and over again I tried. It's not a topic you ever want to address. After the, uhh, other stuff, I didn't want to put anything else on you, especially having to do with the baby. But I can't leave everything indefinitely. I did what was best for everybody. Is that so terrible?"

She sprang from her seat. "Hell yes, it's terrible! You don't get to use the fact that I don't want to deal with your shit as an excuse! I didn't get a say in this arrangement. You did this behind my back. That's not a marriage. Did you talk to her?"

"What?" He understood her question. He stalled, hoping a better answer would come.

"Did you talk about it with her? Is she aware you used *our* money to change her zip code?"

He gave it ten more seconds before succumbing to the reality that he had to tell the truth. "They'll be here in a week."

Angela looked around for something to throw. "Excuse me? I thought you said a week. But you did not say *a week*. You are not sitting here, telling me that not only did you plan this and kept it from me, it was going to happen right under my nose. If I didn't get the mail, I may have bumped into her in the hall. I can't—" She stopped mid-tirade as something clicked in place. "When was this planned? How often have you been talking to her?"

"Angela, calm down." Mitchell left his seat. His goal was to soothe his wife.

She stepped away from him.

"Please understand, I haven't seen the baby in almost a month."

"You haven't seen the baby at all. It's still unborn."

"You know what I mean."

"You mean you haven't seen its mother in almost a month."

"No. That's not what I mean. I'm the baby's father. I'm supposed to be present. I have to talk to her, make sure everything is okay. I have to check with her, to be sure the doctors I'm setting up for her are going to be acceptable. Keira and I have to communicate. Surely you understand that."

She was stunned he couldn't see what he did to her. His every word tore a hole through her. He fathered a child. He's making arrangements for doctors. He's doing things and yearning for his baby. That was a whole world she didn't get to be a part of. She would never know if a prenatal doctor was acceptable or not.

He interpreted her silence as contemplation. He took that for encouragement. "Keira is not my mistress. I wasn't keeping things from you to be secretive. I'm trying to do the right thing here. On one hand, I have a baby. We have a baby. This child is as much yours as it is mine and Keira's." He smiled, liking that idea. "We have to do what will be in the baby's best interest. In this case, his father will supply his needs. Or, her needs." His smile broadened. He was not opposed to a girl. "He or she needs to be where I can take care of him… or her. This child is not getting raised by check." Mitchell moved in again, thrilled when Angela didn't step away. "On the other hand, I have my wife, whom I love very much. I made an unintentional mistake and wronged you. I don't want to hurt you again. I don't want to talk about shit to upset you. It has to be dealt with, but you don't need it shoved down your throat. You need to handle what you can handle and not worry about the rest of it. I'm trying to make it so you don't have it in your face. That's all. If you want Keira to call the house, okay. If you want to be there when I talk to her, I'd love it. I'm happy being transparent, as long as it's not too much for you." He held his arms open.

She sneered.

He let his hands fall to his side. "Honestly, Angela. I'm not lying to you. I want you to be a part of this. I hope you'll pick out some starter furniture so they can settle in and not have to stay up here with us. I'm no good at it and you know what's practical…" He stopped talking when she turned away. "Angie?"

That fast she turned back. Bringing her arm around so forcefully the crack against his cheek echoed. "You have some sick, screwed-up fantasies."

She left him standing there, not understanding at all.

CHAPTER 37

"You look like crap." Deidra opened the door wide enough for Angela to enter.

"Then it's a slight improvement over how I feel. I quit my job." Angela—tear-puffed eyes, without make-up, clad in yoga pants, without a full night's sleep in days—ignored her sister's impeccably clean living room. She bypassed the kitchen and both guest rooms, and made her way to Deidra's bedroom, kicked off her running shoes, and climbed into her sister's queen-sized bed. She pulled the covers over her head for good measure.

Deidra climbed in on the other side, sprawled across the top of the floral spread and said, "I'll be here when you're ready."

They were like that, the sisters: picking up the pieces, cleaning up the mess. When the adoption process fell through, and Angela's heart was broken, it was Deidra's idea to have Lexie plug the wound. They were the best of friends, willing to sacrifice anything for the other.

After a moment of silence, and a deep sigh, Angela's muffled voice sounded from beneath the blanket. "My office has been great, but there's no point in staying. It's not their fault I can't function."

"Why can't you function?"

"Don't tell me 'I told you so.'"

"Did I tell you so?"

"You should have."

Deidra pulled the covers down, revealing Angela's head. "What happened?"

"Where to begin?" Angela turned over, ready to talk.

"Umm... at the beginning?"

"No, not the beginning. How about I start with me coming back home with the man who not only slept with another woman some hours before talking me into it, the asshole used our money to put her in an apartment two floors below us—"

"What?"

"He didn't bother to tell me, either. However, when I found out, he thought I would like to help pick out furniture."

In answer to that, Deidra shifted and scooted beneath the covers, pulling them completely over her own head.

"I've been sleeping in the guest room for the last week and a half."

Deidra stuck her head out. "Why are you sleeping there at all? You have a room here."

Angela sighed. "This isn't a marriage, Deed. I can't tell you what it is, or what it's supposed to be, but it isn't a marriage."

"He wanted you to pick out furniture? For her?"

"She's pregnant. Needs to have the broken, infertile wife supply her luxuries."

"Don't say that. You're not broken. The question is what do you want to do about it?"

"What can I do?"

"What do you want to do?"

There was a long pause.

"Angela? This is your life that's being shredded. You can accept it, stop it, or do something completely different. It's whatever you want, but we can't move until we figure that part out."

"Are you saying I should give up on my marriage?"

"I'm not saying anything. I'm asking you... Yes, in light of what you just said, to hell with your marriage. Go to Florida."

Angela turned over. "I can't go to Florida."

They leaned on their elbows, facing each other.

"Why not? Nolan loves you."

"I'm a married woman, Deidra."

"Are you? Does Mitchell know?"

"I made a choice."

"Change your mind."

"Nolan doesn't want to see me."

"Yes, he does."

"How would you know?"

Deidra moved her braids out of her way. "He loves you, Ange. He misses you."

"I threw that away. Anyway, we're supposed to be talking about Mitchell, not Nolan."

"Mitchell's a dog. We're done with that conversation. Now we can talk about someone good for you… like Nolan."

"You used to love Mitch. Why are you such a Nolan fan?"

"I still love Mitch. I don't like what he's done to you. Honey, you're a train wreck. The last time you were a train wreck, Nolan helped you fix the problem. And let me highlight, when you were a train wreck the first time, all Mitchell did was take you on a boat and trash your life."

Angela's lip trembled. "I'm always a train wreck."

Deidra leaned in and kissed Angela's forehead. "Don't. Who wouldn't be a wreck after what you've dealt with? You've been amazing. The point is you've been through hell. Extra crap because of Mitchell. You put your marriage first, to no avail. Nolan is an angel. It's okay to take a second chance with him. You owe it to yourself and him." When Angela didn't say anything, Deidra continued, "You and Nolan were good. It's heartbreaking to see you both suffering and when it's not necessary."

"Nolan's suffering? Why would you say that?"

Deidra was silent.

Angela arched her eyebrows.

Deidra took a deep breath. "It's wretched of me, talking about this; rubbing salt in your wounds."

"Tell me."

"I was down there last weekend. Rob and I are…" She rocked her head, "kind of dating… somewhat."

"You're dating Rob?" Angela voice was flat. She concentrated on holding back the wave of jealousy and longing that threatened to spew from her core. Her head was pounding, but she wanted to—needed to—be happy for her sister. "He is a hot doctor."

"He is. But it's not going to get too serious. There are a lot of miles between here and Florida. Plus, the race-thing is a thing. I'm gung-ho now, but I don't have that kind of long-term energy."

"Of course, you do. And, the race-thing is only a thing if you don't handle it. Rob's worth it." Her voice cracked. She couldn't hold it together any longer. With a complete loss of energy, Angela plopped down, face first, and gave in to her urge to cry.

Deidra hugged her, crying also. "I'm sorry, Angela. I am. I didn't mean to hurt you. I'll stop seeing him."

"No, no, no. You can't do that." Angela sobbed. "I'm happy for you. I want you and Rob to date. I think it's awesome. Or, at least, I will. This isn't you. I'm just... I'm... I'm just..."

"Miserable," Deidra completed the thought.

CHAPTER 38

"Hello?"

"Angela, this is Keira. Please don't hang up."

Hearing her voice stirred a cauldron of emotion. "And you are calling here, why?"

"Please... I wouldn't... but... but I'm in pain. I'm cramping. Nate and Mitchell are in a meeting. This is important for Nate. I don't want to cause a scene, but I can't reach Mitchell's parents and there's nobody else around here to call. Please..."

The desperation and the obvious fear—she couldn't close off from it. "I'll be there in a minute."

"Thank you." Keira sniffed.

. ■ ■

Angela took the stairs, it was faster. She refused to dwell on it. She wasn't going to wish ill on anybody. She certainly didn't want anything to be wrong with the baby. She would not resent having to be a part of this new drama, at least not yet. This was a woman in trouble who needed her help. Beyond that, she wouldn't dwell on it.

Keira opened the door, hunched over, cradling her slight belly. She looked pasty green. Her eyes were sunken and haunted. Angela hadn't seen her since their encounter at the hotel. She had made it a point not to have anything to do with the occupants in the downstairs apartment. Even haggard and distressed, it was hard to look at her.

Despite her secret outrage, Angela helped Keira to dress and drove her to the hospital. En route she sent Mitchell a text, telling him to call her when he was free. She could have called but she didn't want to talk to him. It was his fault she was involved.

In no time, she received a return call from Adele, Mitchell's secretary.

"Hi Angela, this is Adele. How are you doing?" She sounded full of energy.

"I'm okay—"

"I'm glad. All this craziness in your life, it's good you're still hanging in there, sweetheart. And, speaking of crazy, your husband just stuck his head out. He wanted me to get in touch with you. He said he'd be about a half hour or so, unless you need him."

Angela looked a Keira. "Mitchell's going to be a half hour."

Keira's eyes were squeezed shut in her fight against nausea. "No. Don't interrupt. We won't have any answers by then anyway."

"Fine." She didn't have to care about the details. She put the phone back up to her ear. "Adele, a half hour is fine. But tell him not to linger. We're on our way to the hospital."

"Are you all right?"

"I'm fine. His baby's momma is having problems."

Adele lost her energy. "Oh… well… umm… okay… I'll… uhh… let him know… right away."

Adele was somebody Angela liked. Understanding the weight of what she just conveyed, she brushed past the awkwardness. "Thanks, honey. When this is over, we should have lunch."

"That is definitely a date."

■   ■   ■

From her corner in the waiting room, Angela watched Mitchell and Nate enter and scan the room, presumably searching for her. It did not take them long to find her. She tensed, frowning at Mitchell's approach. He seemed half crazy with worry. It made her angry and jealous to see her husband desperate with anxiety over another woman. A place he would never go to for her because she'd never get pregnant. No. She wasn't going there. She couldn't afford to go there.

He kissed her forehead and took a seat beside her. "How are you, honey?"

She couldn't respond. His first question was concern after her wellbeing? It defied logic. "They're going to keep her overnight, but she's okay. They're putting her in a room now."

"Thank you." Mitchell closed his eyes, relieved. "You didn't answer my question. How are you?"

"Me? Fine. I'm not the one in trouble."

"I know what this is costing you." He took her hand in his. "You're an amazing lady."

They hadn't slept together in weeks. These days, she barely talked to him. She spent more time at Deidra's than she did at home because everything about Mitchell was painful. Yet, here he was, placing her before everything, treating her like she mattered. That was even more painful because she didn't trust it.

Nate slipped into the chair on Angela's other side. Like Mitchell, he wore a tailored suit. He was clean-shaven and his dreads were impeccable, neat coils twisted up to his scalp and tied back into his signature ponytail. He remained silent, his dark eyes watchful. Angela didn't acknowledge him. Neither did he force his presence upon her. But, he wanted to know about Keira.

As if Mitchell read Nate's mind, he said, "Did the doctors tell you anything about her condition?"

"She was trying to do too much. He said her body was under some stress and she'd have to be off her feet for a while."

He nodded and sat back, contemplating.

A confident doctor came over to speak with them. Obviously, he followed the news, because he held his hand out to Mitchell first. "Hello, Mr. Pointe. I'm doctor Osely. Miss Brigham-Hoffman is anxious to see you. If you'll walk with me, I'll take you back. We can talk on the way."

Mitchell shook his hand and followed him back.

Nate chose not to accompany them.

Angela, stung by Mitchell's instant dismissal, got up to leave.

"Mrs. Pointe."

She jerked around, surprised to hear her name.

Nate pushed himself out of his seat.

She thought his locs gave him a sophisticated edge. It was attractive. Not that she cared.

"I realize you don't have anything to say to me. I understand why and I have no intention of troubling you." He coughed to clear his throat, uncertain how to continue. "I wanted to tell you I do understand. This is a shitty situation. Excuse my French, but it is."

Her eyes glossed over.

"I'm sorry. I don't mean to upset you."

She waved it off. "It happens."

He took a deep breath and forced himself to say it. "It seems to me you're the one getting shitted on the most. I'm not against Mitch or Keira or anything. I'm happy about the baby. I am. We're all a mess. I don't have a wife anymore. We're all trying to pick up and make something out of this. It is what it is. This is crazy, and I am sorry for you."

Angela didn't want to break down. She was sick of crying. But this stranger, this person who was there, involved in the events that stole her life was offering her pity. People always say they don't want pity. But she wanted his pity; she needed his pity. She leaned into him and let go of her tears.

He wrapped his arms around her, giving the comfort he volunteered.

Three minutes past. It may have been five. It wasn't long, but it was enough. She raised her head from Nate's chest and took a deep breath. "Thank you."

"Any time. I mean that."

"You too." He didn't need anything from her, but this man—also shipwrecked—wasn't her enemy. "I'm going to go." She stepped away. "Thank you."

"You're welcome. Be careful."

She nodded and left him watching her exit.

CHAPTER 39

Deidra *tsked* as Angela peeked through her curtains again. "Standing at that window isn't going to get them here any sooner." She touched her hair to be sure it was still in place.

"It might."

"This is the happiest I've seen you in ages."

"This is the first time I've seen Lexie in ages." Angela moved away from the window only to approach from the other side. "I didn't notice you crying over the fact that Rob will be here any minute." She glanced at her sister. "You look beautiful."

Deidra touched her hair again. "Thanks. If all goes well, this should be a great weekend."

"What do you mean, if all goes well? As long as they get here, everything will be perfect."

"No offense, but I don't trust Mitch not to ruin it."

"Please. He doesn't have to look at me for three whole days. He can assemble the crib," she sneered, "without the guilt of hanging down there all day."

"Yeah, and when he's done, he could pop up over here to do a headcount."

"He can't count past three. The baby, its mother, and Nathaniel... I don't want to talk about Mitchell. Oh! I see the cab. They're here!"

• • •

A three day weekend with Lexie, Tank, and Rob: for Angela, it wasn't Halloween. It was Christmas. Friday night, Angela and the kids made s'mores and watched Halloween movies. Deidra and Rob went out.

Saturday morning, Angela took the kids shopping for the 'greatest costumes in the world' according to Lexie.

Deidra and Rob stayed in.

In the afternoon, they trick-or-treated at the mall. Early evening, they trick-or-treated at the homes of co-workers and friends. Later came a haunted hayride and a grand Halloween party to attend. Finally, Angela took the sugar-shocked, dead-tired, super-hyper, over-stuffed fairy/pirate team back to Deidra's to detox, while Rob and her sister stayed for the adult after party.

Nobody moved much on Sunday.

Lexie didn't want to pack. She didn't want to leave. She clung to Angela and they hung out on the sofa, procrastinating.

"I like it here."

"I like having you here."

"If my mom and dad okayed it, would you keep me?"

"In a heartbeat. In fact, I would cheat."

Lexie scrunched her face.

"If I got one of them to agree, I'd pretend the other one said yes too and call it a deal."

"That's easy. You can call my mom right now. She'd say yes."

Jackie wasn't the parent Angela wanted to talk with. "I doubt it. Your mom doesn't know me."

"She won't care about that. I was mad because I didn't want to leave Daddy's. When I got home, I ran away. I was gone all day and she didn't even notice."

Angela sat up, breaking the snuggled position she and Lexie formed. "You ran away?"

Lexie shook her head to ward off the worry. "I only ran across the street to the Wineo house. They watch out for me, and Dooney got me a steak sub and gave me a sip of his Manichevitz 'cause he didn't have enough for a soda."

"Okay." Angela pulled Lexie against her and leaned back, pretending to relax. "Do you do that a lot? Run away."

"Not a lot. It doesn't work anyway. That's why I want to stay with Daddy... or live here."

"I see. We're going to have to see if something can be done about that. I want you to promise me if you run away, or if you're just by yourself too long, or something's going on with your mom or anything, you call me. Do you understand?"

Lexie nodded, pleased with the instructions. "I will."

"I mean it. Anytime you're not where you should be, I want to know about it. I'm serious."

Rob chose that moment to make an appearance. "You're bucking to make us late, kiddo. Are you packed?"

Lexie poked her lips out at him. "No. I'm not going."

"She can stay." Angela smiled at his frown.

"See. I'm staying."

Rob exaggerated his sigh. "I'm picking up an attitude of resistance. That would be why we made a deal before we left. Do you remember that? You promised if I made this visit happen, you would not be a pain in my butt when it was time to go."

"I want to renegotiate."

"You want to get off that sofa and get ready unless you want to board the plane in your pajamas. We're leaving in less an hour."

"Uncle Rob—"

"Rob—"

"Less than an hour." He cut off their duel whine.

Lexie stomped off in a huff, pouting while she packed her bag.

Rob made the most of his opportunity. "Are you coming down for Thanksgiving?"

Angela frowned at him. "No. Are you nuts?"

"Nolan misses you. According to Deidra, you miss him too."

"Deidra has a big mouth."

"It's obvious. You've been here all weekend and you've talked to your husband how many times?"

"He knows where I am."

"Do you know where he is? Sorry," Rob amended. "I shouldn't have said that. I was out of line."

"But correct." She didn't flinch. "I have no idea where he is and I don't care. I know where he's supposed to be. But, I can't do anything about it if he isn't."

"If not you, then who?"

Angela's phone rang.

Rob's brow crinkled in confusion. He recognized the ring.

Angela reached for her phone and yelled into the kitchen where Deidra was making Tank a snack for the plane ride. "Unless you want something, quit calling me."

"Not my fault," Deidra yelled back.

＊　　＊　　＊

Mitchell wandered around the condo. It was cold and lifeless. They'd tastefully painted the walls beige and used layers of brown and tan and cream with hints of wine and rose to make their home warm and inviting. It was neither. It didn't look like Halloween. It didn't look like anything.

Angela always decorated and gave out treats. But not this year. This year, she was at Deidra's sharing her holiday with Nolan's kid. She didn't invite him. Angela could have brought the child home... where he could see if she came with her father.

He thought about going over to check, but decided it wouldn't be a good idea for him to appear jealous or mistrusting. He didn't have the track record for that.

Mitchell walked past the guest room. Angela's room. What kind of life were they having? They were out of options. It was time to get some counseling. He hadn't wanted to admit it, not even to himself, but they weren't going to survive without help.

Especially when they had to start working on a nursery. This was his child's home too. They had to get ready for it. Angela slept in the bigger guest room. It should be the nursery. She had her own room... with him. But she wasn't with him. She was with Nolan's kid. Maybe Nolan...

He had too many thoughts. It was too quiet, not at all like a holiday. He'd see what was going on downstairs.

. . .

Mitchell let himself into the condo. "Where is everybody?"

"Baby's room," Keira called out.

Mitchell found her on the floor, lying on her back, rubbing her belly. "What are you doing?"

"We're listing to music." She pointed to her iPhone sitting on the baby's dresser. The room had a forest theme, with soft green walls with darker green accents. The oak furniture gave it a woodsy vibe. A pair of white bunnies hopped along one wall and a robin and two bluebirds flew along another. The accessories were still missing. Adventurer or princess had to wait for the sonogram.

"May I ask why you are on the floor?" Rather than continue to stand over her, Mitchell sat down beside her.

"The baby wanted to be here." She grinned.

"That's your favorite excuse, I'm noticing."

"It's infallible. Who's going to deny the baby?"

He rubbed her stomach. "Who would dare try?"

"Exactly." She closed her eyes, enjoying his massage.

Mitchell enjoyed it too. Watching her lay there, affected by his touch had an immediate effect on him. It had been too long. "Where's Nate?"

"Hmm?" She blinked up at him, almost drowsy.

"Nate? Godfather. Roommate. You've met him." He pulled her shirt up and rolled the top of her maternity pants down to expose the firm roundness of her soft, tight skin. He rubbed her with both hands.

"The baby loves when you do that."

"That's why I do it."

"Nate's gone. He went to a party with Adele and some people from the office."

"Oh yeah." He remembered. Vaguely. He and Angela were invited. Without her, he wasn't interested. He didn't regret it. "I hope he has fun."

"Me too. I was supposed to go, but I—" Keira's breath caught.

Mitchell leaned over and kissed her belly button. "That's my baby," he whispered into the wetness and kissed her again. Traveling beneath her top, Mitchell caressed her breast, weighing the heaviness, lightly teasing the nipple.

Keira moaned and held him to her when his mouth followed his fingers and he suckled her. She was needy. There was no question that she wanted him. What he did was delicious. His fingers worked their way into her pants, pushing aside her panties. She was already wet.

But, no.

Even as she pulled away from him, she yearned for more of his touch. "We are not doing this. Remember what happened the last time." She sat up, adjusting her clothes.

Mitchell took a deep breath that did nothing to calm him. "The doctor said it was okay. We were too rough before. You hadn't been resting. But, it's been a while. You're stronger now. I'll go easy. I promise." He stroked her nipple with his thumb.

"No." She batted his hand away. "I know what the doctor said. I also know what he didn't say. That was a warning. I only need to be told once. I'm not jeopardizing the baby."

"We're not jeopardizing the baby. Couples have sex all the time when they're pregnant."

"Yes. Exactly." Keira tried to get up.

Mitchell was faster. He was on his feet, easily lifting her to an upright position. In two steps, he had her pinned against the crib where he ran his tongue along her neck. "Baby, I need you."

It was delicious. "You're not listening to me." Keira tilted her head back to help him along.

"I'm listening." He kissed her shoulder and squeezed her ass as he pressed into her.

"We're not a couple. Screwing around on your wife is wrong." She let her words clear her head. "Okay, yeah, we did it." She wiggled out of his embrace. "But to keep doing it is wrong. Can you imagine how terrible it was to have her drive me to the hospital because I overdid it giving her husband a quickie before work? Mitchell, that's low, lower than I ever want to be again. I already told you. I am not sleeping with you anymore while you're married." She stepped further away. "And I'm not. Period."

Mitchell studied her. Knowing she was right didn't change his desire to make love to her. Knowing he would say anything to get his way, he kept his mouth closed.

.　.　.

Keira moped. The shower didn't help. The cup of chamomile tea remained untouched. Her evening was ruined. Mitchell ruined it. What the hell was going on? How did she get this life? *Life.* The word made her think of the baby. She rubbed her stomach. Everything made her think of the baby. "Don't tell anybody I said this," she whispered, "but sometimes your daddy's a butt." Sometimes. She glanced around the luxurious condominium. He had manned up. He took care of them in grand style. She didn't lack for any material thing. But emotionally she was sad and tired. It was not all connected to pregnancy hormones either. She was lonely. She didn't like having to share her man. *Humph.* He wasn't her man. If he were her man, she wouldn't be sharing him. Every disrespectful, vile thing Angela thought about her was true. She was the home-wrecking 'ho clinging to the bottom of the social order.

Angela had referred to her as 'his baby's momma.' *Baby-momma.* Never in her wildest imaginings did she ever think she would become a baby-momma. Baby-mommas were supposed to get public assistance because their baby-daddies were irresponsible dogs. Baby-mommas had issues with the other women their baby-daddies were involved with. Baby-mommas did their thing without a man's hand. Apparently, some baby-mommas were equivalent to well-kept call girls. Keira wept. She rubbed her belly for comfort.

CHAPTER 40

Angela waited until she was home alone. She planned it to be that way. Every room in the condo was silent, but she was a bundle of nervous energy. The phone shook in her hand. Her heart pounded a frantic beat. What would she do if he picked up?

She got to ponder for the space of one ring.

"Angela?"

His voice. Her name rolling off his tongue. It overwhelmed her with longing. "Nolan. Hi."

"How are you?"

Missing you. "I'm fine. Thank you so much for letting me have Lexie for the weekend. It was wonderful."

"She thought so too. I'm glad she got the chance." *I'm glad you called. Now, tell me what I want to hear.*

"Good. Good." She let her memories have her mind.

"Angela?"

"Oh. I'm sorry. I do have a reason for calling you. I do."

"I hope so."

As opposed to calling you because I wanted to hear your voice. "Umm. Yes... I wanted to talk to you about Lexie."

That was a cold dose of reality. "What's going on with Lexie?"

"I promise, I am not trying to get into your business or interfere with your life or tell you how to raise your child—"

Regardless of how much I want you too.

"But something is not right with her mother."

She had his full attention. "What do you mean?"

"Are you aware after Lexie went home she ran away?"

"She ran away?"

"My understanding is she does it with some sort of frequency. She hangs out at the Wineo house across the street. According to Lexie, Jackie doesn't notice."

"She doesn't notice her daughter?"

"Lexie doesn't want to be in California. I'm worried about her safety."

"She knows she has a home here. Why wouldn't she tell me if there was a problem with her mother?"

"She didn't exactly tell me. Things came out in conversation. Kids her age can't bring themselves to say they don't want to live with their mother. It's a betrayal. I would suggest you tell her you would like her to stay in Florida and see how she reacts. Or better yet, let her come live with me."

He laughed at her sincerity.

"I wanted to keep her, but you may have some kind of first dibs on her."

"I do have first dibs, but I'm not opposed to sharing."

Everything in her lit up.

"Some things."

And then went dim. She was barred from parts of him. As well, she should be.

He felt the warmth one beat and the chill the next. Apparently, exclusivity with him did not appeal to her.

"Well, thank you for listening to me."

"I always want to hear what you have to say. Especially when it comes to Lexie." *Or us.*

"I love her." *I love you too, but that's beside the point.*

Her, not me. "One thing is certain. If Lexie has a circumstance she needs to run away from, I'll be changing that situation. I'll let you know how it pans out."

"Thank you."

"Thank you." She hadn't said what he wanted to hear, but he was grateful for the sound of her voice anyway.

With nothing else to share and no incentive to linger, they disconnected.

CHAPTER 41

"I'll let them know we're home." Mitchell held the door to their complex open and followed Angela in.

"Whatever." The last thing Angela wanted to focus on was *them*. She ignored him as he pulled out his phone. So far, this was the worst Thanksgiving in her life. Not in any of the group homes she and Deidra grew up in did she ever feel as lonely and uncomfortable as she had spending the afternoon with Mitchell's parents.

Instead of cooking and talking and making eye contact with Deidra whenever her mother-in-law would say something snippy, she was forced to endure Nicolette's condescending attitude, the bitter surprise of seeing the new nursery for the baby, and worst of all, Deidra's absence.

Having no other living relatives, Angela and Deidra always spent the holidays together. But this year, Deidra forewent Mitchell's family, choosing instead to accept Rob's invitation to join him at the Enn. Angela loved that Deidra and Rob appeared to be getting closer, but she hated not having her sister around for support. And, she really hated knowing Nolan was so close, just there, out of reach. Out of sight, but not out of mind. On her mind, more often than she would ever admit.

She wanted to call him, just to say hi. To have someone talk to her as if she was the important one. But she wouldn't. She couldn't. It would hurt too much. In her innermost being, she knew it wouldn't be fair. Not to Nolan, not even to Mitch.

In the rare moments when she was being truthful with herself, Angela had to admit Mitchell was trying. He wanted them to see a counselor. He and Nate trained and planned and worked on projects upstairs, in her line of vision. When he did go down to the other apartment, he told her why and how long he expected to be. He always invited her to accompany him. To the best of her knowledge, he didn't call Keira or Nate without letting telling her beforehand. To the discerning eye, Mitchell seemed to be putting his marriage first.

But, Angela was not discerning. She was not helpful, agreeable, or cooperative. She was numb… and angry. It was wearing on Mitch, but she was too angry to care. Too numb. This thing between them had grown and spread and had begun to harden.

"Are you sure you're okay with Nate's family sleeping upstairs?" Mitchell put his phone away and allowed her to enter the elevator first.

"Why do you always call our condo 'upstairs?'" Angela rolled her eyes. She talked over her shoulder. "Your other apartment isn't a part of our house. We don't have a house. We don't live *upstairs*."

"Angie, it's been a long day. I don't want to fight with you."

"Asking a question is considered fighting?"

"Everything is a fight with you," he muttered.

"Excuse me?"

"I don't want to fight. All I'm asking is if there's going to be a problem with Nate's family sleeping upst—sleeping at our place? If you're uncomfortable with it, I'll get them a room."

"I do remember saying I didn't care. I don't recall saying I had a sudden problem with it. I'm not sure why you're questioning me as if I've given some indication it is now a problem although, I told you it was not a problem." Her words were sharp, having been pushed through her clenched teeth.

"I didn't say you had a problem with it." Outside their door, he jammed his key into the lock. "You didn't have fun today. I'm concerned it might be too much. Forgive me for being considerate."

"Humph." She headed down the hall. "If you wanted to be considerate, we wouldn't have wasted the holiday on your mother."

He didn't follow her; he went toward his bar instead. "Every year, we spend Thanksgiving with my parents. Why would that change?" There were few reasons. One, his mother wanted to have a joint celebration with Nate and Keira and their families, something Angela would have never allowed. Two, his wife and mother didn't get along at the best of times. This was hardly the best of times. Three, he and Angela had enough problems without his mother's interference. Four, his parents were going to Nate and Keira's for the rest of the evening. Five... he could go on, but why bother?

"Things change, people change, sometimes you have to change too." Angela closed the door.

She didn't emerge again until the doorbell sounded. Nate, his mother, and brother arrived bearing dessert.

"Here's the girl I want to see." Latoya was robust and vocal. She held out both arms, hugging Angela as if she were her daughter.

"Hi. Welcome. I'm so glad you came." Angela returned the embrace with genuine affection.

"Trust me, if you couldn't fit us in, I wouldn't be here." She released Angela and looked around. "Now, this is nice, a real home. Where can we get comfortable?"

"Hey, Nate."

"Hey, girl. You remember my brother, Rubin?"

"Hi," Rubin said, "Thanks for—"

"Yeah, yeah, yeah." Latoya talked over him. "You're here. She sees you. Now, leave us alone."

Angela grinned. It had been a while since she'd done that. "Let me show you to your rooms."

"Good. Then we can have some wine, eat some pie, and talk about real stuff. Let me tell you, I have had all the phoniness I can handle."

Nate sighed. Mitchell frowned. Angela's night took a turn for the better.

• • •

"Latoya, I'm telling you, I want to throw something."

"This is wrong." The older woman shook her head. "Even after everything you already told me, I wouldn't have believed it if I wasn't sitting right here."

"What kind of marriage is this?"

"It's not. Whatever it is, it's not a marriage."

The baffling turn of events came a little over an hour into the visit. Latoya and Angela were on the balcony, enjoying the view and each other. Angela brought Nate's mother up to speed. Mitchell, Nate, and Rubin were enjoying the Saints and the Packers when Mitchell got a call from his mother.

Nicolette didn't want to disturb Angela so she requested Mitchell come downstairs for a moment. Mitchell was loud and firm when he reminded his mother she saw him once today, she was disrupting the game, and he would only come down for a minute or two. After which he, flanked by Nate and Rubin, made a beeline for the party downstairs.

"Has he always been a momma's boy?" Latoya held her wine glass up for a refill of Solomon's Island.

Angela obliged, filling her own as well. The Pointes owned an extensive collection of expensive wines, but Angela was partial to the locally manufactured sweet stuff. "He's not a momma's boy. He's an opportunist. His mother supplied him with an excuse. He's down there because that's where he wants to be."

Latoya downed her drink and stood up. "I'm an opportunist. I'm going to take this opportunity to find out what's going on. And who's behind it."

"Who's behind it?"

"Your witch-in-law, your jackass, or his 'ho." She talked as she led the way from the balcony through the living room. "She acts like a nice girl but she gets what she wants."

"I'm not arguing."

"You need to decide what you want. If you want your man, then she needs to go." As they neared the door, Latoya focused her conversation inward. "I'll tell you this, she better not try to settle for Nate. Because that ain't happening." Snapping back to the present, she said, "Do you want to come down? That would teach them all a lesson."

"No. I don't go anywhere near that place."

"You should. We'll talk about that later. I'll be right back. If you go to sleep, I'll wake you."

"I won't be asleep. I'll keep the door unlocked."

And then she was alone. On the day of thanks, she was wretched and lonely. Not a soul in the world cared. She let the tears come. There was nobody around to see, no one to be concerned for her sadness. She wiped her wet cheek with the back of her hand and began collecting dishes and cups. She filled the dishwasher, wiped down the counters, and turned off the kitchen light. Her phone rang. Deidra.

God. Intuition. Whatever. It didn't matter what prompted Deidra to call. Angela needed her sister's comforting voice more than she needed air. "Hey, Deed. Thank you for…" It wasn't Deidra. It was, but she hadn't called Angela. The phone dialed her automatically. Deidra wasn't aware of it.

Angela let the disappointment win. She sobbed, the phone still in her ear, too distraught to disconnect.

She heard them.

CHAPTER 42

"I can't do that."

"Why not?" Deidra asked. "One phone call. What's the harm in one phone call?"

"What's the harm?" Nolan huffed. "What's the good? Is it going to change something?"

"Yes."

"Change what? She's a married woman, Deed. Hearing me say I love her—which she already knows—and confessing I can't get over her is somehow going to erase her marriage?"

"No, but you need to talk about it."

"We can't do anything about this. Why do we need to rehash it?"

"She's miserable. Can we do something about that?"

He answered her with silence.

"Part of her misery is because her marriage is a mess. Part of the reason her marriage is a mess is because of you."

"Me? No. I left her alone. Do you know how many times I've started to call her and hung up? I drove to the airport twice, intending to barge in and kidnap her or something crazy. But I didn't. I've stayed away. I respect marriage. Mine wasn't respected. I know how that ends. I've gone out of my way not to interfere. Because I love her."

"I'm not accusing you of interfering. I'm trying to get you to interfere. All I'm saying is on top of her problems with Mitch, she's holding him accountable for something that's not his fault. She's punishing him for not being you."

"What?"

"For not rescuing her and fixing everything and not being the man she's in love with. It doesn't matter what Mitch does or doesn't do. Angela doesn't want her marriage. Nolan, she wants you."

He said something, but Angela didn't catch it. He must have turned away and back again. His voice was crisp when he uttered his next comment, "What is it, honey?"

"I brought Deidra her phone." Lexie sounded close. The gadget was in her hand. "It might have called Angela 'cause it lit up but it didn't ring."

"Is Angela on the phone?" Panic or excitement drove Deidra's tone up an octave.

Angela wanted to hang up. She wanted to talk, to ask her sister what she thought she was doing. Ask if it were true. She already knew the answer. It was shameful. It was wrong. It was true.

"Nobody's there." The line went dead.

Coincidence? Did Lexie know she was listening and helped her? Did she disconnect? Did it matter?

Angela pulled herself together before Latoya returned. Barely. Her eyes were dry, but her thoughts were distant.

"Are you okay?" Latoya gave Angela's shoulder a matronly caress.

Angela shrugged. "Life is crazy."

"Yeah, and so is your mother-in-law. She brought some vomit-inducing items for the baby's room."

Angela scrunched her nose. "Nothing I needed to see."

"She's trying to push Mitchell and Keira together. I almost wish it would work."

"What?"

Latoya waved her off. "It would solve everybody's problem. They deserve each other. You deserve better and I've been watching the way Nate takes care of her. If I somehow end up stuck with her… No… I do not deserve that."

"I wouldn't worry about it. Nate is so dependable, it's hard not to rely on him. He's such a nice guy, everyone is drawn to him."

"Even better. Move Mitchell downstairs and Nate up here. You'll never have to see your mother-in-law again."

"Latoya, I'm in a crazy mood. Don't tempt me."

.   .   .

Mitchell fished through cabinets. He turned when Nate walked into the kitchen. "Do we have any more pretzels?"

"We? What are you doing?"

It took less than a beat for Mitchell to pick up the undertone. "You have a problem with me eating pretzels?"

"They're in the other cabinet." Nate pointed. "That's not what I'm talking about. *We.* You're more at home here than in your own house. Doesn't that bother you?"

"Should it?" Mitchell got defensive.

"Yes, it should. You're happier down here. Your parents are happier down here. How is that fair to Angela or Keira?"

"When have I been unfair to anybody?"

"What are you talking about? You've been unfair to everybody."

Mitchell waited for comprehension to catch up with his hearing. "All I've done is give and give. You've benefitted, my friend." He thumbed the room beyond. "You were fine out there a minute ago. What am I missing?"

Nate reached for the pretzel bag and helped himself to a handful. "I'm fine now. I intend to continue to benefit from your generosity and more." His smile was sincere. "That doesn't change what you're doing."

Mitchell took the bag back. "What am I doing?"

"Nothing and being unfair about it."

"Is that supposed to make sense?" He crunched loudly. Whatever had riled him up was gone. It was like that with Nate. He never meant harm and he was always honest.

"Are you Angela's husband or Keira's man? They don't know and you haven't told them. How is that fair?"

That wasn't how it was. No. It was… It was… There was no answer, no true explanation. Mitchell pretended it wasn't a question. "What's this have to do with anything? I came in here for pretzels."

"What you came for..." Nate reached into the bag and grabbed a second handful of nuggets. "If you want to get what you want, it might be nice for everyone to know what that is." Whatever Nathaniel had come into the kitchen for was no longer necessary; he returned to the company in the other room.

· ·

Mitchell lay in his bed, pondering. He couldn't recall very much of anything he and Angela talked about over the entire weekend. She talked to Nate's mother. She talked to Deidra, of course. She talked to that kid a lot. She didn't talk to him. They exchanged words. She participated in conversations when her participation was required. She was polite and accommodating. She may have flirted with Nate a few times. Her gentle laughter was noticeable in its newness.

And in its absence. When the door closed behind their company for the last time on Sunday, she retreated to that room of hers as if she was alone and he was invisible.

He wasn't invisible. Damn it. He was her husband. He wanted his wife. He hadn't abstained this long since the shipwreck. No, that wasn't true. He hadn't abstained very long after the shipwreck. If he would have, he wouldn't be missing his wife right now.

But...

The baby kicked. He couldn't wait for the ultrasound. He wouldn't say so to Keira, but he was certain they were having a boy. A linebacker. When he placed his hand on her abdomen and felt the strength, a wave of love and longing washed over him. There was no wrong in the creation of his son. His baby's life was not a shame. He would not treat it as such, nor would he allow anyone else to make that judgment.

On his knees he pressed kisses across Keira's belly, passing love and adoration and pride to his Heisman winner. He never felt more like a man in his life. He wanted to bask in that sensation for as long as possible. He touched her with his hands and lips, drinking in her beauty. He wanted to love her, please her, thank her for the life she was giving him.

Keira pulled him closer. She arched into him, her body responding to his. She wanted him too. Even if she said no, it would only be a token protest. It had been too long. The moment was too perfect.

But…

It had been hell leaving Keira alone, but he had. They were both panting when he stood up. She melted into him when he kissed her. She was hot and he wanted her so bad, he lost his resolve. She broke the contact. She was glassy-eyed and sexy, with her rounded belly protruding. The need was heavy between them.

"Oh, Mitch." She closed her eyes.

He sucked in deep breaths of air, "I want you, Keira."

"We can't."

He kissed her forehead and let himself out.

That had been the Wednesday before Thanksgiving. It was Sunday and his body hadn't cooled yet. He walked, talked and functioned, but beneath the surface, he burned. He chose his wife. He refrained because he loved Angela. He wanted what they had. He wanted counseling. He wanted his life back. What he didn't want was her in the guest room, not talking to him, while he burned.

.   .   .

"Angela." Mitchell knocked once and let himself into her room.

Surprised, Angela clicked off her phone.

It reregistered as suspicious. "Were you busy?"

"No. I'm done."

The silence stretched.

"Did you need something?" she asked.

"You."

"Pardon me?"

"I'm tired of this." He moved forward as he talked. "I want you to move back into our room and I want us to get back on track." He leaned in for a much-needed kiss.

She pushed him away. "Girlfriend busy tonight?"

"What?"

She folded her arms and gave him a look. "Stop it, Mitchell. I know you're still sleeping with her. Let's not pretend, okay."

"I'm not still sleeping with her." Given that he was horny, the accusation angered him.

Her pursed lips expressed her lack of belief.

"Why would I be standing here if I wanted to be with Keira?"

"That's what I'm waiting to find out."

Something was off. "Who were you on the phone with?"

She wouldn't answer. That made her guilty. "Is that why you won't see the counselor? Because you've moved on?"

"Let's not make this about something other than what it is. I'm not going to see a counselor because I don't need to pay someone to tell me the problem is my husband got another woman pregnant."

"That's not the problem."

"Since when?"

He sighed. This wasn't working. "It's not the only problem. That's not something we can do anything about. But, there are other things, other problems we could be working on. If we got some other stuff fixed, dealing with the baby wouldn't be so difficult for you."

"Really?" Angela sat down on her bed hard. Every word he uttered was a weight. "How is that ever not going to be difficult for me? Watching you with your baby and its mother. Would it be easy for you to watch me with someone else's child?"

He heard her: the words and their meaning.

"No. It wouldn't be. It hasn't been. But I allow it. Even though it's a sham, I allow it. Because that's what you need. Angie, I'm letting you have whatever you need." The phone rang in his office. "I have to get that. It's the West Coast office. I've been expecting it."

She waved him away.

"I'm not stopping you from doing what you need to do, Angie. I'm not knocking you for it either. It would be nice if you worked with me a little."

She did not offer further comment.

He retreated.

"What I need to do." She thought about that.

CHAPTER 43

Nolan opened the door and could not close his mouth. The surprise of her visit was nothing compared to his astonishment at her beauty. She was always in his mind's eye, but he never got it quite right. The reality of her was so much more than his imagination could express. Why was she here? He wouldn't dare to hope. "Angela." He opened the door, welcome already brightening his pupils.

"Nolan." He was ruggedly handsome. So confident and comfortable with himself. Even now, he did things to her heart rate and made her breathless. She glided past him into the living room. "How are you?"

Nolan took a deep breath, closed the door, and locked it. He turned around and waited for her to speak.

"I'm sorry. I should have called, but… but nothing. I was scared."

"Of?"

"You. I was scared if I called, you would tell me not to come."

As she spoke, he stepped forward, each word bringing him closer until he invaded her space. "Never." His voice dropped an octave. "But I would ask you why? Why are you here?" He whispered. Without preamble, he claimed her lips, kissing her with uncontrollable desire. She returned his kiss, matching his ferocity with her own need. He stopped caring why. All that mattered was that she was there. She was in his arms. She was his.

She wasn't his. She rejected him. Just like Jackie.

That didn't stop him from wanting her. He crushed her to him, touching her, luxuriating in the feel of her against him. He wanted to take her right there. He would have, except she wasn't his to take. He gave himself a few more precious seconds before he dragged his mouth away. "Why did you come?"

Tears spilled across her cheeks—tears of joy, tears of relief, tears of desire. "I wanted to see you. So bad. I missed you." She reached for him again, needing his mouth moving over hers. Needing his strength, his protection. "Nolan, I don't know what this is, what we are, but it hurts too much being away from you. It hurts."

Responded to her urgency, he met her halfway. "You know why. You do know what this is." He backed her up, lowered her onto the sofa. He had worshipped her body numerous times in his dreams. Now, he would do it in earnest. "It's love, Angela. It's real. I love you."

She wasn't his.

"I love you too, Nolan. I can't not love you." She was still crying, but blissfully euphoric. She hadn't been this happy since she left Florida. She realized when she walked away, she forgot to take her heart with her. Overwhelmed and overjoyed at these revelations and emotions, it took her a moment to realize he didn't pull away to undress. "What?" She reached for him, caressing the steel of his bicep and sighing.

"Where's Mitchell?"

That name coming from his mouth was as chilled as the ocean. She was reminded of the night she plunged into its depths. "To hell with Mitchell."

He arched an eyebrow at her venomous tone but said nothing.

The heat ebbed away. He sat back, giving her room to sit up. She heaved another sigh—this one without passion. She supposed talking should come first, but she wanted him to hold her. "Mitchell is away on a 'business trip.'" She air quoted.

"I take it all is not well in paradise?"

"All will never be well in paradise. We can't get past anything. But, I don't want to get past anything because I can't get over you."

"What are you going to do about it?"

She hunched her shoulders. "I'm here."

"Permanently?"

She didn't answer for a long minute, unable to meet his eyes.

"Hell." Nolan saw his dreams slipping away from him, again. "Angela, why are you screwing with me like this?"

She shook her head. "No, no. I'm not! This is so intense; it's crazy. But is it real? Are we in love? Do you love me?"

He stared at her as if she was insane.

"I came down here to see if we could try. To ask you if you thought we should... try. I'm scared, Nolan. I can't help it. I'm on the verge of adultery, but I'm here."

"Adultery?"

"I can't pretend it's not."

It wasn't so much what she said that irked him. It was what she didn't say. That was the problem. He stood up and moved away from her as fast as possible before he crumbled at her feet.

"Nolan?" She waited for him to turn around. "Talk to me. Please."

"And say what? I'm in love with you Angela. I would do anything for us to be together. Anything. I opened that door and for one split second, I thought you were here because you felt the same way."

She started to slide off the sofa. "I do. I'm here."

He took a step back and raised his hand to halt her and her words. "You don't. That's not why you're here. You're here because you're still in some kind of indecision. You're still on the damned fence. You're still angry with Mitchell. You can't move on like that. Is he off somewhere with Keira? Is that why you're here? How is this any different? Do you want me to screw you, so you can get even?"

"NO! That's not it!" He wasn't getting it. He didn't understand.

"I'm never going to do that because I am in love with you. I won't share. You need to get that through your head."

"Nolan..."

"If I was married, but told another woman I loved her as I attempted to undress her, I would be a dog, a scumbag, a cheater, all those things you call him. What does that make you? You don't love me, Angela. You're stringing me along. You're stringing us both along."

He had never spoken so cruelly to her before. She sat, stunned, unable to accept the truth past the ringing in her ears. The sting was too great.

And he wasn't done.

"I'm only human. How many times are we going to get close before I decide I won't be denied?"

She shook her head. "I-I'm not denying you."

"You ought to. You damn sure shouldn't be offering me something you can't deliver. What do you think this does to me? How long were you planning to stay? A week? A day? I want you here, but if you only came for a visit, go check into the Enn. I'm not going to be strung along, not understanding what the hell is going on."

"I can't explain it. Three hours ago, I wasn't planning to come down here. I tried to remember the last time I was happy, completely content. I thought about you and that night... the night they came back. I had to see you. I don't remember if I bothered to cut off the lights or lock the door. But, I had to see you; I couldn't wait. I should have called. We could have talked. But, but... I needed to see you. I wanted you to..."

"To what? Save you. Is that what I'm good for?"

It didn't occur to her to lie. "Yes."

CHAPTER 44

The Summer Shack's dinner crowd trickled in, but it wasn't enough to qualify as busy. Joey looked up when Nolan walked in. One glance told him enough. He bypassed Nolan's favorite bourbon and filled a glass with vodka. He set it down at the end of the bar, in the far corner, away from everybody.

Nolan followed the alcohol. He slammed himself on the barstool and slammed the entire glass back in one gulp. ·

Joey waited with the bottle in hand. He refilled the glass. "What happened?"

Nolan threw back the second glass. His eyes stung. He blamed it on the vodka. "Nothing. Not a damned thing."

"Uh-huh." Joey filled his glass a third time.

Nolan covered his face with his hands. His shoulders shook from holding in his pain. "This is fucked up. That's what it is."

"You need a minute?"

When Nolan nodded, Joey said, "I'll be back in a sec." He left the bottle.

She left. As fast as she came, she left. He walked out of the house, down to the Willow Inlet to catch his breath. He needed five minutes to wrap his head around her arrival, and her suggestion of adultery. Five minutes. She didn't go to the Enn. She left. She left him again. He wanted to call her, beg her to come back. But he couldn't. It was her choice. Adultery. Not a forever kind of thing. Adultery.

Nolan concentrated on his breathing. When he accomplished that, he thought about the alcohol. It wasn't having the right effect. It wasn't numbing his senses. It wasn't dulling the pain. What was the point in drinking if it wasn't going to change anything?

He was staring into space trying hard to think of nothing when he felt the tension. He didn't look up. The bastard was here.

Although he was sober, Mitchell had the dazed expression of a madman. He staggered like a drunk to Nolan's corner and stood there panting like he'd run a great distance to get there.

Nolan ignored him.

Joey came over with a second glass. "Do you need this?"

Mitchell nodded once. "You know of any other reason I should be here?"

He filled it and refilled Nolan's. "Sit down. Don't start any trouble, Slick. This ain't the time or place."

"Or what?" Mitchell snapped. Still, he did as ordered. He took the stool at the end, next to Nolan's corner. "You going to call the good ol' boys network and attempt some racial profiling?"

"Whipping your ass wouldn't be racial. It'd be a pleasure. Now, take a drink and get your shit together. I mean it. No trouble. From either of you." Joey walked away.

"Aren't you the owner?" Mitchell addressed Nolan. "He can talk to you like that? Disrespectful."

Nolan still hadn't bothered to look at Mitchell. "Shouldn't you be with your wife?"

"Should I?"

"Should you?"

They sat in silence, one scowled while the other sulked.

Nolan reached for his glass. "Is there something you want?"

Likewise, Mitchell took a swig from his glass. "Can I talk to you man to man?"

Nolan rolled his eyes but noted the attitude Mitchell fired at Joey was missing. "What do you want?"

"Did you sleep with my wife?"

Nolan snorted. "Did she tell you I did?"

"I haven't asked her."

"Ask her."

"I'm asking you."

To Nolan's mind, Mitchell's lack of anger was cause for alarm. This was a man who seemed as broken as he was. He lost some of his own anger. "Why are you asking me?"

"Because I want the truth." For the first time, Nolan looked at him. Mitchell wasn't looking for a fight. He was nursing wounds. "Shit ain't making sense. I've got to make it make sense. So I'm starting with this. Did you sleep with my wife?"

Now that Nolan looked at him, he kept looking. He searched for something yet unnamed.

Mitchell was compelled to continue. "She wants to be with you. Is it retaliation or something more? She needs to figure that out. I followed her to your place. I planned to bust in and cap both your asses."

If that bothered Nolan, it didn't show.

"I didn't. I couldn't. So, I waited. I watched her leave in tears, all confused and regretful. I don't understand it. If all she wanted was revenge, she should have been as happy as a lark. Same thing if she wanted to get you out of her system. It seems to me like that wasn't it. If she decided to leave you alone, she wouldn't be here. So, did you two disagree? One time thing versus a drawn-out affair? Did she get here and then backed out of her deal? If she wanted to stay with you, why did she leave? What the hell happened between you two? What should I expect when I see her?" Mitchell raised his hands in surrender. "That's all I'm asking. Just to be clear, the answer doesn't mean shit other than it's an answer. I'm not looking for a fight. This isn't between me and you anyway. I'm here to find out where her mind is; to see if I still have a marriage to save."

"Those are things you need to ask her." Nolan held Mitchell's stare. "We didn't sleep together. She'll have to explain why. I'm not your problem, Mitchell. She came here. You followed her. The problem is in your house. Something back there prompted the exodus. Address that if you want to know if your marriage is salvageable."

They went back to their silence.

"What did you expect?"

Angela glanced at her sister. Deidra was missing the point. "Not that."

"Okay. Not that. Then what?"

"Are you saying rejection should have been my goal?"

"I'm not saying anything. I'm asking you a question. Why won't you answer it?"

Angela thought for a moment. For one thing, it was a stupid question. "I hoped he missed me. I hoped he wanted me to stay."

"Yeah, he told you he wanted you to stay before you left."

Angela side-eyed her.

"Don't take your attitude out on me. I didn't do it."

Angela turned away. "I came here for support. But if you're not going to be helpful, I'll leave."

"Sit down, Ange. You're oversensitive and being dramatic." She tugged on her sister's arm. "This is the way it comes off to me. You and Mitch aren't getting along. You ran back to Nolan. But, you didn't sever your ties with Mitchell. Is Nolan a prop; payback or a fling to boost your ego? I bet whatever you said to him didn't sound like you were ready to spend the rest of your life in Florida. Was he supposed to be thrilled you went there to offer him crumbs?"

"That's not what I did."

"Then tell me, what were you doing? What did you want to happen?"

"I-I... I don't know." She slouched down, withdrawing into herself. "I just wanted somebody to love me. I wanted Nolan to still want me. I wanted to be sure. I left him. I left before we had a full relationship. Can we go back and pick up like nothing ever happened?"

"You wanted a guarantee?"

Angela didn't answer.

"There are no guarantees. But, if you want Nolan to love you, you're going to have to leave Mitch. And vice versa. If you want your marriage to work, you're going to have to walk away from Nolan and never look back."

"What about Keira?"

"This ain't about Keira. Or what Mitch would or should or could do. This is about you, Ange. You have to decide what you want and what you'll do. And you have to decide first."

"That's not fair." She shook her head to prove her point.

"What's fair have to do with anything? You had a great marriage. You did. But just like that boat, you got shipwrecked. All you're doing is floating around waiting for somebody to save you. It ain't happening this time. It's up to you. You can drown, or, you can try to get to the shore—one side or the other." She waved her hand between two imaginary points. "However you look at it, it comes down to you."

"I didn't cause the ship to wreck. I didn't put me in the ocean."

"All the same, that's where you are."

"I don't like boat or water analogies."

"All the same. That's where you are."

CHAPTER 45

Returning from Deidra's, Angela was surprised to see Mitch lounging on the sofa watching her.

"Oh. Uh. Hi. You startled me." She sat her bag down, ignoring her guilt; she was innocent of any wrongdoing.

He made it a point to notice her bag. She was guilty. "Where have you been?"

She closed the front door. Something in his tone put her on edge. "Deidra's. I was under the impression you were going to be gone all week. I didn't want to be alone." Too much. She said too much. She needed to go to her room and get herself together.

"You spent the night with Deidra?"

"Ummhmm." She reached for her bag again but stopped. "Why are you back early? Or should I not ask?"

"I didn't have a meeting. Never did. I knew you were up to something. I wanted to find out what."

Her eyes flared. Anger at everything simmered beneath the surface of her emotions. It wasn't going to take much. She marched over to where he sat, taking a seat in a chair close enough to talk, but not touch. "You were spying on me?"

"You don't talk to me. What other choice do I have?"

She didn't answer him.

"What happened with him?"

Humiliation and shame came over her, less from what he knew than what he witnessed. She responded with bitterness and sarcasm. "You were spying on me. Your gall is amazing."

Her attitude had a negative effect. He leaned forward. "Note, I have yet to make one judgment against you. I don't intend to. But I'll be damned if I'm going to let you blame me. We're not pretending I did something wrong. I'm not the one who ran off to see another man."

"You don't have to, Mitchell." She was falsely pleasant. "You moved your whore downstairs. Made it convenient for yourself."

He didn't acknowledge the whore comment. "No, no. This situation doesn't have anything to do with Keira. This is us, that's all."

"Bullshit." She crossed her arms. "If it was *us, and that's all* we'd be fresh out of problems, wouldn't we?"

"Angela, can we talk? Just talk. Let's figure out what we want."

She knew what she wanted. It was not to be had. There was nothing she could do about it. "Okay, Mitchell. Talk."

.　　.　　.

They'd been at it for hours, but Mitchell would go at it all day if necessary. "Help me out here," he said. "I'm trying. Okay. I'm trying." He let out a wearied breath. "I've put myself in your place. I get it. You thought I was dead. Our life was over. Being with him didn't have anything to do with me, us. It all happened too fast. That's it."

He sounded reasonable, accepting. She didn't trust it. "Okay."

"Okay," he agreed. "Why can't you flip that? I thought you were dead. Keira didn't have anything to do with us. You were dead. It just happened too fast." He held his hands out, surrendering.

"Because I was here watching the news. The coastguard didn't find you. You didn't get pulled out of the water. But, you decided I was gone— with no news—and you couldn't wait to celebrate."

Mitch frowned at the bitterness. "I'm sorry. No, I didn't watch CNN. But I did row the ocean the whole damn night calling your name. You didn't answer."

She could imagine what he suffered, but she didn't want to. "Yes," she admitted, "we both had reasons for what we believed. I befriended Nolan.

After a while, I did allow him to kiss me. But, I have yet to sleep with him. Our marriage meant something to me. Even though I thought you were dead, I didn't hop into the first available bed, like any old substitute would do. I gave you a little more honor than that."

"It wasn't about a substitute. You're my wife, Angela. I love you. You're the most important person in the world to me."

"For how much longer, Mitchell?"

He scrunched his face, not understanding. "Forever. That's not going to change."

"Yes it will, in a couple of months. Where on the list will I fall after you have your baby?"

"Angela…"

"You want a baby as much as I do. The only difference is you're getting one."

"We're getting one! This is a chance for us to have a family. Why can't you see that?"

"I'm not getting anything other than a reminder that you slept with another woman. You have a family I couldn't provide."

.•.•.

It had been a full day and then some. They argued their way from the living room to the kitchen to the balcony and back again—but not the bedroom. Their conversation cycled along the same repeated path.

Mitchell's eyes were on Angela, but he didn't see her; his vision was clouded. His mind locked in some dark, burning place.

"It's not the same thing!" She yelled from her own place of fire. "We did not handle it the same way!"

"No!" The bass in his voice vibrated with sarcasm. "No. Not the same thing at all. I," He poked his finger into his chest—a subconscious attempt to break it, "I didn't think about what I was doing. There wasn't any thinking going on 'cause I had already lost my mind. All I knew was you were dead and I was about to die. Keira offered me solace—"

She made a face.

He didn't see it. "—She tried to help me pull my shit together! If there was something other than the madness in my head, maybe I would have been able to think. Maybe I could have helped us not to die."

"She's a super-do-gooder. Screwing you for the sake of mankind. The Red Cross should take lessons."

Her disdain reached through his haze and made him focus. "Her actions were pure. You can wrap yourself up in your cloak of wounded self-righteousness, but Keira didn't move in with a man and start playing house two days after her husband was pronounced dead."

Angela's mouth dropped. Not only did he misrepresent what took place, he defended the bitch!

Her discomfort encouraged him. "Keira isn't behaving as if *her* actions are all justified and she has some divine right to throw judgment on a situation she can't relate to because she was too busy moving on with her life to concern herself with so much as a prayer for those of us who weren't fortunate enough to be rescued. We had to worry about food and water—"

"Yes, you were roughing it hard in that beach house."

He cleared his throat and leveled his cold gaze. "At least we didn't bother playing games with emotion and lust." He hoped she would cry.

Angela didn't cry. Her pain was way past the point of tears. She held herself stiff, breathing deeply, trying to collect the scattered bits of her pride while maintaining her weak illusion of control.

Mitchell didn't speak either.

Twenty-five breaths later, she unlocked her jaw. "Now I understand. Thank you."

He didn't interrupt.

"Keira was with you and I was not. That is the full gist of your argument. Because of that fact, that one all-consuming ingredient, you and your entire experience are acceptable and above reproach. Whatever happened, happened. There's no judgment. No guilt. For those few weeks, life sucked for you. It did. It sucked. But because it sucked, your choices are all good and I have to like it. If I don't, you're free to attack and blame me. You're free to berate me and throw judgment on my choices. I understand. Keira can do no wrong. It wasn't adultery. It was the thing to do. Survival one-o-one. She worked hard to keep your penis alive. Glad we got our priorities straight."

Real or imagined, Mitch didn't like her accusations. He didn't like her haughtiness. At the moment, he didn't like her. "Get *your* priorities straight. Or, is me sleeping with someone more relevant than me being alive? Or..." He paused as if he were considering a new angle. "Is it that Keira conceived? Is that it? The baby? Something you can't have?"

"I'm done with this conversation." Angela spun on her heel, needing to leave the room. She paused in the hallway to spew a dose of her own venom. "You being alive *is* the most relevant fact, Mitchell. If not for that, all other points would be moot." Her heels echoed against the hardwood.

"Yeah, well," he said to the emptiness, "I'm done."

It had been hours, a full day and then some. Somewhere they stopped talking. The wounds had festered.

CHAPTER 46

Mitchell let himself into the downstairs condo. It would be a pleasure to see Keira. She was always beautiful, always welcoming. He needed to be welcomed. The house smelled good. She must have made something amazing for dinner. He'd find out what it was and have some. After.

The table hadn't been cleared. Odd. Keira kept on top of things. As much as he would allow. He'd have to ask Nate if she was overdoing it. If she was resting now—which Mitchell suspected—she was overdoing it. He walked past Nate's room and knocked once in greeting. *The lazy bum.* He joked to himself. In reality, Nate was far from lazy. Nathaniel Dovey was the most astute person Mitchel had ever had the pleasure of working with. Not only was he a hard worker, he was a loyal friend... She wasn't in her room. "Keira?"

His first reaction was to worry. He checked his phone to see if he had missed a call. He hadn't. He went back through the condo, looking in the baby's room, the guest room, and the den. She wasn't there. Sweeping his eyes around the main room, he saw what he failed to notice earlier.

Two people were eating, but dinner had been interrupted. The lights were low and... *What the hell?*

He picked up the offending article of clothing and waited for a different answer. He didn't like the one that came to mind.

"Hey, Mitch."

Mitchell turned. Keira leaned against the wall, watching him. He wanted to ask where she had been but didn't see the point.

"When did you get back?"

She had some nerve. Standing there—beautiful with her hair mussed and skin glowing—making small talk, like he gave a damn about that shit. "When were you going to tell me?"

"It just happened. We haven't had a chance to work our heads around it yet."

"This is wrong. It doesn't make sense."

She studied him as if he were an unknown object. "Are you kidding me? This is about the only thing that does make sense. Aren't you married? Didn't you decide to work on your marriage? Isn't that where you've been?"

"I did try. It didn't work."

"Pffffhhh." She brushed past him to find a comfortable place to sit. "So on to plan B. Is that what you thought?"

"I thought I was coming to tell you I love you and I wanted to get married. But I see you have other ideas."

"Like I said, on to Plan B. Mitch, I'm not a contingency. And, more important, I'm not your mistress. I told you at the beginning I wasn't going to be your mistress."

He did not want to argue. He'd done too much of that already. "Didn't you hear me? I said I wanted to marry you."

"Now? Come on, Mitchell. I deserve better than that. You're down here, talking marriage because things didn't go the way you wanted with Angela."

Mitchell let it go. Keira did deserve better than that. "What do you want me to say?"

"Say you're a reasonable man. You can accept the truth."

"The truth being you got tired of waiting for me to figure this out and slept with Nate? Or, he took advantage of the situation?"

"I meant the actual truth. You wanted us both. The reality is you were waiting to see which one of us hung around the longest. You figured since I'm having your baby, I would always be near, just in case."

"You're supposed to be near. I am the baby's father."

"No one is disputing that. But you're not my husband. You're not even my man."

"And Nate is?"

"Yes. Yes, he is. In every way that matters." She ignored the face Mitchell made. "Nate's been here with me the whole time. Right here."

"I've been with you the whole time. I haven't missed a doctor's appointment. I've purchased two of everything a child needs."

"You've been here for the baby. You don't get a prize for that. You're supposed to be. Nate has been here for me. Nate is the one rubbing my feet and my back. And helping me get up and sit down. He watches silly movies with me and endures my hormonal mood swings. He's the one taking me to dinner and bringing me flowers and making me laugh." She pointed to the dining room table. "This was me realizing how much Nate loves me. The other night, I ate something the baby didn't like. I laid down and got nauseous. I couldn't get up fast enough. I ended up throwing up in the bed."

Instinctively, Mitchell made a 'yuck' face.

Keira shook her head. "Nate took care of it. He put me in the tub and brought me a cup of soup to settle my stomach. While I was soaking he changed the sheets. Then he washed my hair. My hair." She tugged her tresses for proof. "I didn't care about him seeing me naked because he took such good care of me. He put me to bed and tucked me in like I was important. Because, to him I am. I thought, here is the kind of man I could love. Here's the kind of man I want to spend the rest of my life with. And then it clicked. He is the man I want to spend the rest of my life with."

Mitchell didn't say anything for a while. In all the scenarios that played out in his mind, never had there been one in which Keira left him for Nate. Only, it made sense. Nate was his go-to guy. Mitchell burdened Nate to be the back-up husband—one without the perks. Mitchell moved them in together expecting Nate to take care of her in his absence. He hadn't realized how absent he had been. "Is this why you stopped sleeping with me?"

"I stopped sleeping with you because it was wrong."

"Nate tell you that?"

"Yes, he did, as a matter of fact. It wasn't news, but there's nothing like getting hit with the truth upside your head." She shrugged.

"Like now," he mumbled. Louder, he asked, "Did it ever occur to you this might be why? Maybe he had reasons for wanting to talk you out of waiting for me."

"As long as it's the truth, what difference does my alleged motivation make?"

Nathaniel entered the room without them noticing. Clad in gray sweatpants, his dreads hung free down his bare back. He walked past them into the kitchen. A short moment later, he returned with two beers and a glass of grape juice. Keira thanked him. Mitchell accepted the offering without comment. Nate made himself comfortable on the couch. Likewise, Mitchell finally took a seat. He was angry but he hadn't placed it yet.

"Sleeping with a married man who supposedly wants his marriage back is whorish activity. Keira is not a whore; she didn't need to act like one. Angela certainly didn't deserve it."

"Was that a call you needed to make?"

"It was a call somebody needed to make." Nate chugged a big gulp of Blue Moon. "I know you feel like shit. You might want to fight or fire me. You want to kick me out? It doesn't matter. I didn't steal your girl. I didn't wreck your life or ruin our friendship. None of that typical shit. This isn't a typical situation. Keira is the mother of your baby. That's it. She's the girl you slept with when you were grieving. That's it. You were going to do right by her. For the most part, you have. But it was never love. Not the lasting kind, anyway. You were looking out for the team, but you didn't choose her because you don't love her. Not like that."

"Shut the hell up," Mitchell said it because he didn't have anything else to say.

"Drink your beer so we can figure out what we're supposed to do with this new pile of crap."

Mitchell's shoulders dropped. Like a whipped dog, he drank his beer.

.   .   .

Hours later, Mitchell sat alone, contemplating. In the end, it had been his choice. Angela walked out on the conversation, but he walked out on her. Tired of the fighting and the loss, he chose Keira. If only. If only she had chosen him. If only she had waited. If only he would have come to that decision sooner. If only.

Keira had chosen Nate, and Mitchell couldn't be mad about it. But he was mad. And sad, and hurt, and confused, and betrayed, but only in his emotions. On another day, when his logic regained control, he wouldn't be mad. But, he had to get there. If only.

If only he would have stuck to his plan to fight it out with Angela. If only he would have stayed there and waited for her to come out of her room—out of her wounded funk. If he wouldn't have run to Keira, Angela wouldn't have found him gone. She wouldn't have left him. If only.

CHAPTER 47

Nolan continued wiping down the bar even after Rob walked over. These days, Rob was almost always happy so his frown was noticeably out of place. "Something happen? Do you need a drink?"

"No." Rob shook his head. "Need to talk to you."

Nolan laid his cleaning cloth aside.

"Tank's first Christmas; Lexie back permanently. This is going to be a special holiday."

"Agreed."

"We should all be together. Mom is like a kid… Well, Mom is always like a kid. At least now, she's a well-behaved kid. It's going to be great."

"I sense a *but* in there."

"But it won't be great if I don't get to spend it with Deidra. I want her to come down here."

"Why wouldn't she? She's family."

"Because she doesn't want to leave Angela alone for another holiday. She won't come unless Angela comes with her." He fixed his gaze on his brother.

Nolan ignored the tightening in his chest. "What's that have to do with me?"

"Angela is not feeling welcomed."

"Angela is always welcomed. She knows that. But why is it even a consideration? Why wouldn't she want to spend the holiday with her husband and let her sister do whatever she pleases… Wait a minute… Are you suggesting Angela and Mitchell come down here and pretend it's normal like we're all some big happy family of misfits?"

Rob crinkled his forehead. "No. You idiot. Not Mitchell. Who gives a shit about him?"

"You're the one making asinine suggestions."

"That's the whole point. Since Angela and Mitchell split, Deidra doesn't want Angela to be alone. What's difficult to understand about that? You do comprehend English, don't you?"

Nolan didn't understand anything. He thought Rob said Angela and Mitchell were separated, but Christmas wasn't for a few days yet. "Split?"

Rob nodded. The brothers stared at one another for a long minute, confused. Suddenly, it made sense. "She didn't tell you? Wow. Sorry. I thought you knew, seeing as you were the cause. Well, not entirely. Her surprise trip down here was the last bit. She came home and moved in with Deidra. Why didn't you know any of this?"

Nolan picked up his cloth and vigorously re-cleaned the counter. "It wasn't my business." His agitation was so evident, Rob moved away without further comment.

■　■　■

"No way!" Angela held up her hand to ward off Deidra's next comment. "I am not going down there for Christmas."

"I'm not leaving you here alone."

"Why not? I'm a big girl. I'll be fine."

"You've been saying that for days." Deidra crossed her arms.

"I've been fine for days."

"You do realize living here means I get to see you every day? You have not been fine."

"Let me assure you, going to Florida isn't going to help that."

"Why not? Nolan is in Florida."

"Yes, I know where Nolan lives."

"You're in love with him. Mitchell is not a factor. What am I missing?"

"A few screws if you think I'm going to spend Christmas with a man who doesn't want me."

"He does want you."

"Not the way I remember it. Besides, I've got plans."

"Which are?"

"Job hunting." Angela tapped the screen on the tablet she'd been reading. "I'm tired of being depressed. I'm getting on my own nerves. If I'm going to move on with my life, I actually have to get my butt moving."

"Agreed. Start by moving your butt into your bedroom and pack. We're going to Florida."

"I'm not—"

This time, Deidra's hand shot up, warding off comments. "Yes, you are. Nolan is not the only person there. If not for yourself, or me, do it for Lexie and Tank. After all the junk you shipped down there, don't you want to see their faces when they open it?"

Any mention of Lexie gave her pause. "I wasn't invited."

"I dare you to say that to Hilda. Let's call her."

"If I go down there, I'll be miserable and I'll ruin the holiday."

"If you stay here, you'll be miserable. It's Christmas. Make it my present. Besides, I already bought the tickets."

"You are a conniving witch. And, a manipulator. And, I don't want to go."

"I do, but I'm not going without you. Start packing."

"You didn't give me any warning."

"No. If I did, you would have figured a way out by now."

"The day isn't over yet."

"For you, it is. If I have to leave without you, I'm calling Mitchell and telling him you're here alone pining for him and he needs to come and talk to you."

"Deidra!"

"Mitch or Nolan. Your choice."

"Since when?"

CHAPTER 48

Nolan took his boat out without anticipation or desire. He used the time to brood. Angela was coming, today. Before, they had a chance as a couple, but not anymore. It wasn't her marriage; it was them. They stopped talking and there was no way to get it back. When Jackie left him, he let her go. Married ten years, and he didn't hesitate to dissolve it. She cheated; he was done.

This should be easier; he and Angela were only together a short while. They were never official. He'd been nothing if not respectful. If she didn't want a relationship, he'd accept it.

The worst part about his morning boat ride was coming back. His life was empty. He had Lexie. He had Hilda, Rob, and Tank. They meant everything. He had a great family. Angela would be close—even if he couldn't touch her. It was going to be a great Christmas. Still, he was empty.

Nolan came around the corner of the house and stopped short. Hilda snuck out of his garage, looking left and right, imitating a thief. "What are you doing?"

Hilda jumped. When she identified the speaker, she put a hand over her heart. "You scared me to death." With her other hand, she pulled the garage door closed.

"What are you up to?"

"I could ask the same of you, but I know what you're up to. A big fat nothing."

He arched an eyebrow.

"Angela and Deidra will be here soon. When are you going to get out of your funk and find some Christmas spirit?"

"I wasn't aware I was in a funk."

"That makes you the only one. You weren't this bad over Jackie. That should tell you something."

It did. It told him Hilda was voicing the same thoughts he contemplated.

"Rather than pout because you lost your squeezie-doll, why don't you quit stalling and get her back? You'll have a golden opportunity this afternoon."

Nolan sighed. He wasn't in a funk, and he wasn't pouting. "Despite whatever it is you think I should be doing, Angela and I are done. I love her, but she made a choice. I can't make her change her mind. Neither will I destroy the holiday trying."

Hilda folded her arms. "If you were a real man, you would. You would at least give it a shot, instead of slinking around pouting all day. That will ruin the holiday for sure. I swear, you remind me of Lexie after the divorce. At least, she had a reason to be angry. It wasn't her fault."

"This is my fault?"

"Absolutely." Hilda strode past him, presumably back to the Enn.

Nolan stood there a long minute with Hilda's reprimand echoing in his head before he dialed Rob.

"Yep."

"You at work?"

"Just left. What's up?"

"Can Mom get to her motorcycle?"

"Not unless she's a magician. It's under more than lock and key. Why do you ask?"

"I caught her coming out of my garage looking guiltier than usual. I'm guessing she somehow acquired a new one."

"Are you kidding?"

Nolan opened the door and flicked on the light. "No. I was wrong."

"Good. After that last fiasco, I can't imagine anybody stupid enough to sell her one."

"She didn't need to buy one. She stole yours."

"Son of a—"

"Yeah, you are. Can I ask you a question?"

"Why not? Anything to keep me from calling the police on my own mother."

"Do you think I'm like Lexie?"

"I'd go with the other way around; you being here first and all. But yes, you and Lexie are a lot alike. You're both quiet and observant. Lexie is smarter than you are, but you both could use a little help with your problem-solving skills. Angela's influence made a tremendous difference for Lex. I'm sorry I can't say the same for you."

He said enough. "Was I like that before?"

"Nolan. You caught Jackie screwing Travis, your half brother, who is a whole dick. What did you do?"

"I tossed him out of the window."

"Not him. What did you do about Jackie?"

Nolan made a face. "I wasn't going to toss a woman out of a window."

"You let her leave with Lexie. You let her take whatever she wanted. You did the divorce without a comment. You left everything up to her."

"She threw our marriage away. That was her choice, and everything that went with it."

"But it was your life. If anybody has something to say about what goes on in your life, it should be you. At least, in part. When Lexie was mad at the world, it was because everything was different. That's scary for a kid. She wanted somebody to fix it, to put it back together. You're not a kid, Nolan. Nobody is fixing it for you. No matter how much you pout. I have to go. The plane lands in two hours. I have to run some errands before the girls get here."

Nolan didn't need the reminder. "If I can wrangle the key away from mom, I'll ride your bike to the Shack. You can pick it up from there."

"You might want to remind her she's still on probation."

"Do you think it will help?"

"No, but remind her anyway."

Nolan disconnected. That was twice he'd been accused of pouting. He didn't pout. He may be slightly obsessing over Angela, but he wasn't pouting. His morning was ruined. His mother was a reckless driver and a thief. He wanted Angela. Rob was right, he was smart. Not as smart as Lexie, but smart enough to see the truth. Angela wasn't his, because he hadn't done a damned thing to get her.

CHAPTER 49

Nolan spent the day at the Summer Shack. If Angela didn't want to resume a relationship with him, he would be respectful.

Angela knew what Nolan's absence meant. He did not want to see her. They were not going to become a couple, and he was not going to allow her an opportunity to change his mind. It was his choice; she would respect it. She may be at his house, but she was going to stay out of his way.

It hurt knowing she was so close and not for him. When she didn't come around to say hello, he pretended it didn't matter. He gave himself to the fantasy of Angela waiting at his house. She put her things in *her* room, waiting to surprise him in his. The imagery was an aphrodisiac. Seeing the house cold and dark was the bucket of ocean-water that forced him to stop dreaming.

Angela hung out, caught up, baked cookies, and wrapped presents. She posted herself close to the front window and kept an eye out for Nolan's car. He hadn't come to a complete stop before she excused herself for the night.

He was up and gone before she dared to venture from her bedroom.

They *respectfully* avoided one another until the Christmas Eve Mass, in which they exchanged a few tight words and sat at opposite ends of the pew.

Christmas morning was a different story. Between Lexie and Tank's enthusiasm and Rob and Deidra's romance, it was impossible not to enjoy the magic. Caught in the moment, Nolan and Angela let go of the tension.

There was laughter and banter; innuendos passed between them. It felt promising. It made them hopeful, and their hearts yearned… A different kind of tension began to build. Their eyes met, and he held her gaze, shared her longing, and needed a deep breath.

The pause was long enough for him to decide he would ask her to take a walk with him.

The pause was long enough for her to remember he already refused her.

She turned away.

Her rejection silenced him.

■　■　■

Angela parked the rental car and wondered what she was doing. Before that, she hadn't given her actions consideration. Unable to sleep, she took a drive, not concerning herself with where she might end up, and found herself wandering around a Circle K. The cashiers watched her. She was black, at an ungodly hour. That was bound to make them nervous. She debated the merits of a cup of coffee versus leaving.

Joey walked into the store. "Angela."

"Hey. What are you doing here?" She asked Nolan's bartender.

"Ran out of sugar," the big grizzly man said. "What are you up to?"

She wanted to divert, but the truth came out. "Running." She walked with him to find the sugar.

He grabbed a five-pound bag. "Can't say I blame you. But you're running from the wrong things, hon."

She didn't answer.

"We're up and out. Let's get some coffee."

"It won't taste like yours." She led the way to the Styrofoam cups.

They got vanilla lattés, and he walked her to her car. "What's going on in that head of yours?"

"Oh, the usual—husband, wife, girlfriend, baby, boyfriend… err… ex-boyfriend."

"Nolan? He's not your ex."

She sipped her latté. "Where have you've been?"

"Watching Nolan. He's not over you."

"I left him to save my marriage—my doomed marriage." She paused, seeing it. "It was doomed. It was always doomed," she confessed. "I didn't try before the accident. Neither of us did. Mitch wanted an image, and I sabotaged it. That's what we were working on." She looked at Joey as if he had given her the key to life.

He nodded, taking big gulps of the hot liquid. "You guys had different goals from the beginning. That's why everything else happened."

"No image, no pressure. No pressure, no depression," she made a continuous circle with her hand. "Depression, cruise, wreck, Nolan... baby... me holding you up in a parking lot on Christmas to blurt out the obvious."

He laughed. "There's nowhere else I'd rather be."

Joey's gentle spirit was a balm, and the latté was good. "This is my fault, isn't it?"

He got serious, but the warmth never left his eyes. "A lot of it, but not all. The only one who is innocent is the baby. The rest of you made choices. Sometimes living with them is hell. Sometimes, living with other peoples' choices is worse."

She got serious too. "He hates me, doesn't he?"

"That's bullshit." He finished his drink. "Nolan loves you. That's irrevocable."

"Past tense. He can't stand to be around me now."

"He's raw right now. Ange, he'd rescue you in a heartbeat if you needed rescuing. But that's not what you need."

"What do I need?" She sloshed the remains of her coffee around the cup.

Joey hunched his shoulders. "You're the only one who can answer that."

. . .

"Come in."

The knock was light in case she was still asleep. Angela let herself into her sister's room. "Hey. Sorry to disturb you so early, but I can't do this anymore. I need to go."

"My sentiments exactly." Deidra was dressed and in the process of packing her bag.

"This is unexpected. I was prepared for another fight."

"Nope. You've been better than brave. I shouldn't have asked so much of you."

Something wasn't right. "It wasn't that big of a hardship... Yes, it was, but it had its perks."

"Regardless, I'm sorry I dragged you down here. Let's go home."

"All for it. Right after you tell me what's wrong."

Deidra raised her head for the first time. "Am I that obvious?"

"You packed one of Hilda's pillows."

She removed the unnecessary object. "Ugghh. I've got to get out of here."

Angela sat on the edge of the bed. "What happened?"

Deidra sat beside her and hugged the pillow. "Rob didn't get me anything for Christmas."

"You sound petty. I'm sure there's a reason for it."

"It's not about gifts. He had a gift for me. A *particular* gift."

"A particular..." It only took a moment for Angela to understand. "He was going to give you a ring?"

Deidra brushed the hair off her face. "If I weren't sure of it, I wouldn't have forced you to come down here. I wanted you to be here when we got engaged."

Inside, Angela was elated. Rob and Deidra belonged together. "What happened?"

"Thanksgiving." She pointed to a small emerald she wore on her right hand. "This somehow got lost. I'm pretty sure he stole it because he found it the next day in the exact place I laid it. I checked ten times. It wasn't there. I can't tell you how many jewelry catalogs were strewn around his house. He would *randomly* pick up one and ask my opinion. Which do I prefer: round diamonds or oval? What's prettier: white or yellow gold? Is a double band elegant, or ostentatious? All kinds of obvious crap. Yesterday, Tank was holding my hand when he asked Rob if he had forgotten to give me my gift. Rob hemmed and hawed around an answer. He hinted it was coming later."

"Okay. Your assumptions are reasonable."

"Except later never came. He got reserved and avoid-y. I can only conclude he changed his mind."

"Nerves?"

"Possibly. Or, maybe he changed his mind. Which would be fine, but talk to me. Don't make me feel like I've done something wrong, and now I'm no longer good enough. If there was never a ring, why didn't he buy me something? A scarf, earrings, gloves. It is Christmas. Any token would have sufficed."

Angela blew the air. "I'm sorry Deed. I don't know what his problem is, but it's obvious Rob loves you."

"He can love me over the phone. I want to go home."

"I want to go home."

"I'm sorry I put you through this. I thought if you and Nolan were in the same place, you'd both realize how much you love and miss each other, and we'd all be happy. What was I thinking?"

"No idea."

"What happened?"

"No idea. Whatever we thought we had isn't there."

"Yes, it is."

Angela shook her head. "Not enough of it is there for us to get around this gigantic mountain between us."

"I thought Mitch was the mountain. But he's gone. He is gone, isn't he?"

"He's gone. By his own choice." She waved that thought away. "I can't go there. Not today. Nolan is gone too. By his own choice. I can't do anything about that either."

"Did you try?"

Angela leveled Deidra a nasty glance. "I'm here, aren't I?"

"Did you tell him how you feel?"

"I don't know how I feel. Did you tell Rob how you feel?"

"He'll find out exactly how I feel because I'm going to demonstrate. I feel like leaving."

"I'm already packed."

CHAPTER 50

To hell with it. Nolan's morning ride was spoiled. Thoughts of Angela cluttered every crevice of his brain. He couldn't concentrate. He needed to hear it. He needed closure. If she didn't want a relationship, a friendship, any kind of *ship* with him, she would have to say so. She couldn't keep pulling him along, the possibility hovering just beyond his reach. She had to tell him to stop, to let go. Otherwise, he'd wait on her forever.

He docked his boat and ignored his daily maintenance. He needed to talk to Angela. It couldn't wait. Coming around the side of the house, he met Rob climbing the steps to the Enn.

"You look like crap."

"I feel like crap. You're one to talk. Skip your morning ride?"

"Cut it short. I need to talk to Angela."

"About time."

Nolan didn't bother to comment. Rob wasn't who he wanted to talk to. Hilda was baking cinnamon rolls when they entered the kitchen.

"What room is Angela in?"

She turned, tossed something in the refrigerator, and slammed the door closed. "Good morning to you too." Hilda rolled her eyes at her sons. "She's not in any room. They left twenty minutes ago."

Nolan sat down hard. He heard what she said, understood what it meant, and was physically ill.

Rob was slower to comprehend, mostly because he didn't want to. "What do you mean, they're gone? Who's gone?"

"Don't be an idiot. Deidra left too." Her words were short, and her movements were stiff.

Rob took a second seat. "All right. How about why?" He knew why.

"Ummm... Let me see." Hilda shoved the pan into the oven. "Because you two are idiots. That's why. I don't blame them one bit. How could you be so callous?"

"How was I callous?"

"I didn't have a choice."

They talked at the same time, realized it, and stopped.

"You first." Rob pointed to Nolan.

"I didn't do anything."

"No shit, Sherlock," Hilda snapped. "Do you think she came all the way down here for you not to do anything?"

"She didn't say anything to me. She didn't tell me what she wanted. She didn't bother telling me she was separated."

"You're an idiot. Did you ask her? Not like you needed to. She came, didn't she? She waited on you, didn't she? What else did you need? A neon sign flashing with A to Z instructions on how to claim a woman who wants you? Did you need specific directions saying DO NOT reject the woman who loves you?"

Apparently, he did. Hilda's rant wasn't wrong. He never considered while he was busy feeling rejected, so was she. He wanted to believe so badly, it sounded true. But it couldn't be that simple. Nothing was simple with Angela. It was pure desperation to blame it on a miscommunication, but this wasn't a sitcom. Angela had always been easy for him to read. When she wanted him, she came to his house. She didn't hide in the Enn waiting for him to figure it out. She threw herself at him. No, Hilda's rant meant nothing. Angela was gone.

Hilda wasn't done. "You." She hit Rob with her dish towel. "What in the hell is wrong with you? What possessed you not to propose?"

Nolan's head snapped up. "Propose?"

Rob squirmed, seeming very uncomfortable. "It wasn't the right time."

"The hell it wasn't. She knew you were going to do it. Now, all she knows is you are a chickenshit coward messing with her heart."

Hilda hadn't cursed this much in a while. Somewhere between the layers of mutilated thoughts and crippled dreams, Nolan noted the profanity and hoped she would curb it before the kids came down.

"I wasn't messing with her heart. I love Deidra. I want to marry her. But now isn't the right time. We have to talk about some things first."

"You should have thought about that before you led her to believe you loved her enough to propose. Oh, wait. You didn't. You had her come down here so you could give her nothing. Not even the truth. Do you even know the truth? Why did you back out, you punk?" She hit him with the dish towel again and swatted Nolan for good measure.

Rob didn't speak. He leaned forward with his elbows on the table. A second later, he leaned back, slouching down. He rubbed his hands through his hair. Deidra's absence had a serious effect.

"Well? I don't have all day. You can tell us what the hell is wrong with you, or you can get out of my kitchen. I don't want to see you right now."

"I didn't propose because of Nolan and Angela."

"What?" Nolan joined them in the present.

"Do what?" Hilda's oven timer buzzed, but she ignored it.

Rob used the opportunity to move around. He grabbed a potholder and extracted the buns while he talked.

"Mom, if Deidra and I get married… No. When Deidra and I get married, Nolan and Angela are going to be seeing a lot of each other."

"So? Angela and Nolan are grown. Angela is, anyway."

"I didn't get the impression they could handle it, not yet. I'd rather not have the maid of honor and the best man wrecking my wedding because they can't function around each other. This was their first meeting since everything happened. I didn't want my proposal to be marred by the realization they are going to be stuck with each other. Deidra was worried about Angela. I was worried about you, Nolan. It wasn't appropriate to say, 'Hey, our siblings are suffering, why don't I mess up our moment by compounding their stress?' Didn't seem like a great plan to me."

Hilda was silent for a while, absorbing the information.

Nolan sighed. One more thing for him to feel bad about. "I appreciate your concern. I do. But, telling Deidra how you feel supersedes everything."

Rob nodded. "It does. But whatever was in the air superseded me and my plans. Now, she's gone."

"Robert Woods, you are a good man," Hilda said. "You're also a coward. You used Nolan as an excuse because you were afraid."

He didn't bother to disagree.

Lexie tapped Nolan's shoulder. No one saw her come into the kitchen. Clad in her new pajamas with Ollie tucked under her arm, she wanted to sit on his lap.

He lifted her. "Good morning, sweetheart."

"Morning, Daddy. Morning, Mammaw. Morning, Uncle Rob."

"Good morning, peanut."

"Morning, sweetie. You want a cinnamon bun?"

They sounded as if small talk had been what she interrupted. "Yes, please. Daddy, I have something to tell you and Uncle Rob."

"What's that?"

"Sometimes grownups do stupid stuff. They make a mess out of their lives. Sometimes the only thing left to do is clean it up and start over again. And, stop being stupid. And you, Mammaw, stop using swear words. You're a bad influence on Tank and Ollie."

"Tell Ollie to cover his ears. My sons are stupid grownups who make me say bad words. That's good advice, by the way."

"Did you call me?" Tank joined them in the kitchen. "I'm hungry. I smell cinnamon."

"I didn't call you," Lexie said. "Food called you."

CHAPTER 51

"It was in my bag. I must have dropped it."

All activity in the kitchen stopped when they heard Deidra's voice.

"Bedrooms, kitchen, we didn't go anywhere else," Angela said.

Nolan and Rob looked at one another, trading disbelief and hope.

"Hilda," Deidra led the way into the kitchen. "Have you seen my…" She stopped.

Angela bumped into her, took a step back, and stopped.

Nolan and Rob stood up.

"…wallet?" Deidra finished her sentence.

"Deidra," Rob began.

She held up a hand, not interested.

Hilda's mood improved. "Yes, I have it," she grinned. "I took it out of your bag while you were bitching. Angela was moping. Neither of you were paying attention to anything but your complaints. They were valid," she added, "but distracting."

Not wanting her sister to curse at an elderly person, Angela responded first. "You did what?"

Hilda put a second bun on Tank's plate. "I couldn't stop my sons from being idiots, but I saw an opportunity to stop you two from making a mistake. You can thank me later."

Lexie went to Angela. "You didn't say goodbye."

Angela hugged the child. "I left you a note. And, I would have called you from the airport."

"Would you have called me?" Nolan spoke his first words since seeing her.

"And say what?"

The question hung in the air.

The tension did nothing to Tank's appetite. "Can I have another one?"

Deidra seized the opportunity. "Can I have my wallet?"

"Later," Hilda said. "After you talk. Rob has something to tell you."

"Yes," Rob said. "Can we go somewhere and talk, please?" He reached for her hand.

Deidra pulled her fingers back.

Hilda hit him with a potholder. "No. You said it once. You can say it again. Right here."

Deidra folded her arms, liking that idea.

Nolan tried to help. "I'll take the kids. Angela?"

"No, you chicken-shit, punk. You're not escaping." Hilda made a face. "You didn't cut your ride short just to run out now." Done with him, she turned back to her younger son. "Robert, why didn't you propose?"

"Thanks, Mom." Rob cut Hilda a mean look. "That's exactly how I wanted her to hear it."

"Glad you got your wish. Get on with it."

Deidra struggled not to laugh. She covered it with attitude. "Yes, get on with it."

Rob sighed. This time, he captured Deidra's hand. "I love you, Deidra. I want to marry you more than anything." He reached into his pocket and showed her the ring. "May I put it on you? Will you marry me?" He pleaded.

Deidra's breath caught when she saw the three-carat diamond and accelerated when she saw the raw emotion in his eyes. It was hard to form the words. "Why? Why didn't you ask me before?"

"It wasn't because I didn't want to."

He gathered her close and was grateful she didn't pull away. He almost had the ring on before she closed her hand.

The truth or nothing.

"I was scared. Not of us. We belong together."

"Scared of what?"

"Scared for Nolan and Angela." He looked at her sister—whose eyes went wide—and his brother—who nodded encouragingly. "This holiday was a disaster for them. I didn't want our day, our plans, marred by their misery. I didn't want to say it. I didn't want to hurt anybody. Especially, not you."

"I get it. I do." Deidra opened her palm.

He slid the ring on.

Angela blocked the sound of her ears ringing. "Rob. I'm fine." She glanced at Nolan. "We're fine. It's good. Nothing matters more than this." She hugged them both. She prayed they couldn't hear her heart pounding.

"Are you sure?" Deidra asked.

"Nothing could be better." Angela's voice was an octave high, but only noticeable to Nolan.

He joined their huddle. "This is the best news ever. Angela and I will get our kinks out, won't we?" His smile was soft and sincere.

"We will." Her tone carried enough quiet doubt to temper his hopes.

"They'll try hard not to be stupid." Lexie squeezed in to hug her soon-to-be-aunt.

"Precisely."

Angela and Nolan said the same word at the same time. Their eyes locked, and something sparked.

Deidra felt the sizzle. "Seriously, Ange. Are you sure you can handle this?"

"Deed. Do you see this ring!" She grabbed her sister's hand. "Don't make me steal it. Because I will."

Hilda joined them to get a look at the ring. "I'll show you how. Only took a second to grab her wallet."

"Woman, where is my wallet?"

"It's in the fridge," Tank announced. " I saw it when I was getting the stuff for breakfast." While the adults talked, he made use of the time. A carton of eggs, a pack of sausage, a loaf of bread, and a stick of butter were on the counter waiting.

. . .

The morning got busy with happiness. Nolan and Angela made sure to laugh, smile, and pretend to relax. No one pressured them to talk—it was Rob and Deidra day— but the unspoken assumption was there.

Angela took long bathroom breaks and hidden moments to balance her composure. It was a relief for Nolan to go to work. Contrary to her tough-talk, she was miserable. The potential. The possibilities. Of all the things she and Nolan might have been, *buddies* wasn't the option she would have chosen.

He came home for dinner and confused the hell out of her with a bouquet of flowers.

"Thank you." She eyed the Canna Lilies and coneflowers, and ignored her embarrassment. "They're beautiful. What are they for?"

"Because you're beautiful." He held her gaze.

"Are those from my greenhouse?" Rob pointed.

"Nope. They're from Deidria's." Nolan went to wash up.

Deidra cackled.

.　　.　　.

Sitting around the dinner table, Angela wondered if they wandered into another dimension. Nolan put her on edge, and no one cared to notice her new wave of awkwardness. It was a good thing wedding-talk dominated the conversation. Her brain couldn't function beyond that.

Wait. What? Did he help himself to a bite of my blueberry pie?

Nolan chewed slowly, staring at her, to be certain she saw him.

"Did you eat my pie?"

"It's delicious." He grinned.

She was at a loss for how to respond.

His grin broadened.

She pushed the plate toward him. "Help yourself." She couldn't eat anything after that anyway.

"I will." He scooped up another forkful and watched for her reaction.

Embarrassment raced up her face. He rendered he speechless.

"Angela, angel," Hilda said, "I'm putting you on dish duty tonight. Do you mind?"

Angela wanted to kiss Hilda. "Sure. My pleasure." She hopped up and collected dessert dishes and cups. They rattled as she stacked them because her hands were shaking.

Hilda continued to talk. "I told the Martians, after dinner, we would search the attic for some cool stuff to decorate their new treehouse. Besides, I don't want to be responsible for the bride messing up her new engagement ring."

"If a little water hurts that ring, Rob's in big trouble," Nolan teased.

"You got that right," Deidra answered. "But, I'm going to milk that excuse anyway—anything to get out of housework.

"Only until the honeymoon's over," Hilda warned. "That's what the phrase 'honeymoon's over' means."

"Hey," Rob said. "No negatives."

CHAPTER 52

In the kitchen, Angela breathed long and deep. *This is nuts.* If she couldn't hold it together for one day, how would she make it 'til the wedding? They can't be in the same family; they couldn't be in the same house. She was flustered and crazy, unable to collect her composure. "This is nuts." She turned on the water and opened the dishwasher, willing her fingers to stop trembling with each piece rinsed and loaded.

The running water drowned out his footsteps. She didn't hear his approach. She felt his presence. She turned as his shadow reached her. He stood there with a few leftover plates and forks. Her imagination was vivid. He reminded her of a lion poised to pounce. She had nowhere to hide. "Thank you." She reached for the dishes.

"I thought I'd keep your company while you worked." He gave her the items he held in one hand.

A hazy memory tried to surface. Didn't she tell him once she wanted someone to keep her company while she did the dishes? She was too nervous to hold the thought. She was too nervous to do anything. Reaching for the dirty dishes in his other hand, she hoped he couldn't see her trembling. Or at the very least, he would pretend not to notice.

Nolan didn't give her the plates. He set them on the counter and grasped her outstretched fingers. With no warning, he pulled her in and claimed her lips. The kiss wasn't gentle. It wasn't a light brush of friendship. He *was* a lion pouncing. A powerful and dangerous force, taking everything from her: her mind, her resistance, her will. He didn't stop there. He made her respond. Made her desire him, want to kiss him back. Her body reacted according to his will with a need she thought she suppressed.

He whispered into her mouth, "I've been waiting, dreaming of this." He backed her into the sink and left off the conversation.

Angela cried. It felt so good. He tasted wonderful. She needed him; she needed this. But it didn't make sense. She was falling, drowning, lost. She couldn't breathe. There was no air, just him. He was solid; she could feel him, hold him. He touched her, everywhere. Shooting arcs of electricity through her, causing her to come alive with need. She pressed into him. No mind. No thought. Just need.

Nolan had to make a decision: release her or make love to her in his mother's kitchen. He chose the latter. He would do the former, but making love to Angela, anywhere, would always be his first choice. He broke the kiss, but not the contact. She had a tear he needed to taste. An eyelash to brush his lip across. An ear he wanted to nibble. A jawbone to run his tongue along. "Do you want to take a ride with me? We can grab some beer and talk."

She had no mind, no ability to function. Her response was automatic, produced by magic. The breath that spoke it wasn't even hers. It was just the natural answer to any question he asked. "Yes."

He kissed her again, less forceful but no less urgent. He had to or die.

There was a rush of cold air when he backed away from her. But the heat returned when he took hold of her hand and led her out the back door. Angela was dazed. She didn't have a mind, no ability to function. *Yes.*

Nolan yelled, "ROB. DISHES."

.　.　.

Angela couldn't recall if the motorcycle Nolan led her to belonged to Rob or Hilda. Maybe it was his. She'd never seen Nolan ride, but the ease in which he fit into his helmet gave her the impression he wasn't a novice. Her wide-eye stare fixated on his electric blue orbs as he placed a second helmet over her hair. With deft fingers, he adjusted the chin strap, all the while returning her gaze.

"Damn, you're beautiful." He kissed her nose and straddled the bike, holding it steady for her to climb on.

It was fortunate he didn't appear to be expecting a response; the only thing in Angela's head was *yes*.

He gunned the engine. She wrapped her arms around his waist, and they both felt the thrill. They drove into the night and nothing else mattered. The wind in his face and Angela pressed against him—Nolan had found his recipe for heaven. The faster they drove, the tighter she held him. Nolan noticed and accelerated.

They could have gotten beer from the Summer Shack. The Quik Mart sold alcohol as well. The nearest liquor store was just over the bridge. They passed them all, chasing stars instead. Angela's heart thundered. She clung to Nolan, hoping they had enough gas to make it to the moon.

Their ten-minute trip took more than an hour, and they savored every second of it. Nolan slowed and turned into the drive. He didn't stop at the house; instead, he slow-rolled them down the small incline to the Willow Inlet. He parked and helped Angela slide off. They made their way to the oversized tree stump. He sat the six-pack on the ground and popped a beer for each of them. They silently watched the waves and drank. Nolan reflected. Since her arrival, they hadn't talked much. A lot of misdirection and confusion but no heart to heart; it was time to stop dancing, and deal with it. "When did you stop loving me?"

She waited her whole life for him to ask that question. Her answer was there, ready to be spoken without her having to pause or ponder. "I never stopped loving you."

Nolan took a long swig from his beer and set the bottle down. "If either of us has done anything wrong, I'm sorry. If you're hurting, like I am, I'm sorry. If there is a way to fix this, I promise, I will do it. I love you."

She remained quiet while he talked, but she couldn't help the tiny gasp that escaped when she heard his declaration. He'd said it before, but this time was different. It meant something else. Something more.

"I'm always going to love you. Angela, I need you to marry me."

The answer was already on her lips, her mouth forming the word. "Yes—Nolan? What are you saying?"

"I'm saying what I should have said when you came to me before. I'm saying, I'm in love with you, and I want to get married. I need to marry you."

Yes. It was right there, fighting to leap off her tongue. "So-so much has happened. Married? We haven't talked or figured out anything."

"Do you still love me?"

It had to be spoken. She couldn't keep it in any longer. "Yes."

He removed her beer from her hand, entwined his fingers with hers, and pulled her to him. "Marry me."

CHAPTER 53

Angela stirred. It wasn't dawn yet. Bits of jumbled memory flitted into her consciousness. They were in Nolan's bed, but they hadn't started there. It began at the inlet. Nolan's proposal, a passion-fueled kiss, and all their pent-up emotions erupted.

As if sensing her state of semi-awareness, Nolan moved. She lay on her side, while he was flat on his stomach with an arm draped across her waist. He shifted, so they were spooning and held her against his chest. "You promised to marry me," his husky whisper made her neck tingle.

"I did." She snuggled into his warmth.

Comfortable, sated, and high on happiness, they drifted back to sleep.

■ ■ ■

"Ohhhhhh noooooooo...." Angela opened her eyes, covered her ears, and banged her head against the pillow. She was alone. Nolan was more than likely on his morning ride. Or, "Oh no..." It was almost ten. Everybody was awake by now. Her whereabouts, without doubt, common knowledge. Nothing would make this right. She didn't know how it happened. She didn't know what happened. She was in Nolan's bed; of course, she knew what happened. She knew how it happened and how many times. She just didn't understand why it happened. Sleeping with Nolan was *not* on the itinerary. Nolan. Beyond her shock, inside her guilt, hidden within the rapid beat of her heart, Angela remembered his hands, his lips, the way he undressed her. How strong he felt moving inside her made her exhale and glow.

▪ ▪ ▪

There was a mountain of bacon on the counter beside a half pot of coffee. Nolan had gone, come, and gone again. Just as well, she didn't want to see him while she was wearing yesterday's clothes. She grabbed a cup and a handful of bacon and made a beeline for the Enn. "Morning," Angela waved and kept her head down. "Be out in a little while." Rob and Tank were painting the treehouse. They'd want her to inspect it. She'd stop by on her way out... of town.

The voices were in the dining room. Angela was glad. Straight up the steps without a confrontation. She'd see people when she was ready.

It took her a half hour to bathe and dress. She still wasn't ready to see people, but she ran out ways to procrastinate. *Fine. Get it over with*. She used attitude to propel herself back into the world.

Deidra and Hilda made lists. The dining room table was littered with bridal magazines Hilda picked up from the Quik Mart. Deidra had Rob's laptop open while they talked and planned.

"Hey, Ange." Deidra glanced up from the screen. "Get over here. We need a tiebreaker opinion."

Hilda jotted something on a to-do list. "About time you showed up. I wondered if he had you tied to the bed."

Angela's jaw dropped.

Deidra snickered.

Hilda flipped a magazine page.

Hilda was Hilda. Best to get on with it. "Yes, I slept with him."

"I hope he did something more exciting than missionary."

"Hilda!"

"You don't look like you got much sleep. That's encouraging."

"This is your fault. If you hadn't snatched Deidra's wallet, none of this would have happened." Despite herself, Angela relaxed.

"I got you laid. Go me."

Deidra laughed outright then asked. "What now?"

"I go away. Far away."

"You are not messing up my engagement celebration, you chicken."

"Deed. We haven't figured out anything. We're not a couple, but I had sex with him…a lot. That entitles me to be a chicken. I should already be gone."

"He should have tied you to the bed," Hilda mused.

Deidra nodded. "I want the absolute truth, Ange. My engagement-bliss is on the line here. Before I make an executive decision, I need answers."

A long minute passed. Then Angela released the truth. "It was a dream come true—the greatest night of my life. I love him so much I'm numb. I'm never going to get over him and I'm never going to be able to tell him no."

The back door opened. Angela's declaration hung in the air as all three women turned toward the sound. Nolan and Rob laughed as they came down the hall.

"Breathe," Deidra quietly commanded her sister.

Angela sucked in a breath and forced herself to exhale.

"There you are." Nolan entered the room, golden in his splendor. His brilliant blue eyes took in everything. "Everybody's here. Good. That makes it easy." Lexie and Tank bounced around behind their dads. Rob moved beside Deidra, and Nolan stood toe to toe with Angela. From the possessive way he assessed her, his thoughts were clear. "You promised," he said. "Lex," he held out his hand.

Lexie reached into the small jewelry bag she held. She produced a fancy ring box, removed the top, and proudly offered it to her father.

"Thanks, hon." Nolan took the ring in one hand and Angela's trembling fingers in the other. He gave his full attention to her and locked her in the intensity of his gaze. "Did you mean it?"

She was never going to be able to tell him no. "Yes."

"I love you, Angela." He slipped the ring on her finger. Amid the cheers, the exclamations, and Hilda pointing out Angela neglected to mention the part about the 'promise' to them, Nolan gave in to his all too obvious desire to kiss his intended.

With a happy shriek, Deidra threw herself against the entangled couple. "Let me see the ring!"

"I picked it out," Lexie announced.

Deidra pawed at Angela's hand. "Oh, it's beautiful. You've got good taste, kiddo. Hey! I have a great idea. We should get married together."

"No!" Angela shook her head. "I'm not messing up your day."

Deidra made a face. "You were willing to mess it up a few minutes ago."

"Shut up."

"Anyway, it's perfect... unless you want your own day."

Hilda said, "You're going to have the same people. It would save some bucks. Besides, it's a nice corny-theme: two sisters marrying two brothers."

"As far as corny-themes go, sisters and brothers get my vote." Rob made a ridiculous puppy face at Angela.

"Mine too." Nolan offered her a crooked smile. His happiness was so, so obvious.

Angela didn't want her own day. She wanted Nolan. She wanted him forever. She wanted him now.

Lexie discussed their good fortune with Tank. "We both get a mom and an aunt."

"At the same time!" Tank added.

"Best. Christmas. Ever!"

CHAPTER 54

Three months later…

Nolan squeezed her hand. "Are you okay?"

"Yes." She brought his fingers to her lips and kissed them. "I won't linger."

"No, you won't. Otherwise, I'll come up to hurry you along."

Nolan in D.C.; it was hard to imagine. He came to help with her final packing and be with her when she served Mitchell their divorce papers. After this, she would leave Washington—and her old life—for good.

Nolan's presence made all things possible, but they agreed it might be in poor taste for him to accompany her into Mitch's condo.

He waited in the car, close and at the ready.

. . .

It was weird to ring the doorbell. Angela had the keys in her pocket. For the whole of her marriage, this was her home. But, she couldn't walk in like she lived there. It wasn't her home anymore. As of today, she wasn't married. She was Ms. Jefferies again.

The door opened. "Hi." Mitchell held it wide. "Why didn't you come in?"

"I wouldn't do that. I'll leave you my keys."

"I don't want the keys, Ange. Keep them." She looked skeptical, so he added, "I may get locked out or fall and break my leg. Your access might be the only way to save me."

She doubted that. Not only were Nate and Keira a lot closer than she would be—in Florida—she couldn't imagine anything she'd be capable of saving him from. However, he was pleasant; there was no reason to pick a fight. "Try not to fall."

He chuckled. "I'll keep that in mind. By the way, thanks for bringing them over. I appreciate it."

"It's the least I could do. You made everything so easy; I'm almost offended." She smiled as she removed the divorce papers from her purse.

"Don't. That was the least *I* could do. I messed us up, babe. No pretending otherwise."

"Yeah, well, my anger didn't help matters." She left it at that. She didn't want to dwell on her anger. Parts of it were still there.

"I guess the piper is paid now. It's nice for us to be able—"

The cry of an uncomfortable infant disrupted the last of his sentence.

"Hold that thought." Mitchell turned away. "I shouldn't have to tell you to sit down and make yourself comfortable." He called over his shoulder as he answered Ladarius's summons.

Angela didn't want to get comfortable; she wanted to leave. Nolan was waiting. She wasn't mentally prepared to deal with Mitchell's baby. His baby was the main reason she handed him copies of their divorce papers to sign. She didn't want to see a baby. Not his baby. His living proof she failed as a woman.

He came back before she could run.

"Daddy's got somebody for you to meet."

She couldn't breathe watching him carrying that tiny bundle as if it contained the entire world. For Mitchell, it did.

"Ange." His eyes, his smile, his whole being lit with pride. "This is my son, Ladarius. LP, say hi to Miss Angela." He offered the child to her.

She took a step back, tears brimming, accusation dilating her pupils.

Mitchell smiled. It was a sad smile, full of disappointment. "Someday, Angela, you're going to have to get over it. I'm sorry if that sounds harsh to you. I don't mean it to be. But the truth of the matter is life is shitty...and awesome in varying levels at different times for everybody. It's nobody's fault you can't have natural children. It's one of those things that falls on the shitty side." He kissed LP, for his comfort as much as the baby's. "I never meant for any of this to happen. It wasn't my intention to cause you pain. I love you. Always have, always will. What happened with us was a series of incidents, not some evil plot. It is what it is. If you expect to be happy, you have to A: accept it with grace, not a grudge. And B: get over it. It's not changing. I accept all the responsibility, but don't look at me like I'm a villain. I'm not a villain. When I look into my son's eyes, I know I'm not a villain." He offered her the baby again.

Having no other recourse, Angela took the baby. She looked at the tiny face and felt his worth in her soul. He was wonderful and precious. He smiled at her, and she couldn't hold on to her anger. Her pain didn't fit the moment. "H-He's... beautiful."

"Thank you." Watching the emotion play across her features triggered his. They were both teary-eyed. "Everything else might have been messed up, but not him. He's the awesome part."

"You are, little man," she talked to the child. "And handsome, aren't you?" LP kicked his legs and cooed in response to her voice. "Does that mean you agree?"

"Of course, he does. He's a genius, and he looks like his father."

"You're not proud at all, are you?"

"Can't deny the truth." Mitchell stopped talking. He took in the image of Angela holding his baby.

She caught his look and wondered. "What?"

"This had been the original plan: you, me, and LP. I've had this image in my head since college. Fate changed everything, but here's the image, just like I saw it. It defies logic. But it's an incredible picture, all the same."

Angela rocked LP, amazed at what it did to her. "If I wouldn't have been so angry, we may have been able to achieve some form of this image sooner. Divorce day is an inopportune time for clarity," she chuckled.

"I concur," he laughed with her.

"I wouldn't have gotten the clarity if not for the process."

"We had to get something out of it."

"Thank you, Mitchell." She kissed Ladarius's head. He was too irresistible.

"Thank you, Angela. I will always regret losing you."

Now that she no longer had such a tight hold on her anger, other emotions surfaced: peace, forgiveness, and healing.

There was a tap on the door.

Mitchell arched an eyebrow.

Angela kept a blank expression.

Mitchell opened the door. His body clenched, but he forced himself to speak. "Woods."

"I'm just making sure everything is okay." Nolan glanced in, saw Angela holding LP, and relaxed his stance.

An echo of the advice Mitchell gave Angela filtered back to his consciousness. He opened the door for Nolan to enter.

Nolan went to the baby, peeked, and said, "Congratulations. Handsome fellow." He checked Angela for signs of stress.

"Thank you."

Angela grinned. "He is. He's perfect." She cuddled the baby and let the last of her tension ebb away.

They left Mitchell's condo with Angela smiling. Her mood was light and her energy a little stronger. It was as if her feet had touched solid ground. She finally reached that other shore.

EPILOGUE

Nolan Woods loved the morning. The predawn hour before sunrise belonged to him. He took his speedboat out where he was at peace.

These days he was hardly ever at peace. He cut his ride down to thirty minutes. Before, it was always an hour, at least. He couldn't afford it, not right now. He would get back to it, but not any time soon. He only did it because he promised. Apparently, he was an annoying bear if he didn't get some quiet time in the morning.

Jackie never understood that. There was a lot about him Jackie never understood. For example, he was a slow reactor. Or, that in most instances, he didn't take to change well. He was great at stability, not so great at flexibility. She was flighty and needed flexibility. Lexie was like him—big on stability.

He didn't have to worry about Jackie anymore. But it was nice to have some objectivity.

More than fifteen minutes out—farther than he intended. But the blue and gold morning was beautiful. The sunrise over the water was a thing not to be missed. His phone blared. Every nerve in his body jumped to life. Rather than cut the engine, he turned the boat and talked loud. "Is it time?"

Hearing the engine roar, Lexie talked even louder. "Yep. Come home. Mom's water broke. The contractions are closer."

"On my way. Did you call Rob?"

"I'm supposed to call Aunt Deidra and then Mammaw after I call you."

"What?"

"Mom said Aunt Deidra would tell Uncle Rob."

"Call Rob!" Nolan hung up and took the boat to its maximum speed. The sunrise was forgotten. Angela was in labor. He wasn't going to miss it.

NOTE FROM THE AUTHOR

Word-of-mouth is crucial for any author to succeed. If you enjoyed *The Other Shore*, please leave a review online—anywhere you are able. Even if it's just a sentence or two. It would make all the difference and would be very much appreciated.

Thanks!
Tracy

ABOUT THE AUTHOR

Made entirely of rum and snacks—International Bestselling Author, Tracy A. Ball is a native Baltimorean and veteran West Virginian, whose family is a mashup of cultures. She writes real and raw interracial romance with an intensity that burns because she has been busting stereotypes while teaching interracial/generational healing for more than a quarter of a century.

Tracy engages with folks from every twist of fate and all manner of experience. She has hung out with murderers and dined with people who have dined with the Pope, which is why she needs the rum…and a nap.

Thank you so much for reading one of **Tracy A. Ball's** novels.
If you enjoyed the experience, please check out our recommended
title for your next great read!

Civil Warriors by Tracy A. Ball

"A tragic and heroic story that readers will love."

–LOST IN A BOOK REVIEW

View other Black Rose Writing titles at
www.blackrosewriting.com/books and use promo code
PRINT to receive a **20% discount** when purchasing.